中文详注剑桥莎士比亚精选

仲夏夜之梦

原版创始主编：[英] 瑞克斯·吉布森（Rex Gibson）
原版主编：[英] 瑞查德·安褚斯（Richard Andrews）
　　　　　[英] 维姬·维南德（Vicki Wienand）
原版编注：[英] 琳苾·巴克尔（Linda Buckle）
总主编：陈国华
分册主编：胡岑卉

社图号 20142

Cambridge School Shakespeare: A Midsummer Night's Dream [Fourth edition] [978-1-107-61545-8] was first published by Cambridge University Press in 2014. All rights reserved.

This Simplified Chinese edition for the People's Republic of China is published by arrangement with the Press Syndicate of the University of Cambridge, Cambridge, United Kingdom.

© Cambridge University Press & Beijing Language and Culture University Press 2020.

This book is in copyright. No reproduction of any part may take place without the written permission of Cambridge University Press or Beijing Language and Culture University Press.

本书版权由剑桥大学出版社和北京语言大学出版社共同所有。本书任何部分之文字及图片，如未获得出版者书面同意，不得用任何方式抄袭、节录或翻印。

This edition is for sale in the People's Republic of China (excluding Hong Kong SAR, Macao SAR and Taiwan Province) only.
此版本仅限在中华人民共和国境内销售。

北京市版权局著作权合同登记图字：01-2020-4101 号

图书在版编目（CIP）数据

中文详注剑桥莎士比亚精选．仲夏夜之梦 ／ 陈国华总主编；胡岑卉分册主编． -- 北京：北京语言大学出版社，2020.10
 书名原文：Cambridge School Shakespeare：A Midsummer Night's Dream
 ISBN 978-7-5619-5748-6

Ⅰ.①中⋯　Ⅱ.①陈⋯　②胡⋯　Ⅲ.①多幕剧－剧本－英国－中世纪　Ⅳ.① I561.33

中国版本图书馆 CIP 数据核字（2020）第 169653 号

中文详注剑桥莎士比亚精选：仲夏夜之梦
ZHONGWEN XIANG ZHU JIANQIAO SHASHIBIYA JINGXUAN: ZHONGXIAYE ZHI MENG

项目策划：李　亮		**责任编辑**：孙冠群	
封面设计：乔　剑		**排版制作**：北京创艺涵文化发展有限公司	
责任印制：武晓东			

出版发行：北京语言大学出版社
社　　址：北京市海淀区学院路 15 号，100083
网　　址：www.blcup.com
电子信箱：service@blcup.com
电　　话：编辑部　8610-82301019/0178
　　　　　　发行部　8610-82303650/3591/3648
　　　　　　北语书店　8610-82303653
　　　　　　网购咨询　8610-82303908
印　　刷：北京中科印刷有限公司

版　次：2020 年 10 月第 1 版		**印　次**：2020 年 10 月第 1 次印刷	
开　本：787 毫米 × 1092 毫米　1/16		**印　张**：12.25	
字　数：372 千字			
定　价：65.00 元			

PRINTED IN CHINA

序

由于观察角度不同，评判标准不同，关于哪个国家哪位诗人或小说家的成就最大，世人可能难以达成一致；可是说到剧作家，大家的共识是，莎士比亚不仅是英语国家有史以来最伟大的剧作家，也是全世界最伟大的剧作家，在知名度、影响力和传世作品的数量上，没有任何一位剧作家可以与之比肩。正是由于其公认的文学成就和人文精神，在过去400多年里，莎士比亚戏剧的演出在英语国家和许多非英语国家经久不衰，莎剧的阅读和鉴赏已成为这些国家英文教学的必选内容。

莎剧进入中国，已经有100多年历史，莎士比亚全集已经有了四个中文译本。不懂英文的人可以通过译本来欣赏莎士比亚剧作。然而文学作品的语言，尤其是诗歌的语言，具有相当程度的不可译性，而几乎所有莎剧的大部分台词都是素体诗（blank verse）。例如《哈慕雷》（*Hamlet*）里主人翁的名言"To be, or not to be, that is the question"，不论怎样译，都难以完全再现原文的深刻内涵和形式特点。要想真正欣赏莎士比亚的语言和戏剧艺术，还得阅读其英文原作。最早由剑桥大学出版社出版的这套莎剧精选，收录了最受读者和观众喜爱的14部剧目，涵盖莎剧的各个类别，以其独具匠心的设计和编排，成为所有英文原版莎剧中最适合英语学习者阅读、最适合戏剧爱好者排演的莎剧选集。

本选集的创始主编瑞克斯·吉布森（Rex Gibson）在本书引言（Introduction）里指出："不论做什么，都要记住，莎士比亚写下他的剧本是为了演出、观看和享受的。"秉承这一宗旨，这一新版莎剧选集有四个鲜明的区别性特点：

一、书的开本和页面的宽高比例特别适合学校的老师和学生以及剧团的导演和演员在排练莎剧时把书打开，拿在手里，随时参阅，而且左边页面上有许多有关排演活动的建议。

二、书中配有大量世界各国莎剧演出的彩色剧照，为莎剧爱好者和剧团排演莎剧提供了灵感。

三、书的正文部分打开后，右页是未经删减、原汁原味的剧本原文，左页是多种不同栏目，包括导演技巧（Stagecraft）、剧中语言（Language in the play）、人物分析（Characters）、主题分析（Themes）、写作练习（Write about it）及词语注释等。每幕之间（本幕回顾）和最后一幕后（本剧回顾）有与剧情相关的各种思考题。

四、在剧本之后有各种针对全剧的专题论述，以《哈慕雷》为例，包括视角与主题（Perspectives and themes）、人物分析（Characters）、《哈慕雷》的语言（The language of *Hamlet*）、《哈慕雷》的演出（*Hamlet* in performance）、笔论莎士比亚（Writing about Shakespeare）、笔论《哈慕雷》（Writing about *Hamlet*），还有一份莎翁年表（William Shakespeare 1564–1616）。

左页上的栏目对于解读和排演莎剧特别有帮助，剧本后面的专题论述对于撰写有关莎士比亚的文章特别有帮助，而参加莎剧排演，背诵台词，撰写论文，又是提高英语水平的极好途径。

为了方便更多的中国读者阅读、欣赏、排演莎士比亚原作，北京语言大学出版社携手剑桥大学出版社，将这套莎剧精选引入中国。我有幸应邀担任这套书的中文版总主编，组织起一个团队，对原版进行一定程度的改编和汉化，以适应中国读者的需求。我们不仅将原版提供的关键注释基本译成了中文，而且针对中国英语学习者和莎剧爱好者阅读理解上的难点，主要做了以下四件事：

　　一、参考 The Oxford Dictionary of Original Shakespearean Pronunciation (David Crystal 2016)、Oxford Dictionary of Pronunciation for Current English (Clive Upton 2003) 和 Shakespeare's Names: A Pronouncing Dictionary (Helge Kökeritz 1950)，给每个剧本前面人物表里的人名加上了国际音标。为了便于读者识别，我们将第一本发音词典里一般中国读者不认识的个别音标替换成了大家熟悉的近似音标。

　　二、为左页顶端的剧情简介添加中文译文。

　　三、左页中以及剧本后面论文部分里有一些具有挑战性的词和术语（如tableau），我们为其中的大部分添加了相应的中文释义。

　　四、适当增加了原版里没有的词语注释。

　　给剧中人物的名字加了国际音标之后，我们发现，现有莎剧中文译本里一些人名的中文译名与原文的读音差别较大且互不相同。根据定名不咎、译音循本、音义兼顾、音系对应的原则，我们给出了新译名。根据前两个原则，我们将剧本 Julius Caesar /ˈdʒuːliəs ˈsiːzə(r)/ 译成《儒略·恺撒》，而没有采用《尤利/力乌斯·恺撒》《裘利/力斯·凯撒》《居里厄斯·恺撒》等现成译名中的任何一个，因为从公元前1世纪到公元16世纪西方使用的儒略历（Julian calendar）就是以这位 Julius Caesar（拉丁文读音是 /ˈjuːlɪ.ʊs ˈkae̯sar/）命名的。根据音义兼顾的原则，我们将剧本 Hamlet /ˈ(h)amlət/ 译成《哈慕雷》而不是《哈姆莱特》或《哈姆雷特》，因为"慕雷"比"姆莱"或"姆雷"更适合用来给男子起名，结尾的辅音 /t/ 在实际说话中往往不发音。根据音系对应的原则，我们借鉴了曹禺的译法，将剧本 Romeo and Juliet 译成《柔密欧与朱丽叶》，没有将 Romeo 译成更常见的"罗密欧"，因为"柔 /rou/"比"罗 /luo/"更接近原名 Romeo /ˈroːmɪoː/ 的读音；同时我们将 Juliet /ˈdʒuːlɪət/ 译成"朱丽叶"而不是"朱丽叶"，因为这样做不容易让人误以为这个女孩姓"朱"。

　　这套经过改编并且带中文注释的《中文详注剑桥莎士比亚精选》不仅可以用作中国高中和大学的英文教材，而且适合中国所有具有较高英语能力的莎剧爱好者阅读和欣赏，将戏剧从书中提升到自己心中，将剧本从课堂搬演到戏台。

　　相信《中文详注剑桥莎士比亚精选》会带给中国广大英语爱好者一个惊喜。

陈国华

北京外国语大学

2020年5月于英国剑桥家中

Contents 目录

Introduction 引言	iv
Photo gallery 剧照精选	v
A Midsummer Night's Dream 《仲夏夜之梦》	
List of characters 人物表	1
Act 1 第 1 幕	3
Act 2 第 2 幕	27
Act 3 第 3 幕	57
Act 4 第 4 幕	101
Act 5 第 5 幕	119
Perspectives and themes 视角与主题	150
The contexts of *A Midsummer Night's Dream* 《仲夏夜之梦》的创作背景	153
Characters 人物分析	156
The language of *A Midsummer Night's Dream* 《仲夏夜之梦》的语言	162
A Midsummer Night's Dream in performance 《仲夏夜之梦》的演出	166
Writing about Shakespeare 笔论莎士比亚	174
Writing about *A Midsummer Night's Dream* 笔论《仲夏夜之梦》	176
William Shakespeare 1564–1616 莎翁年表	178
Acknowledgements 鸣谢	179

Introduction 引言

This *A Midsummer Night's Dream* is part of the **Cambridge School Shakespeare** series. Like every other play in the series, it has been specially prepared to help all students in schools and colleges.

The **Cambridge School Shakespeare** *A Midsummer Night's Dream* aims to be different. It invites you to lift the words from the page and to bring the play to life in your classroom, hall or drama studio. Through enjoyable and focused activities, you will increase your understanding of the play. Actors have created their different interpretations of the play over the centuries. Similarly, you are invited to make up your own mind about *A Midsummer Night's Dream*, rather than having someone else's interpretation handed down to you.

Cambridge School Shakespeare does not offer you a cut-down or simplified version of the play. This is Shakespeare's language, filled with imaginative possibilities. You will find on every left-hand page: a summary of the action, an explanation of unfamiliar words, and a choice of activities on Shakespeare's stagecraft, characters, themes and language.

Between each act, and in the pages at the end of the play, you will find notes, illustrations and activities. These will help to encourage reflection after every act and give you insights into the background and context of the play as a whole.

This edition will be of value to you whether you are studying for an examination, reading for pleasure or thinking of putting on the play to entertain others. You can work on the activities on your own or in groups. Many of the activities suggest a particular group size, but don't be afraid to make up larger or smaller groups to suit your own purposes. Please don't think you have to do every activity: choose those that will help you most.

Although you are invited to treat *A Midsummer Night's Dream* as a play, you don't need special dramatic or theatrical skills to do the activities. By choosing your activities, and by exploring and experimenting, you can make your own interpretations of Shakespeare's language, characters and stories.

Whatever you do, remember that Shakespeare wrote his plays to be acted, watched and enjoyed.

Rex Gibson
Founding editor

This new edition contains more photographs, more diversity and more supporting material than previous editions, whilst remaining true to Rex's original vision. Specifically, it contains more activities and commentary on stagecraft and writing about Shakespeare, to reflect contemporary interest. The glossary has been enlarged, too. Finally, this edition aims to reflect the best teaching and learning possible, and to represent not only Shakespeare through the ages, but also the relevance and excitement of Shakespeare today.

Richard Andrews and Vicki Wienand
Series editors

This edition of *A Midsummer Night's Dream* uses the text of the play established by R.A. Foakes in **The New Cambridge Shakespeare**.

Theseus, Duke of Athens, and Hippolyta, Queen of the Amazons, are anticipating their wedding. Their plans are interrupted by Egeus, who is having a problem with his daughter, Hermia. Egeus wants to marry Hermia to Demetrius, but she is not co-operating because she is in love with Lysander. Egeus appeals to the duke to support him with a legal judgment, and Theseus decides that Hermia must abide by her father's wishes. Her punishment for disobedience will be a death sentence or a lifetime spent in a nunnery (女修道院).

The 'course of true love never did run smooth'. Lysander and Hermia plan to avoid the harsh Athenian law and meet in the wood at night, then to elope (私奔) and marry. Will this solve the problem, or will the jealousy of Demetrius and his ex-love Helena, who plan to follow them, spoil everything?

▼ 'Ill met by moonlight, proud Titania!' The wood is the domain of the fairies, ruled by Oberon and Titania. These powerful beings are in conflict over a changeling boy whom they both wish to have in their service. Their power struggles have reached a critical point, causing a deep rift in their relationship and in the natural world.

▲ The Mechanicals, a group of working men, are rehearsing a play in the wood that night. Their dramatics are decidedly amateur and Puck, Oberon's meddlesome fairy servant, does not think much of them: 'What hempen homespuns have we swaggering here?' Puck mischievously puts an ass's head on Bottom, the individual with the most bravado (外强中干).

◀ Oberon plans to use a magic love potion on Titania as revenge and to make her more compliant. The potion will 'make or man or woman madly dote / Upon the next live creature that it sees'. By this time, the mortal lovers have all arrived in the forest and Oberon has overheard the discord between Helena and Demetrius. Oberon involves Puck in his plan to resolve the lovers' problems.

Newly transformed into an ass and alone in the forest, Bottom sings to raise his spirits. His awful voice wakes Titania, who immediately falls in love with him: 'O, how I love thee! How I dote on thee!'

▲ In attempting to sort out the lovers' tangle with the magic potion, Puck inadvertently makes things worse. Under the influence of the potion, Lysander abandons Hermia and transfers his affections to Helena. Scenes of jealousy, abuse and rage ensue.

▼ 'Lord, what fools these mortals be!' Directors often make the most of the confusion, anger and hurt to present a crazy world in which love has gone badly wrong.

▼ Puck has been instructed by Oberon to put things right with the four lovers, and all their love problems are magically resolved. 'Are you sure / That we are awake? It seems to me / That yet we sleep, we dream.' Hermia and Lysander, Demetrius and Helena, Theseus and Hippolyta all express confusion about the nature of dreams and reality. However, all are to marry and be happy.

▼ 'My Oberon, what visions have I seen!' Titania is awakened by Oberon as he administers a 'herb' on her eyes and she is able to 'See as thou wast want to see.' She looks with horror on the ass she was 'enamoured of' and is happily united with Oberon in love and harmony.

▼ The Mechanicals perform their play about the tragic love of Pyramus and Thisbe at the wedding, with all the seriousness of amateur theatre. To some extent their play is a parody* of the problems faced by the young lovers. Their performance is comic, sad and surreal (怪诞，离奇), providing an opportunity for slapstick (恶搞式) humour. Fantasy and reality continue to merge as the theatre audience observes the onstage audience watching the comic performance.

* *parody* 戏仿，指对一部作品进行借用，以达到调侃、嘲讽甚至致敬的目的，例如周星驰的《大话西游》。

▼ 'This is the silliest stuff that I ever heard.' The audience of newlywed lovers watch the Mechanicals' performance, wide eyed with disbelief.

xi

▼ The performance over, the three couples retire to bed at the end of their wedding day. Oberon and Titania and their attendants arrive to bless the couples with loving marriages and perfect children: 'To the best bride-bed will we, / Which by us shall blessèd be'.

▼ Shakespeare gives Puck the final word. He asks the audience for a round of applause: 'Give me your hands, if we be friends, / And Robin shall restore amends.'

List of characters 人物表

The court 宫廷
HIPPOLYTA /hɪˈpɒlɪtə/ (希炮丽塔) Queen of the Amazons /ˈaməˌzɒn/ (阿玛宗人), engaged to Theseus
THESEUS /ˈθiːsɪəs/ (提修) Duke of Athens, engaged to Hippolyta
EGEUS /ɪˈdʒiːəs/ (伊杰) father of Hermia
PHILOSTRATE /ˈfɪləˌstreɪt/ (菲勒斯垂) master of the revels (狂欢) to the Athenian court

The lovers 恋人
HERMIA /ˈhɑː(r)mɪə/ (哈蜜娅) in love with Lysander
HELENA /ˈhelənə/ (海乐娜) in love with Demetrius
LYSANDER /lɪˈsandə(r)/ (理善德) in love with Hermia
DEMETRIUS /dɪˈmiːtrɪəs/ (迪米垂耶) Egeus's choice as a husband for Hermia

The Mechanicals 工匠
(workers who put on a play)

NICK BOTTOM /nɪk ˈbɒtəm/ (尼克·包臀) a weaver who plays Pyramus /ˈpɪrəməs/ (丕若莫)
PETER QUINCE /ˈpiːtə(r) kwɪns/ (皮特·木棍) a carpenter who speaks the Prologue (开场词)
FRANCIS FLUTE /ˈfransɪs fluːt/ (福冉希·福笛) a bellows-mender who plays Thisbe /ˈθɪzbiː/ (提兹碧)
TOM SNOUT /tɒm snaʊt/ (汤穆·壶嘴) a tinker who plays Wall
ROBIN STARVELING /ˈrɒbɪn ˈstɑː(r)vlɪŋ/ (若宾·麻秆) a tailor who plays Moonshine
SNUG /snʌg/ (榫卯) a joiner (细木匠) who plays Lion

The fairies 仙子
PUCK /pʌk/ (捣蛋精帕克) (or Robin Goodfellow)(也叫好人若宾) Oberon's attendant
OBERON /ˈoːbərɒn/ (欧博让) King of the Fairies
TITANIA /tɪˈtanɪə/ (提坦妮娅) Queen of the Fairies
PEASEBLOSSOM /ˈpiːzˌblɒsəm/ (豌豆花)
COBWEB /ˈkɒbweb/ (蛛网)
MOTH /mɒθ/ (飞蛾)
MUSTARDSEED /ˈmʌstə(r)dˌsiːd/ (芥菜籽)
} Titania's fairy attendants
A FAIRY (仙子) in Titania's service

Hippolyta and Theseus have been at war and are now to marry to cement the new peace. Theseus regrets that time is moving slowly before he can marry Hippolyta, and orders preparations for their wedding.

 剧情简介：希袍丽塔与提修曾有过大战，如今二人将用婚姻来巩固新的和平。提修不甘度日如年般等着迎娶希袍丽塔，于是下令准备婚礼。

Stagecraft 导演技巧
Theseus and Hippolyta

Shakespeare chooses to use two characters from a myth that was well known in his day. Theseus, Duke of Athens, fought a battle with the Amazons (a group of warrior women) and then married Hippolyta, their queen. The opening scene of the play is set in Athens, in Theseus's palace.

Imagine you are planning to direct a performance of *A Midsummer Night's Dream*. Start your own Director's Journal and record your ideas as you go through the play. For this opening scene, consider the following questions:

- How do you want the stage to look as the curtain rises and members of the audience get their first glimpse of this world?
- How would you position your two actors? Think about their relationship, their past and the impact you want their first appearance to have on the audience.

1	nuptial hour	婚礼的时刻
2	Draws on apace	很快到来
3	wanes	（月）亏
4	Like to = Like	
5	step-dame	继母
6	dowager	有遗产的寡妇
7	revenue	财富
8	steep	潜入，没入
9	solemnities	正式典礼
10	pert	欢快
11	pale companion	灰白脸的伙计（指melancholy [忧郁]）
12	pomp	庆典
13	key	基调
14	triumph	欢庆
15	revelling	狂欢

1 Key words and images (in pairs)

Write down key words and images in lines 1–19 and look for patterns (such as those to do with the moon, or 'slow' versus 'quickly'). These patterns and the discussion between Theseus and Hippolyta give an idea of what the play is about.

a Make a list of what you consider to be the three most important words or phrases that Theseus uses, while your partner chooses Hippolyta's key words or phrases. Share your ideas and then write a few sentences describing what they reveal about the characters and their situation.

b With your partner, try to predict what might happen in the play. Consider how imagery and symbolism (see pp. 162–4) could foreshadow (预示) events.

Write about it 写作练习
The moon, the night and dreams

Think about the title of the play and the focus on the moon, night and dreams in the opening speeches. Write two or three paragraphs on the emotions, associations and ideas that this imagery evokes for you.

A Midsummer Night's Dream

Act 1 Scene 1
Athens Theseus' palace

Enter THESEUS, HIPPOLYTA, PHILOSTRATE, *with others.*

THESEUS
Now, fair Hippolyta, our nuptial hour[1]
Draws on apace[2]; four happy days bring in
Another moon – but O, methinks, how slow
This old moon wanes[3]! She lingers my desires,
Like to[4] a step-dame[5] or a dowager[6]   5
Long withering out a young man's revenue[7].

HIPPOLYTA
Four days will quickly steep[8] themselves in night;
Four nights will quickly dream away the time;
And then the moon, like to a silver bow
New bent in heaven, shall behold the night   10
Of our solemnities[9].

THESEUS
                Go, Philostrate,
Stir up the Athenian youth to merriments,
Awake the pert[10] and nimble spirit of mirth;
Turn melancholy forth to funerals;
The pale companion[11] is not for our pomp[12].   15

                                                          [Exit Philostrate]

Hippolyta, I wooed thee with my sword,
And won thy love doing thee injuries;
But I will wed thee in another key[13],
With pomp, with triumph[14], and with revelling[15].

Egeus enters with his daughter Hermia and her two suitors, Lysander (whom she loves) and Demetrius (whom she dislikes). He appeals to Theseus to support his right to decide between them.

 剧情简介：伊杰携女儿哈蜜娅及其两位追求者，即理善德（女儿所爱的）和迪米垂耶（女儿所不爱的）一同登场。伊杰恳请提修赞同他有权为女儿择婿。

1 What kind of father? (in fours)

Is Egeus being totally unreasonable, or is he a responsible Athenian father who is justifiably taking control of Hermia's future and choices? Let one member of your group become Egeus, and the others form a 'court' of justice. Each member of the 'court' prepares one question to ask Egeus, who can then defend and explain himself.

▶ Hippolyta listens intently to Egeus's complaint and watches Hermia's response; she does not speak, but her face is expressive. What might she be thinking? Prepare her thoughts in note form. Then practise these ideas as a monologue (独白). Try voicing them in character to the class.

1 renownèd　声名赫赫
2 vexation　烦恼，恼怒
3 bewitched　迷惑
4 interchanged　彼此交换
5 feigning　虚假
6 stolen … fantasy　偷走了她一片痴情
7 gauds, conceits　不值钱的花哨玩意儿
8 Knacks　哄人的小玩意儿
9 nosegays　花束
10 sweetmeats　甜点
11 prevailment　影响力
12 filched　偷窃
13 Be it so　如果是这样
14 Immediately　明确

Language in the play 剧中语言

Language of love (in pairs)

Egeus uses very different language from Theseus and Hippolyta to present love. In pairs, pick out five words that show his attitudes and describe an alternative picture of love from that painted by Hippolyta and Theseus at the start of the scene.

A Midsummer Night's Dream Act 1 Scene 1
仲夏夜之梦

Enter EGEUS *and his daughter* HERMIA, LYSANDER *and* DEMETRIUS.

EGEUS	Happy be Theseus, our renownèd[1] Duke!	20
THESEUS	Thanks, good Egeus. What's the news with thee?	
EGEUS	Full of vexation[2] come I, with complaint	
	Against my child, my daughter Hermia.	
	Stand forth, Demetrius! – My noble lord,	
	This man hath my consent to marry her.	25
	Stand forth, Lysander! – And, my gracious Duke,	
	This man hath bewitched[3] the bosom of my child.	
	Thou, thou, Lysander, thou hast given her rhymes,	
	And interchanged[4] love-tokens with my child.	
	Thou hast by moonlight at her window sung	30
	With feigning[5] voice verses of feigning love,	
	And stolen the impression of her fantasy[6],	
	With bracelets of thy hair, rings, gauds, conceits[7],	
	Knacks[8], trifles, nosegays[9], sweetmeats[10] – messengers	
	Of strong prevailment[11] in unhardened youth;	35
	With cunning hast thou filched[12] my daughter's heart,	
	Turned her obedience, which is due to me,	
	To stubborn harshness. And, my gracious Duke,	
	Be it so[13] she will not here, before your grace,	
	Consent to marry with Demetrius,	40
	I beg the ancient privilege of Athens;	
	As she is mine, I may dispose of her;	
	Which shall be either to this gentleman	
	Or to her death, according to our law	
	Immediately[14] provided in that case.	45

Hermia pleads to be allowed to choose Lysander for a husband. Theseus warns her to abide by Egeus's decision, otherwise she risks being sent to a convent or to her death.

 剧情简介：哈蜜娅恳求允许她选理善德做丈夫。提修告诫她，要服从伊杰的决定，否则她将陷入危险，要么被送至修道院，要么被处死。

Themes 主题分析
Gender and power (in pairs)

The themes of conflict, power and gender are beginning to emerge.

a Who is the most powerful character at this point in the play? Where do our sympathies lie, and why?

b In what ways would life for men and women, and the nature of their relationship, have been different in 1594 (when this play was written) from today? With a partner, draw up a list of your ideas and consider if Shakespeare's contemporaries would have approved of Hermia's confidence in the defence of her choice. Be prepared to share your ideas with the class.

1 Sisterhood

Hermia stands up for herself as a lone female figure, surrounded by squabbling men. Yet she is not alone: Hippolyta, the other female on the stage, says nothing. Why? What is she thinking? Shakespeare has decided to leave her silent. As director, would you have some recognition pass between Hermia and Hippolyta? If so, suggest how it would be done.

Language in the play 剧中语言
Close analysis

HERMIA *I would my father looked but with my eyes.*
THESEUS *Rather your eyes must with his judgement look.*

Write out these quotations at the centre of a blank sheet of paper, and then make brief notes on your analysis of:

- how language is being used
- how character is being developed
- which themes are being explored.

2 Male dominance (in fours)

Already there has been a 'forced' engagement. Go through the play so far, finding any images, **similes** (明喻) and **metaphors** (隐喻) (see p. 164) that imply male dominance – for example, 'your father should be as a god' (line 47). Read the images about males, then those about females, and say which you find acceptable and which you find offensive – and why.

1 imprinted 塑造
2 leave 放过
3 wanting 没有，缺少
4 entreat 请求
5 modesty 节操
6 beseech 恳求
7 befall 降临
8 abjure 放弃
9 the society of men 与男子的来往
10 blood 血性
11 livery 装束（修女的道袍；泛指修道院的规矩）
12 For aye = For ever
13 cloister 回廊
14 mewed 禁闭的
15 barren sister 没有子嗣的修女
16 distilled 提炼过（喻指已婚女子）
17 Ere = Before （此处表示否定，即"也不愿"）
18 unwishèd yoke 不情愿的婚配
19 sovereignty 自主权

THESEUS	What say you, Hermia? Be advised, fair maid.
	To you your father should be as a god,
	One that composed your beauties; yea, and one
	To whom you are but as a form in wax
	By him imprinted[1], and within his power 50
	To leave[2] the figure, or disfigure it.
	Demetrius is a worthy gentleman.
HERMIA	So is Lysander.
THESEUS	In himself he is;
	But in this kind, wanting[3] your father's voice,
	The other must be held the worthier. 55
HERMIA	I would my father looked but with my eyes.
THESEUS	Rather your eyes must with his judgement look.
HERMIA	I do entreat[4] your grace to pardon me.
	I know not by what power I am made bold,
	Nor how it may concern my modesty[5] 60
	In such a presence here to plead my thoughts;
	But I beseech[6] your grace that I may know
	The worst that may befall[7] me in this case,
	If I refuse to wed Demetrius.
THESEUS	Either to die the death, or to abjure[8] 65
	For ever the society of men[9].
	Therefore, fair Hermia, question your desires,
	Know of your youth, examine well your blood[10],
	Whether, if you yield not to your father's choice,
	You can endure the livery[11] of a nun, 70
	For aye[12] to be in shady cloister[13] mewed[14],
	To live a barren sister[15] all your life,
	Chanting faint hymns to the cold fruitless moon.
	Thrice blessèd they that master so their blood
	To undergo such maiden pilgrimage; 75
	But earthlier happy is the rose distilled[16]
	Than that which, withering on the virgin thorn,
	Grows, lives, and dies in single blessedness.
HERMIA	So will I grow, so live, so die, my lord,
	Ere[17] I will yield my virgin patent up 80
	Unto his lordship, whose unwishèd yoke[18]
	My soul consents not to give sovereignty[19].

Theseus orders Hermia to make her decision before his wedding to Hippolyta. Lysander argues his case and points out that Demetrius loved Helena before Hermia, and that Helena still loves Demetrius.

剧情简介：提修命令哈蜜娅必须在他与希炮丽塔举办婚礼之前做出决定。理善德为此辩解，指出迪米垂耶先是向海乐娜求爱，然后又移情别恋哈蜜娅，而海乐娜仍爱着迪米垂耶。

1 Hermia's dilemma – what would you do? (in pairs)

Would you rather die or be imprisoned than marry someone you disliked? (Assume there is no possibility of divorce.) Give reasons for your reply. Make notes on your ideas and then write them up as a paragraph of structured argument. Share your paragraph with a partner.

Themes 主题分析
Reality and illusion (in pairs)

When Hermia says 'I would my father looked but with my eyes' (line 56), she means that she wishes Egeus could 'see' Lysander as she sees him. The people watching 'see' the debates in this scene very differently.

One of you makes notes about where the sympathies of a Shakespearean audience might lie in this situation. The other makes notes on where a modern audience's sympathies may be. Compare your notes and discuss the different perspectives.

2 'Love' and 'dote' (迷恋) (in small groups)

There has been a good deal of talk about feelings. Talk with your group about which characters are sensitive to others' feelings, and which are not. Compile a list of all the words and phrases so far that describe or explore emotion.

Characters 人物分析
Lysander

Lysander is beginning to emerge as an interesting character. Consider his response to Demetrius in lines 93–4:

> *You have her father's love, Demetrius;*
> *Let me have Hermia's – do you marry him.*

How do these lines help us to understand Lysander's character? How would you advise an actor to play them? Write some briefing ideas for an actor who has been cast in the role of Lysander. (For more information on Lysander, see p. 160.)

1	pause	三思
2	sealing-day	婚礼日
3	betwixt	= between
4	Diana	荻阿娜（月亮和狩猎女神，也象征着贞节）
5	austerity	严格自律，禁欲
6	Relent	屈从吧
7	crazèd title	疯癫的名号
8	estate unto	授予
9	as well-derived	出身同样高贵
10	well-possessed	富有
11	with vantage	更胜一等
12	prosecute	行使
13	avouch	证实，发誓
14	to his head	当着他的面
15	in idolatry	像崇拜偶像般
16	spotted	（道德上）劣迹斑斑

THESEUS	Take time to pause¹, and by the next new moon,	
	The sealing-day² betwixt³ my love and me	
	For everlasting bond of fellowship,	85
	Upon that day either prepare to die	
	For disobedience to your father's will,	
	Or else to wed Demetrius, as he would,	
	Or on Diana's⁴ altar to protest	
	For aye austerity⁵ and single life.	90
DEMETRIUS	Relent⁶, sweet Hermia; and, Lysander, yield	
	Thy crazèd title⁷ to my certain right.	
LYSANDER	You have her father's love, Demetrius;	
	Let me have Hermia's – do you marry him.	
EGEUS	Scornful Lysander, true, he hath my love,	95
	And what is mine my love shall render him;	
	And she is mine, and all my right of her	
	I do estate unto⁸ Demetrius.	
LYSANDER	I am, my lord, as well-derived⁹ as he,	
	As well-possessed¹⁰: my love is more than his,	100
	My fortunes every way as fairly ranked,	
	If not with vantage¹¹, as Demetrius';	
	And, which is more than all these boasts can be,	
	I am beloved of beauteous Hermia.	
	Why should not I then prosecute¹² my right?	105
	Demetrius, I'll avouch¹³ it to his head¹⁴,	
	Made love to Nedar's daughter, Helena,	
	And won her soul; and she, sweet lady, dotes,	
	Devoutly dotes, dotes in idolatry¹⁵,	
	Upon this spotted¹⁶ and inconstant man.	110

With a final warning to Hermia, Theseus takes Demetrius and Egeus away to talk to them. Left alone, Lysander and Hermia lament the problems of lovers.

 剧情简介：提修向哈蜜娅发出最后警告，随后领着迪米垂耶和伊杰到别处商谈。只剩下理善德和哈蜜娅在哀叹天下有情人的各种苦恼。

Language in the play 剧中语言
Love, 'short as any dream' (whole class)

a In lines 141–9, Lysander paints love as a temporary thing: 'momentany' (momentary), 'Swift', 'short', 'Brief', surrounded by a hostile world. Talk about what he compares love to, and whether you think the comparisons are suitable.

b Lysander connects love with sinister (险恶) imagery of 'collied night' and 'The jaws of darkness'. Why do you think this is? He is, after all, a man in love. Do you agree with him? Does love always have a shadowy, dark side? Reflect on your response to these questions. Make brief notes and then share your ideas in a class discussion.

Themes 主题分析
'The course of true love never did run smooth' (in small groups)

Line 134 has become a commonplace saying. How true is it? Think about what it might suggest about the rest of the play. Make a list of movies, novels, poems and TV series that explore this theme. Then update your list with ideas from everyone in your group. See which group in the class can compile the longest list.

1 private schooling 个别辅导
2 fancies 心愿
3 yields you up 迫使您服从
4 extenuate 缓和，减轻
5 what cheer 你还好吧？
6 Against 为了准备
7 nearly 密切
8 *Exeunt* （剧本中的说明，两个以上演员）退场，下场
9 Belike 可能
10 Beteem 赠予，给予
11 tempest of my eyes 暴风雨般的泪水
12 aught = anything
13 blood 血统，家世背景
14 enthralled 束缚
15 misgraffèd 不相称，不合
16 sympathy 共情，心心相印
17 momentany = momentary （转瞬即逝）
18 collied 炭黑
19 spleen 发脾气
20 confusion 毁灭

1 The dance of the lovers – who loves whom? (I)

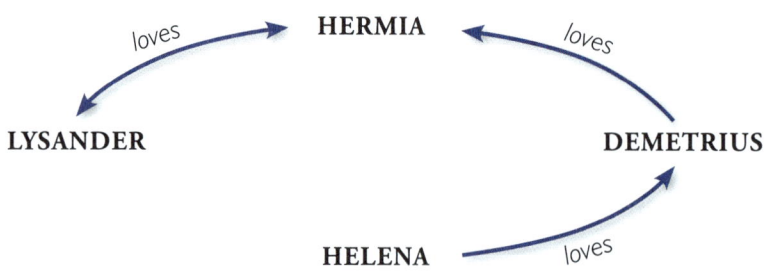

▲ Discuss this diagram with a partner, then individually write a brief description of what it shows.

A Midsummer Night's Dream Act 1 Scene 1
仲夏夜之梦

THESEUS	I must confess that I have heard so much,
	And with Demetrius thought to have spoke thereof;
	But, being overfull of self-affairs,
	My mind did lose it. But Demetrius, come,
	And come, Egeus. You shall go with me; 115
	I have some private schooling[1] for you both.
	For you, fair Hermia, look you arm yourself
	To fit your fancies[2] to your father's will;
	Or else the law of Athens yields you up[3]
	(Which by no means we may extenuate[4]) 120
	To death, or to a vow of single life.
	Come, my Hippolyta; what cheer[5], my love?
	Demetrius and Egeus, go along;
	I must employ you in some business
	Against[6] our nuptial, and confer with you 125
	Of something nearly[7] that concerns yourselves.
EGEUS	With duty and desire we follow you.

Exeunt[8] all but Lysander and Hermia

LYSANDER	How now, my love? Why is your cheek so pale?
	How chance the roses there do fade so fast?
HERMIA	Belike[9] for want of rain, which I could well 130
	Beteem[10] them from the tempest of my eyes[11].
LYSANDER	Ay me! For aught[12] that I could ever read,
	Could ever hear by tale or history,
	The course of true love never did run smooth;
	But either it was different in blood[13] – 135
HERMIA	O cross! too high to be enthralled[14] to low.
LYSANDER	Or else misgraffed[15] in respect of years –
HERMIA	O spite! too old to be engaged to young.
LYSANDER	Or else it stood upon the choice of friends –
HERMIA	O hell, to choose love by another's eyes! 140
LYSANDER	Or, if there were a sympathy[16] in choice,
	War, death, or sickness did lay siege to it,
	Making it momentany[17] as a sound,
	Swift as a shadow, short as any dream,
	Brief as the lightning in the collied[18] night, 145
	That in a spleen[19] unfolds both heaven and earth,
	And, ere a man hath power to say 'Behold!',
	The jaws of darkness do devour it up.
	So quick bright things come to confusion[20].

Lysander and Hermia plan to elope: to run away to Lysander's widowed aunt who lives beyond the reach of the Athenian law. They arrange to meet 'tomorrow night' in the wood outside the city.

 剧情简介：理善德与哈蜜娅计划私奔：逃往理善德的寡居姑母家，姑母的住处超出了雅典法律的管理范围。他俩准备"明晚"在城外树林会合。

1 How old? (in threes)

Because of their behaviour, perhaps Shakespeare is suggesting that the lovers are very young (remember that Juliet in *Romeo and Juliet* was not quite fourteen). Suggest how old you think Hermia, Lysander and Demetrius are. Consequently, how old are Theseus and Hippolyta? Give reasons for your opinions.

1 crossed 挫折，阻挠
2 edict 法令，判决
3 fancy's followers 随爱而来的结果
4 persuasion 见解
5 leagues 里格（1里格约为3英里）
6 respects me 视我（为）
7 without 在……之外
8 do observance 庆祝过……节
9 morn of May 五月节（英格兰传统节日）早上
10 simplicity 纯洁，真诚
11 doves （鸽子代表爱与忠诚）
12 Carthage queen 迦太基女王（即荻朵 [Dido]，与特洛伊王子埃涅阿斯 [Aeneas，即下文的 false Trojan] 相爱，后者弃她扬帆而去，致使她悲痛过度自焚而死）

Language in the play 剧中语言

What do lovers dream? (in pairs)

Hermia speaks of features of love ('fancy's followers') such as thoughts and wishes and dreams. Talk with a partner about what sort of dreams lovers have (being together, freedom from restrictions, happiness, sex, and so on). Hermia also swears oaths by the goddess of love (Venus) and other lovers (Dido, Queen of Carthage, who loved Aeneas, the false Trojan). For Hermia, love is like a dream in which she lives all the time. With your partner, analyse your favourite quotation from Hermia on this page. Then write down your ideas about the following questions:

- Is this what love is like?
- Are people who are in love inhabiting a dream world?
- Is love a fantasy or a reality?

Share your ideas with another pair.

HERMIA	If then true lovers have been ever crossed[1]	150
	It stands as an edict[2] in destiny.	
	Then let us teach our trial patience,	
	Because it is a customary cross,	
	As due to love as thoughts, and dreams, and sighs,	
	Wishes, and tears – poor fancy's followers[3].	155
LYSANDER	A good persuasion[4]. Therefore hear me, Hermia:	
	I have a widow aunt, a dowager,	
	Of great revenue, and she hath no child.	
	From Athens is her house remote seven leagues[5];	
	And she respects me[6] as her only son.	160
	There, gentle Hermia, may I marry thee;	
	And to that place the sharp Athenian law	
	Cannot pursue us. If thou lov'st me, then	
	Steal forth thy father's house tomorrow night,	
	And in the wood, a league without[7] the town	165
	(Where I did meet thee once with Helena	
	To do observance[8] to a morn of May[9]),	
	There will I stay for thee.	
HERMIA	My good Lysander,	
	I swear to thee by Cupid's strongest bow,	
	By his best arrow with the golden head,	170
	By the simplicity[10] of Venus' doves[11],	
	By that which knitteth souls and prospers loves,	
	And by that fire which burned the Carthage queen[12]	
	When the false Trojan under sail was seen,	
	By all the vows that ever men have broke	175
	(In number more than ever women spoke),	
	In that same place thou hast appointed me,	
	Tomorrow truly will I meet with thee.	
LYSANDER	Keep promise, love. Look, here comes Helena.	

Helena enters and talks of Demetrius's love for Hermia. She wishes she were like Hermia. To console her, Hermia and Lysander tell her of their plan to elope.

 剧情简介：海乐娜上场，诉说着迪米垂耶对哈蜜娅的爱慕，她多么希望自己就是哈蜜娅。为了安抚海乐娜，哈蜜娅和理善德将他俩要私奔的计划告知海乐娜。

1 What do you make of Helena? (in pairs)

a Read through Helena's and Hermia's lines 180–207, then identify key words and phrases that reveal Helena's character. Act out the dialogue with your partner, emphasising those key words and phrases.

b What is your first impression of Helena? From her opening speeches, describe her character in three words.

2 How might it end?

Shakespeare has set up an extremely difficult situation for his lovers (remember that Helena is in love too, though it is unrequited). If the play is a Shakespearean comedy, in the sense that there is a happy ending for all the lovers (see p. 150), it's difficult to see how the situation will be resolved. Invent a plotline that might bring all the couples together at the end.

Language in the play 剧中语言
Patterns of language

Look at the 'Language' section on pages 162–5, which describes some of the language features in the play. Use this information to write notes on the patterns of language in lines 180–207. Consider the effects of **blank verse** (素体诗), imagery, simile and metaphor. Find examples of devices such as repetition of words or sounds, **juxtapositions** (并置)(the placement of contrasting words or ideas next to each other), romantic **diction** (choice of words) and classical **allusions** (典故)(see p. 153). What do these patterns suggest about the relationship between Helena and Hermia?

Themes 主题分析
Change and translation

Shakespeare introduces the theme of change and the idea of being 'translated' when (in lines 192–3) Helena pleads with Hermia to:

> teach me how you look, and with what art
> You sway the motion of Demetrius' heart.

This becomes an increasingly important theme, so look out for further exploration of these ideas as you progress through the play. Have there been any changes or translations already?

---

1 God speed （告别语）上帝保佑你（也暗含对speed的文字游戏：海乐娜正巧撞见他俩，正欲快速躲开）
2 Whither away? 你去哪里？
3 fair 美丽
4 lodestars 北斗星
5 air 曲调
6 catching 传染
7 favour 美貌
8 tongue's sweet melody 声音，旋律
9 bated 除外（与baited谐音）
10 fly = flee（逃跑，逃离）
11 graces 幸运的、天佑的特质
12 Phoebe 福碧（希腊神话中的月亮女神，即获阿娜；见第8页注解4）
13 visage 面容

A Midsummer Night's Dream Act 1 Scene 1
仲夏夜之梦

Enter HELENA.

HERMIA	God speed[1], fair Helena! Whither away?[2]	180
HELENA	Call you me fair[3]? That 'fair' again unsay.	
	Demetrius loves your fair: O happy fair!	
	Your eyes are lodestars[4], and your tongue's sweet air[5]	
	More tuneable than lark to shepherd's ear	
	When wheat is green, when hawthorn buds appear.	185
	Sickness is catching[6]. O, were favour[7] so,	
	Yours would I catch, fair Hermia, ere I go;	
	My ear should catch your voice, my eye your eye,	
	My tongue should catch your tongue's sweet melody[8].	
	Were the world mine, Demetrius being bated[9],	190
	The rest I'd give to be to you translated.	
	O, teach me how you look, and with what art	
	You sway the motion of Demetrius' heart.	
HERMIA	I frown upon him; yet he loves me still.	
HELENA	O that your frowns would teach my smiles such skill!	195
HERMIA	I give him curses; yet he gives me love.	
HELENA	O that my prayers could such affection move!	
HERMIA	The more I hate, the more he follows me.	
HELENA	The more I love, the more he hateth me.	
HERMIA	His folly, Helena, is no fault of mine.	200
HELENA	None but your beauty; would that fault were mine!	
HERMIA	Take comfort: he no more shall see my face;	
	Lysander and myself will fly[10] this place.	
	Before the time I did Lysander see,	
	Seemed Athens as a paradise to me.	205
	O then, what graces[11] in my love do dwell,	
	That he hath turned a heaven unto a hell?	
LYSANDER	Helen, to you our minds we will unfold:	
	Tomorrow night, when Phoebe[12] doth behold	
	Her silver visage[13] in the watery glass,	210
	Decking with liquid pearl the bladed grass	
	(A time that lovers' flights doth still conceal),	
	Through Athens' gates have we devised to steal.	

Hermia and Lysander leave, wishing Helena luck with Demetrius. Helena reflects on the transforming and deceiving nature of love, and decides to tell Demetrius of the elopement in order to win his thanks.

剧情简介：哈蜜娅和理善德离开，临别时祝福海乐娜从迪米垂耶那里有好运。海乐娜省悟到爱情的本质不过是善变和欺骗，于是决定告诉迪米垂耶私奔之事，以赢取迪米垂耶对自己的感恩。

Write about it 写作练习

Your view of the lovers (in fours)

Each group member chooses one of the four lovers.

a Individually, write a paragraph on your character, analysing what you consider to be their most important or powerful quotation so far. In turn, read your paragraphs aloud to your group.

b Together, reach a consensus. How are the lovers different or similar? Which one do you like best (and least)? Who speaks most convincingly about love? Share the group's consensus with the class.

1 Love – 'winged Cupid' – Helena's view
(in small groups)

Helena explains what she thinks of love in lines 232–9, using the comparison of Cupid (the mythical god of love, a young child with wings, who was sometimes presented as being blind).
Helena says, in lines 234–5:

> Love looks not with the eyes, but with the mind,
> And therefore is winged Cupid painted blind.

Shakespeare is exploring some interesting and complex ideas here in relation to love. Why do you think Cupid has become a symbol of love? Is the mind more important than the eyes when in love? In what ways could love be said to make a person blind? Talk about these questions with your group in preparation for a class discussion.

1 were wont 过去经常
2 counsel sweet 贴心话
3 Keep word 信守诺言，保持忠诚
4 adieu 再见
5 How … be! 一些人比起另一些人是多么幸福啊！(o'er = over)
6 holding no quantity 没有价值，一无是处
7 transpose 改变
8 Things … dignity = Love can transpose things base and vile to form and dignity (form在这里的意思是"美貌")
9 figure 象征
10 unheedy 鲁莽
11 oft = often
12 beguiled 被哄骗
13 waggish 顽皮淘气
14 game 游戏
15 forswear 许空愿
16 perjured 被做伪证
17 eyne = eyes
18 intelligence 消息
19 dear expense 高昂的代价
20 thither = to or towards that place

HERMIA	And in the wood, where often you and I	
	Upon faint primrose beds were wont[1] to lie,	215
	Emptying our bosoms of their counsel sweet[2],	
	There my Lysander and myself shall meet,	
	And thence from Athens turn away our eyes	
	To seek new friends and stranger companies.	
	Farewell, sweet playfellow; pray thou for us,	220
	And good luck grant thee thy Demetrius.	
	Keep word[3], Lysander; we must starve our sight	
	From lovers' food till morrow deep midnight.	
LYSANDER	I will, my Hermia.	
		Exit Hermia
	Helena, adieu[4]!	
	As you on him, Demetrius dote on you.	*Exit Lysander* 225
HELENA	How happy some o'er other some can be![5]	
	Through Athens I am thought as fair as she.	
	But what of that? Demetrius thinks not so;	
	He will not know what all but he do know.	
	And as he errs, doting on Hermia's eyes,	230
	So I, admiring of his qualities.	
	Things base and vile, holding no quantity[6],	
	Love can transpose[7] to form and dignity[8].	
	Love looks not with the eyes, but with the mind,	
	And therefore is winged Cupid painted blind.	235
	Nor hath love's mind of any judgement taste;	
	Wings, and no eyes, figure[9] unheedy[10] haste;	
	And therefore is love said to be a child	
	Because in choice he is so oft[11] beguiled[12].	
	As waggish[13] boys in game[14] themselves forswear[15],	240
	So the boy Love is perjured[16] everywhere;	
	For, ere Demetrius looked on Hermia's eyne[17],	
	He hailed down oaths that he was only mine,	
	And when this hail some heat from Hermia felt,	
	So he dissolved, and showers of oaths did melt.	245
	I will go tell him of fair Hermia's flight:	
	Then to the wood will he, tomorrow night,	
	Pursue her; and for this intelligence[18],	
	If I have thanks it is a dear expense[19];	
	But herein mean I to enrich my pain,	250
	To have his sight thither[20], and back again.	*Exit*

A group of workers (the Mechanicals) – Quince, Snug, Bottom, Flute, Snout and Starveling – meet to allocate the parts for a play, which they hope to perform at Duke Theseus's wedding.

剧情简介：一群工匠——木棍、榫卯、包臀、福笛、壶嘴和麻秆——聚在一起分派一出戏的角色，他们希望能在提修大公的婚礼上表演这出戏。

1 Who have we here? (in sixes)

To gain an impression of the Mechanicals, take a character each and act out the whole scene. Then work on one or both of the following activities.

Characters 人物分析
The Mechanicals (in sixes)

Shakespeare gives these characters distinctive names and trades. Consider how the name and trade of each helps establish character. Choose a character and work for a little while on your own, reading your character's lines and thinking about how to develop your part. Come back together in your group to act out this scene again.

Stagecraft 导演技巧
The court and the workmen (in small groups)

The Mechanicals provide a real contrast with the mythical court of Athens, if only because they are so clearly of Shakespeare's time and place.

a In your group, talk about the differences between the court and the workmen, and why Shakespeare might have included the Mechanicals and their very different world.

b How could you reveal this different world on stage? Consider the choices a set and costume designer, a lighting engineer and an actor might make. Write your ideas in your Director's Journal.

1 scrip = script （脚本）
2 interlude 幕间表演的滑稽短剧
3 treats on 是关于
4 grow to a point 进入正题，言归正传
5 Marry 圣母马利亚在上（一种温和的赌咒语）
6 lamentable 悲惨，痛苦
7 Pyramus and Thisbe 丕若莫和提兹碧（希腊神话中，女孩提兹碧家住巴比伦，与隔壁男孩丕若莫透过墙缝相爱，因父母阻挠，最后二人殉情而死）
8 look to their eyes 当心他们的眼睛，别哭坏了
9 condole 表现出伤感
10 To the rest 接着说吧
11 chief humour 主要的性情、偏好
12 Ercles （Ercles是Hercules[赫丘力]的不标准读音；赫丘力是希腊神话中的大力神）
13 rarely 精彩地
14 to tear a cat in "撕裂一只猫"为莎士比亚时代戏剧中的习语，意为"大声嚷嚷，咆哮"，泛指暴力的肢体动作（包臀适合表演什么类型的角色、什么类型的戏？）
15 make all split 扮演鲁莽咆哮的角色
16 Phibbus （Phibbus是Phoebus[福玻斯]的讹变；福玻斯是罗马神话中太阳神阿波罗的别称[包臀又搞错名字]，太阳神每天驾马车[car]驶过天空，给世界带来光明）
17 mar 玷污，破坏

A Midsummer Night's Dream Act 1 Scene 2

仲夏夜之梦

Act 1 Scene 2
Athens

Enter QUINCE *the Carpenter, and* SNUG *the Joiner, and* BOTTOM *the Weaver, and* FLUTE *the Bellows-mender, and* SNOUT *the Tinker and* STARVELING *the Tailor.*

QUINCE Is all our company here?
BOTTOM You were best to call them generally, man by man, according to the scrip[1].
QUINCE Here is the scroll of every man's name which is thought fit through all Athens to play in our interlude[2] before the Duke and the Duchess on his wedding day at night.
BOTTOM First, good Peter Quince, say what the play treats on[3]; then read the names of the actors; and so grow to a point[4].
QUINCE Marry[5], our play is 'The most lamentable[6] comedy and most cruel death of Pyramus and Thisbe[7]'.
BOTTOM A very good piece of work, I assure you, and a merry. Now, good Peter Quince, call forth your actors by the scroll. Masters, spread yourselves.
QUINCE Answer as I call you. Nick Bottom, the weaver?
BOTTOM Ready. Name what part I am for, and proceed.
QUINCE You, Nick Bottom, are set down for Pyramus.
BOTTOM What is Pyramus? A lover or a tyrant?
QUINCE A lover that kills himself, most gallant, for love.
BOTTOM That will ask some tears in the true performing of it. If I do it, let the audience look to their eyes[8]: I will move storms, I will condole[9], in some measure. To the rest[10] – yet my chief humour[11] is for a tyrant. I could play Ercles[12] rarely[13], or a part to tear a cat in[14], to make all split[15]:

    The raging rocks
    And shivering shocks
    Shall break the locks
      Of prison gates,
    And Phibbus'[16] car
    Shall shine from far,
    And make and mar[17]
      The foolish Fates.

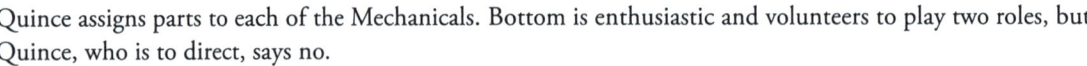

Quince assigns parts to each of the Mechanicals. Bottom is enthusiastic and volunteers to play two roles, but Quince, who is to direct, says no.

剧情简介：木棍给每位工匠分派角色。包臀兴奋不已，自告奋勇要分饰两角，但是导演木棍不同意。

Stagecraft 导演技巧

Physical and verbal humour (in pairs)

How would you direct this scene to make the most of the comic opportunities? Consider the following:

- **'a monstrous little voice'** The problem of Flute playing a woman (lines 36–44) is partly solved, so the Mechanicals believe, by Flute speaking in a high-pitched voice. How could voice, manner and gesture produce comedy?
- **'let not me play a woman'** On Shakespeare's stage, all the actors were male. How could you make the most of the comic value of a man playing a woman?
- **'I have a beard coming'** Flute could be played by a young actor who has not yet started shaving, or an actor with a beard who is using this excuse to avoid playing the part. Consider which would be the most amusing for the audience. Do you have any other suggestions on how to make this line funny?
- **'they would shriek'** The Mechanicals seem to think that if Bottom played the lion's part he would frighten the women in the audience. They clearly have very little experience of acting. Suggest how you would make their amateur attempts humorous.

Write your ideas on all these points in your Director's Journal.

1	Ercles' vein	赫丘力的风格
2	condoling	感人
3	That's a all one	完全是一回事
4	small	嗓音尖细，音调高
5	fitted	定形了，角色分配完毕

Themes 主题分析

More transformations (in fours)

The Mechanicals are attempting to transform themselves into actors playing classical characters. Flute has to pretend to be a woman. This is very much a play about change. For the audience, Shakespeare has transformed the setting from a court, with a duke and a queen, into a wood with a comical group of workers.

a Speak the Mechanicals' dialogue in a way that will highlight this change. For example, you could experiment with different accents. The Mechanicals' lines are written in prose (散文；散体) and the court speeches in poetry. How would this sound different for the audience? Again, play with tone and emphasis.

b Watch out for more transformations as the play progresses, and make a note of each one you spot.

	This was lofty. Now name the rest of the players. – This is Ercles' vein[1], a tyrant's vein; a lover is more condoling[2].
QUINCE	Francis Flute, the bellows-mender?
FLUTE	Here, Peter Quince.
QUINCE	Flute, you must take Thisbe on you.
FLUTE	What is Thisbe? A wandering knight?
QUINCE	It is the lady that Pyramus must love.
FLUTE	Nay, faith, let not me play a woman: I have a beard coming.
QUINCE	That's all one[3]: you shall play it in a mask, and you may speak as small[4] as you will.
BOTTOM	And I may hide my face, let me play Thisbe too. I'll speak in a monstrous little voice: 'Thisne, Thisne!' – 'Ah, Pyramus, my lover dear; thy Thisbe dear, and lady dear.'
QUINCE	No, no; you must play Pyramus; and Flute, you Thisbe.
BOTTOM	Well, proceed.
QUINCE	Robin Starveling, the tailor?
STARVELING	Here, Peter Quince.
QUINCE	Robin Starveling, you must play Thisbe's mother. Tom Snout, the tinker?
SNOUT	Here, Peter Quince.
QUINCE	You, Pyramus' father; myself, Thisbe's father; Snug, the joiner, you the lion's part; and I hope here is a play fitted[5].

Quince completes the arrangements for the play, despite Bottom's interruptions. They plan to meet in the wood 'tomorrow night' for a private rehearsal.

剧情简介：尽管包臀总是打岔，木棍还是完成了这出戏的角色分派。他们计划"明晚"在树林里会合，私下排演。

▲ What line might Bottom (in the pink shirt) be speaking here?

1 extempore 即兴
2 Let him roar again （包臀本想用观众喝彩时说的法语词 Encore [再来一个]，无奈胸无点墨，只好用大白话将就）
3 discretion 酌情裁量权
4 aggravate 加重（包臀想说 moderate [减轻]）
5 and 'twere = as if （好像是）
6 proper 英俊，优美
7 discharge 表演
8 French-crown 法币；秃瓢（双关语，French可指法国病，即花柳病，其患者会秃顶）
9 con 背熟，熟记
10 be dogged with company 被人追随、烦扰
11 devices 计策
12 draw a bill of properties 整理出一份道具清单
13 obscenely （包臀想说 obscurely [秘密地]）
14 hold, or cut bowstrings 不论发生什么

Language in the play 剧中语言
The Mechanicals' language
The Mechanicals' language is very different from that of the court characters. Make a list of contradictions, mistakes and odd things they say in Scene 2. Then choose two or three examples of speech from the court characters in Scene 1. Use these quotations as a starting point for an analysis of similarities and differences.

Write about it 写作练习
A Mechanical's reflection (by yourself)
Imagine you are one of the Mechanicals reflecting on your first rehearsal after you have arrived home. Write a diary account of the rehearsal, the allocation of parts and Bottom's behaviour.

SNUG	Have you the lion's part written? Pray you, if it be, give it me; for I am slow of study.
QUINCE	You may do it extempore[1]; for it is nothing but roaring.
BOTTOM	Let me play the lion too. I will roar that I will do any man's heart good to hear me. I will roar that I will make the Duke say 'Let him roar again[2], let him roar again!'
QUINCE	And you should do it too terribly, you would fright the Duchess and the ladies that they would shriek; and that were enough to hang us all.
ALL	That would hang us, every mother's son.
BOTTOM	I grant you, friends, if you should fright the ladies out of their wits they would have no more discretion[3] but to hang us; but I will aggravate[4] my voice so that I will roar you as gently as any sucking dove. I will roar you and 'twere[5] any nightingale.
QUINCE	You can play no part but Pyramus; for Pyramus is a sweet-faced man, a proper[6] man as one shall see in a summer's day, a most lovely, gentlemanlike man: therefore you must needs play Pyramus.
BOTTOM	Well, I will undertake it. What beard were I best to play it in?
QUINCE	Why, what you will.
BOTTOM	I will discharge[7] it in either your straw-colour beard, your orange-tawny beard, your purple-in-grain beard, or your French-crown[8]-colour beard, your perfect yellow.
QUINCE	Some of your French crowns have no hair at all, and then you will play bare-faced. But, masters, here are your parts, and I am to entreat you, request you, and desire you to con[9] them by tomorrow night, and meet me in the palace wood, a mile without the town, by moonlight; there will we rehearse, for if we meet in the city we shall be dogged with company[10], and our devices[11] known. In the meantime I will draw a bill of properties[12], such as our play wants. I pray you, fail me not.
BOTTOM	We will meet, and there we may rehearse most obscenely[13] and courageously. Take pains, be perfect: adieu!
QUINCE	At the Duke's oak we meet.
BOTTOM	Enough; hold, or cut bowstrings[14].

Exeunt

 A MIDSUMMER NIGHT'S DREAM
仲夏夜之梦

Looking back at Act 1 第1幕回顾
Activities for groups or individuals

1 Emotional hooks

Look again at the decisions Shakespeare has made for the start of this play. Now that you have finished the first act, consider how his choices engage the audience emotionally with the characters and the action.

a   List the decisions Shakespeare makes with regard to setting, staging, introduction of characters and their situation, plot, language and dialogue.

b   With each dramatic technique you have listed, decide how successful you think it is at emotionally engaging the audience, and note down the reasons for your decision.

2 Egeus: a bully, or something else?

Egeus may appear simply as an egotistical (傲慢自负) bully. But he can be played to present a different impression. Explain your opinion of Egeus in three or four sentences.

3 Love

A Midsummer Night's Dream is a play very much about love. Yet in one of the harsher moments in the play, Egeus describes love as 'feigning' and 'cunning' (Act 1 Scene 1, lines 31 and 36).

In pairs, talk together about 'love' and what you think it is. Identify what the play suggests are the problems love can cause and consider what solutions there might be to these problems. Then, with the same partner, improvise a chat-show interview. Partner A plays one of the lovers and Partner B the chat-show host who asks about their relationship, the nature of their love and the problems they are encountering. Partner A answers in role.

4 Hippolyta – and Queen Elizabeth I

The photograph below shows the character of Hippolyta dressed to look like Queen Elizabeth I. Hippolyta is the queen of the Amazons, yet says very little in the play. Elizabeth I chose to remain unmarried and had been queen for over thirty years when *A Midsummer Night's Dream* was written. How do you think the Elizabethan audience would have interpreted the character of Hippolyta? Find a quotation from Act 1 to support your ideas.

Looking back at Act 1

5 More history – Bottom's version

The Mechanicals' fear of bringing on a lion may be based on an actual incident. Just before Shakespeare wrote the play, a lion was excluded from celebrations in the Scottish court because it 'might have brought some fear'. The story was well known.

a Imagine Bottom tells that tale to the other Mechanicals. Write him a speech of ten lines – in his own unique style.

b Write about your reaction to this context. What does it add to our understanding of Shakespeare's purpose with Bottom and an Elizabethan audience's response to him?

6 Word pictures – verbal imagery

The words characters speak often create 'word pictures', or images in your mind. Some phrases conjure up clear visual pictures – for example, 'Chanting faint hymns to the cold fruitless moon' (Scene 1, line 73). Other expressions are more complex and are difficult to visualise, such as 'Swift as a shadow, short as any dream' (Scene 1, line 144).

All imagery can contribute a great deal to your imaginative understanding of the play. Identify five images in the first act. Discuss which are visual and which are not.

7 Stage pictures – visual imagery

A play combines verbal imagery with visual images (e.g. the actors' gestures and actions). Sometimes the visual images match the verbal imagery. For example, when Hermia says 'I swear to thee by Cupid's strongest bow, / By his best arrow with the golden head,' (Scene 1, lines 169–70), what gesture might she make to express the image physically?

Pick a short passage with an interesting verbal image from Act 1 and rehearse it with physical actions. You may want to show this performance to the class, or take a photograph and use the verbal image as a caption.

▶ In a 2002 production at Shakespeare's Globe, Snug's mane was made of a bathmat! In what other ways could you use costume and gesture to highlight the comedy of this supposedly terrifying lion?

A fairy in the service of Titania, Queen of the Fairies, meets Puck. Puck explains the conflict over an Indian boy between Oberon, King of the Fairies, and Titania.

 剧情简介：服侍仙后提坦妮娅的小仙子偶遇捣蛋精帕克。捣蛋精讲述仙王欧博让与提坦妮娅正因争抢一个印度小男孩而闹别扭。

Stagecraft 导演技巧

'*Enter a* FAIRY'

One of Shakespeare's favourite dramatic techniques is to contrast one scene with another. Here, after presenting the worlds of the court and the Mechanicals to the audience, he introduces a third world: the fairy kingdom. Try one or both of the following activities to gain a first impression of the fairy world.

a **Mind movie** Relax and close your eyes as your teacher reads the poetry (lines 2–31) aloud to you. Imagine or draw this world as vividly as you can. Share your picture with a partner.

b **Comparisons and contrasts** Compare and contrast this fairy world with the two worlds presented in Act 1. In your Director's Journal draw up a table of the three worlds, like the one below.

Features	The court	The Mechanicals	The fairies
Characters		e.g. Bottom	
Nature of conflicts	e.g. marriage		
Setting			e.g. wood

c Add additional features that it would be useful to compare – for example, the language that is used and the themes that are introduced and explored in each of the three worlds. Decide on the key similarities and differences between the worlds.

Language in the play 剧中语言

What does the audience see? (in pairs)

Both speeches in the script opposite create visions (or dreams) in the audience's mind of things that happen in the fairy world. Some images would be very difficult to put on a stage – for example, 'elves for fear / Creep into acorn cups' (lines 30–1).

Discuss how much help the audience needs to imagine what is described by the actors. Make some suggestions about props (道具), staging, set and how the actors engage with and respond to the language. Write up your suggestions.

1 **whither** = to what place; to which place; to whatever place
2 **Thorough** = Through
3 **briar** 荆棘
4 **pale** 栅栏
5 **sphere**（托勒密天文学认为，月亮和其他星球都嵌在穹顶，围绕地球旋转；星体在天穹[sphere]的路线也叫sphere)
6 **orbs** 仙人圈（传说是仙女在月夜跳舞所致，实为一种蕈类，繁殖迅速，一夜之间便可在草地上形成环状斑纹）
7 **cowslips tall** 挺立的黄花九轮草（报春花科）
8 **pensioners** 皇家侍卫队（常身着华丽的金色制服）
9 **favours** 皇家恩宠的象征
10 **savours** 余香
11 **seek … ear**（伊丽莎白时代的人认为珍珠源自露珠，珍珠在当时是非常时髦的饰品；莎士比亚在此将伊丽莎白女王的宫廷与仙后的宫廷相关联）
12 **lob** 土包子，大木瓜（精灵对帕克的戏称；也指淘气鬼）
13 **anon** 很快
14 **revels** 狂欢作乐
15 **fell** 凶恶，暴躁
16 **passing fell and wrath** 极其生气
17 **changeling** 调包孩儿（传说被精灵调包的人类的孩子）
18 **Knight of his train** 他的侍从骑士
19 **trace** 漫游，穿越
20 **perforce** 强行，偏要
21 **starlight sheen** 闪耀的星光
22 **square** 争吵

Act 2 Scene 1
The wood

Enter a FAIRY *at one door, and* PUCK, *or* ROBIN GOODFELLOW *at another.*

PUCK How now, spirit; whither[1] wander you?
FAIRY Over hill, over dale,
    Thorough[2] bush, thorough briar[3],
Over park, over pale[4],
    Thorough flood, thorough fire; 5
I do wander everywhere
Swifter than the moon's sphere[5];
And I serve the Fairy Queen,
To dew her orbs[6] upon the green.
The cowslips tall[7] her pensioners[8] be; 10
In their gold coats spots you see –
Those be rubies, fairy favours[9],
In those freckles live their savours[10].
    I must go seek some dewdrops here,
    And hang a pearl in every cowslip's ear[11]. 15
Farewell, thou lob[12] of spirits; I'll be gone.
Our Queen and all her elves come here anon[13].
PUCK The King doth keep his revels[14] here tonight.
Take heed the Queen come not within his sight,
For Oberon is passing fell[15] and wrath[16], 20
Because that she as her attendant hath
A lovely boy stol'n from an Indian king;
She never had so sweet a changeling[17],
And jealous Oberon would have the child
Knight of his train[18], to trace[19] the forests wild 25
But she perforce[20] withholds the lovèd boy,
Crowns him with flowers, and makes him all her joy.
And now they never meet in grove or green,
By fountain clear or spangled starlight sheen[21],
But they do square[22], that all their elves for fear 30
Creep into acorn cups and hide them there.

Puck and the fairy talk about the sort of 'sprite' Puck is. In both descriptions, he is mischievous and plays tricks.

剧情简介：捣蛋精与仙子谈论起捣蛋精是哪种"精"。二位口中的捣蛋精都调皮捣蛋，爱玩恶作剧。

1 The Cottingley (英国一小镇) fairies (whole class)

People have long wanted to believe in the existence of fairies. In 1917, two girls took five photographs of themselves with 'fairies' in the woods near their house. For decades, even eminent scientists and scholars believed these to be authentic. In their old age, the two girls finally admitted that the photographs were faked. Debate why you think fairies continue to have such a hold on the imagination.

1	making	身形；外表
2	shrewd	捣蛋，顽皮
3	knavish	淘气
4	sprite	= spirit（精灵）
5	Skim milk	撇去乳脂皮（这样就做不出黄油）
6	labour in the quern	在磨盘上捣乱
7	bootless	徒劳
8	barm	啤酒沫
9	harm	苦恼；窘迫
10	Hobgoblin	淘气妖精
11	jest	开……的玩笑
12	a fat … foal	模仿小母马嘶鸣，来戏弄一匹用豆子喂养的肥马（bean-fed = well-fed）
13	gossip's bowl	长舌妇的酒碗
14	crab	海棠果（常用于啤酒调味）
15	dewlap	下垂的下巴肉
16	aunt	老妇人
17	for … she	误把我当成三脚凳，然后我一抽身，她便摔个屁股墩
18	'Tailor'	（摔了屁股墩的人习惯喊的一个词）
19	loffe	= laugh（此处捣蛋精故意模仿农村方言和口音，类似的词还有后面的waxen和neeze）
20	waxen	= wax（增加，变得更响亮）
21	neeze	= sneeze
22	room	= make room（让开地方）

Write about it 写作练习

Puck (in pairs)

a Look carefully at the presentations of Puck shown in the images throughout this book (see pp. 36, 68, 96, 142, 146, 148, 149 and 158). Think about costumes, make-up, positioning on stage, body language, facial expression, characterisation and so on. With a partner, discuss the presentations one by one and write down one observation on each.

b Individually, pick one presentation that represents your personal response to Puck. Using this image as a starting point, write one paragraph that analyses how Shakespeare introduces Puck at the start of Act 2, and the initial impact this character has on an audience. Integrate at least three short quotations into your writing.

FAIRY	Either I mistake your shape and making[1] quite,
	Or else you are that shrewd[2] and knavish[3] sprite[4]
	Called Robin Goodfellow. Are not you he
	That frights the maidens of the villagery, 35
	Skim milk[5], and sometimes labour in the quern[6],
	And bootless[7] make the breathless housewife churn,
	And sometime make the drink to bear no barm[8],
	Mislead night-wanderers, laughing at their harm[9]?
	Those that 'Hobgoblin'[10] call you, and 'Sweet Puck', 40
	You do their work, and they shall have good luck.
	Are not you he?
PUCK	Thou speakest aright;
	I am that merry wanderer of the night.
	I jest[11] to Oberon, and make him smile
	When I a fat and bean-fed horse beguile, 45
	Neighing in likeness of a filly foal[12];
	And sometime lurk I in a gossip's bowl[13]
	In very likeness of a roasted crab[14],
	And when she drinks, against her lips I bob,
	And on her withered dewlap[15] pour the ale. 50
	The wisest aunt[16], telling the saddest tale,
	Sometime for threefoot stool mistaketh me;
	Then slip I from her bum, down topples she[17],
	And 'Tailor'[18] cries, and falls into a cough;
	And then the whole choir hold their hips and loffe[19], 55
	And waxen[20] in their mirth, and neeze[21], and swear
	A merrier hour was never wasted there.
	But room[22], Fairy: here comes Oberon.
FAIRY	And here my mistress. Would that he were gone!

Oberon and Titania enter with their attendants. They accuse each other of being attracted to the mortals Theseus and Hippolyta.

剧情简介：欧博让与提坦妮娅带着各自的侍从上场。他们互相指责对方迷恋上凡人提修和希炮丽塔。

Stagecraft 导演技巧

Introducing Titania and Oberon (in pairs)

The entrance of Titania and Oberon, King and Queen of the Fairies, is an important and memorable moment for most audiences. A director has many options for how to introduce these dramatic characters with their attendants.

With your partner, consider the mood and tone of the initial conversation between Titania and Oberon, what it reveals of their relationship and why they are in conflict. Then devise a list of suggestions for the director of a new stage production to consider when introducing these two characters. Think about music, lighting, method of entry, positioning on stage, costume, make-up, props and so on. Write your ideas in your Director's Journal and be prepared to share them with the class.

1 Ill met （well met的反说，相当于"冤家路窄"）
2 forsworn his bed and company 发誓断绝关系，决定不再与他同寝共处
3 Tarry 且慢
4 rash wanton 荡妇，泼妇
5 lord … lady （他们是夫妻）
6 Corin 考润（牧羊人的名字；后文的Phillida是牧羊女的名字，牧歌里常指牧羊人与其妻子）
7 pipes of corn 麦秆做的笛子
8 versing love 诵读情诗
9 step = steep （高山）
10 But that 不过是因为
11 forsooth 实际上
12 buskined 穿着猎靴（以示希炮丽塔狩猎时的英勇）
13 To give … prosperity （据说婴儿降生、受洗和婚典时若仙人光临便有好运）
14 Glance at my credit 中伤我的名声
15 Perigenia 珀蕊格妮（暴徒辛尼 [Sinis] 之女，父亲被提修杀死后，她被提修强暴并抛弃）
16 Aegles 艾格丽（一名仙女，传说提修为了她而抛弃了阿蕊阿德妮）
17 Ariadne 阿蕊阿德妮（克里特国王米诺 [Minos] 之女，对提修有救命之恩）
18 Antiopa 安苔娥娌（即希炮丽塔）

Enter [OBERON,] *the King of Fairies, at one door, with his train; and* [TITANIA,] *the Queen, at another with hers.*

OBERON Ill met[1] by moonlight, proud Titania! 60
TITANIA What, jealous Oberon? Fairies, skip hence.
I have forsworn his bed and company[2].
OBERON Tarry[3], rash wanton[4]! Am not I thy lord?
TITANIA Then I must be thy lady[5]. But I know
When thou hast stol'n away from Fairyland, 65
And in the shape of Corin[6] sat all day
Playing on pipes of corn[7], and versing love[8]
To amorous Phillida. Why art thou here
Come from the farthest step[9] of India? —
But that[10], forsooth[11], the bouncing Amazon, 70
Your buskined[12] mistress and your warrior love,
To Theseus must be wedded; and you come
To give their bed joy and prosperity[13].
OBERON How canst thou thus, for shame, Titania,
Glance at my credit[14] with Hippolyta, 75
Knowing I know thy love to Theseus?
Didst not thou lead him through the glimmering night
From Perigenia[15], whom he ravishèd,
And make him with fair Aegles[16] break his faith,
With Ariadne[17], and Antiopa[18]? 80

Titania claims that the dispute with Oberon has changed the natural patterns of the climate and the seasons.
剧情简介：提坦妮娅声称，与欧博让的这场争吵已经改变了气候与季节的自然规律。

Language in the play 剧中语言
Changing world – changing language

Our world is always changing, and so is our language. You can see some of these changes by comparing Shakespeare's words and phrases with the way we speak and write today.

a Use Titania's lines 81–117 to look for evidence of an older way of life ('ox … stretched his yoke') and beliefs ('Contagious fogs'). You can see how writing about an older way of life means using different language.

b Make a list of what we can learn from these lines about the similarities and differences between Elizabethan times and today. Remember, though, that these are fairies talking. Reflect on how Shakespeare is presenting this as an unreal world with magical powers. For example, Titania describes the disruption of the natural world because of the conflict between her and Oberon (this suggests their power in and over nature). Look for other examples and make a note of them.

Write about it 写作练习
Relationships: fairy world, court world

a Think about the relationship between Titania and Oberon, as shown in lines 60–117, and the sexual nature of their conversation. Write notes on the parallels you see here with the relationships in Act 1.

b What does Titania mean when she says 'These are the forgeries of jealousy' (line 81)? Write two or three paragraphs about power, conflict and jealousy within the relationships in this play. Consider Hippolyta and Theseus, Lysander and Hermia, Demetrius and Helena and Titania and Oberon. Pick two couples to compare and contrast.

1 forgeries 捏造；谎言
2 middle summer's spring 仲夏之初
3 mead = meadow（草场）
4 pavèd fountain 池底铺了石子的喷泉
5 beachèd margent 有卵石的海滨
6 ringlets 圆圈舞
7 brawls 争吵（也可能指一种舞蹈）
8 sport 娱乐消遣
9 Contagious fogs 导致疾病的毒雾（伊丽莎白时代的人认为疾病经空气传播）
10 pelting 微不足道
11 murrion flock 瘟死的羊群
12 nine-men's-morris （一种两人下的九子棋，men指棋子，棋盘可在田野或草坪上挖制，易为泥水淹没）
13 quaint mazes 复杂的迷宫
14 wanton green 茂盛的草地
15 want their winter cheer 不能享受冬季的娱乐活动
16 Pale … air 因为无人对月亮唱赞美诗，天就下起雨来（月亮发白被认为是下雨的征兆）
17 rheumatic diseases 风湿病
18 distemperature 气候异常（也可解释为欧博让和提坦妮娅怄气）
19 hoary-headed frosts 白发苍苍的冰霜
20 old Hiems 老冬神
21 odorous chaplet 芳香的花冠
22 childing 多产，硕果累累
23 wonted liveries 惯常的装束
24 increase 收成，结果
25 progeny 后代，后果
26 debate 争吵
27 dissension 不和

A Midsummer Night's Dream Act 2 Scene 1
仲夏夜之梦

TITANIA These are the forgeries[1] of jealousy:
And never since the middle summer's spring[2]
Met we on hill, in dale, forest, or mead[3],
By pavèd fountain[4] or by rushy brook,
Or in the beachèd margent[5] of the sea   85
To dance our ringlets[6] to the whistling wind,
But with thy brawls[7] thou hast disturbed our sport[8].
Therefore the winds, piping to us in vain,
As in revenge have sucked up from the sea
Contagious fogs[9]; which, falling in the land,   90
Hath every pelting[10] river made so proud
That they have overborne their continents.
The ox hath therefore stretched his yoke in vain,
The ploughman lost his sweat, and the green corn
Hath rotted ere his youth attained a beard.   95
The fold stands empty in the drownèd field,
And crows are fatted with the murrion flock[11];
The nine-men's-morris[12] is filled up with mud,
And the quaint mazes[13] in the wanton green[14]
For lack of tread are undistinguishable.   100
The human mortals want their winter cheer[15];
No night is now with hymn or carol blessed.
Therefore the moon, the governess of floods,
Pale in her anger, washes all the air[16],
That rheumatic diseases[17] do abound;   105
And through this distemperature[18] we see
The seasons alter; hoary-headed frosts[19]
Fall in the fresh lap of the crimson rose,
And on old Hiems'[20] thin and icy crown
An odorous chaplet[21] of sweet summer buds   110
Is, as in mockery, set. The spring, the summer,
The childing[22] autumn, angry winter change
Their wonted liveries[23], and the mazèd world
By their increase[24] now knows not which is which.
And this same progeny[25] of evils comes   115
From our debate[26], from our dissension[27].
We are their parents and original.

Oberon asks Titania to give up her 'changeling boy', the subject of the quarrel. She explains why she is going to keep him, and Oberon promises to be revenged.

剧情简介：欧博让要提坦妮娅放弃她的"调包孩儿"，这是他们争吵的缘由。提坦妮娅解释她为何要把他留在身边，而欧博让决意报复。

1 Titania refuses a male command (in pairs)

With a partner, look carefully at Titania's reasons for keeping the boy (lines 123–37). Once again, a male character is trying to dominate a female character. How persuasive do you think Titania's argument is? Together, choose the most compelling line.

▶ Michelle Pfeiffer played Titania in the 1999 movie of *A Midsummer Night's Dream*. Who would you cast (选角) if you had the choice?

1	cross	与……作对
2	henchman	男侍从
3	votress	女信徒
4	Neptune	尼普顿（罗马神话中的海神）
5	embarkèd traders	上船启航的商人
6	flood	大海
7	wanton	肆意
8	swimming gait	流畅轻盈的步态
9	sail upon	步态轻盈地行走于
10	trifles	琐碎的小东西
11	Perchance	也许
12	spare	避开
13	haunts	经常去的地方
14	chide downright	公然争吵

Themes 主题分析

Mirroring mortals

Shakespeare seems to be presenting the fairy world as mirroring relationships in the mortal world. Much of the behaviour and language of the fairies is evocative (唤起的) of human arguments.

Identify the thematic and linguistic echoes of the lovers. For example, the conflict between Helena and Demetrius and its consequences in the lives of others is mirrored in the extreme consequences of Oberon and Titania's disagreement. See if you can find other examples. Suggest why you think Shakespeare structured the play in this way.

Stagecraft 导演技巧

Dual roles

Hippolyta and Titania, and Theseus and Oberon, are quite often played by the same two actors. What problems might an actor encounter playing two characters? Decide on one piece of advice you would give someone who is cast to play both Oberon and Theseus. Write it in your Director's Journal.

OBERON	Do you amend it, then: it lies in you.	
	Why should Titania cross[1] her Oberon?	
	I do but beg a little changeling boy	120
	To be my henchman[2].	
TITANIA	Set your heart at rest.	
	The fairy land buys not the child of me.	
	His mother was a votress[3] of my order,	
	And in the spicèd Indian air by night	
	Full often hath she gossiped by my side,	125
	And sat with me on Neptune's[4] yellow sands	
	Marking th'embarkèd traders[5] on the flood[6],	
	When we have laughed to see the sails conceive	
	And grow big-bellied with the wanton[7] wind;	
	Which she, with pretty and with swimming gait[8]	130
	Following (her womb then rich with my young squire),	
	Would imitate, and sail upon[9] the land	
	To fetch me trifles[10], and return again	
	As from a voyage, rich with merchandise.	
	But she, being mortal, of that boy did die,	135
	And for her sake do I rear up her boy;	
	And for her sake I will not part with him.	
OBERON	How long within this wood intend you stay?	
TITANIA	Perchance[11] till after Theseus' wedding day.	
	If you will patiently dance in our round,	140
	And see our moonlight revels, go with us:	
	If not, shun me, and I will spare[12] your haunts[13].	
OBERON	Give me that boy, and I will go with thee.	
TITANIA	Not for thy fairy kingdom! Fairies, away.	
	We shall chide downright[14] if I longer stay.	145

                                        Exeunt [*Titania and her train*]

OBERON	Well, go thy way. Thou shalt not from this grove
	Till I torment thee for this injury.

Oberon tells Puck to fetch him 'love-in-idleness' (a flower touched by Cupid's arrow). When the juice of the flower is put on the eyelids of the sleeping, it makes them fall in love with whatever they first see when they awake.

剧情简介：欧博让叫捣蛋精为他取来"三色堇"（一种被丘比特之箭射中的花）。将这种花的汁液滴在沉睡者的眼睑上，他们醒来时第一眼看到什么，便会爱上什么。

1 Actions and reactions (in pairs)

The director has asked you to choreograph (设计舞蹈动作) a pacey (快速) and action-packed presentation of Oberon's speech. One of you takes the role of Oberon and the other of Puck. Dramatise Oberon's narrative for the audience. Work out a series of actions for Oberon and reactions for Puck. Present your performance to another pair, or to the class.

1 hither = to this place
2 Since = When（那时）
3 promontory 海角，岬
4 dulcet 悦耳，美妙
5 breath 歌声
6 rude 狂暴，汹涌
7 certain 固定不动
8 vestal 处女（可能暗指女王伊丽莎白一世）
9 thronèd by the west 坐在西边的王位上
10 Cupid's fiery shaft 丘比特之火箭（据称能使被射中的人陷入恋爱之中）
11 chaste 贞洁
12 imperial votress 具有帝王气质的女献身者
13 In maiden meditation 思索着年轻姑娘的心事
14 fancy-free 不受恋爱的牵绊
15 bolt 箭
16 leviathan 巨鲸海怪
17 put a girdle round about 绕……一周

My gentle Puck, come hither[1]. Thou rememberest
Since[2] once I sat upon a promontory[3],
And heard a mermaid on a dolphin's back 150
Uttering such dulcet[4] and harmonious breath[5]
That the rude[6] sea grew civil at her song,
And certain[7] stars shot madly from their spheres
To hear the sea-maid's music?

PUCK   I remember.

OBERON That very time I saw (but thou couldst not) 155
Flying between the cold moon and the earth
Cupid all armed: a certain aim he took
At a fair vestal[8] thronèd by the west[9],
And loosed his loveshaft smartly from his bow
As it should pierce a hundred thousand hearts; 160
But I might see young Cupid's fiery shaft[10]
Quenched in the chaste[11] beams of the watery moon;
And the imperial votress[12] passèd on
In maiden meditation[13], fancy-free[14].
Yet marked I where the bolt[15] of Cupid fell: 165
It fell upon a little western flower,
Before, milk-white; now purple with love's wound:
And maidens call it 'love-in-idleness'.
Fetch me that flower, the herb I showed thee once;
The juice of it on sleeping eyelids laid 170
Will make or man or woman madly dote
Upon the next live creature that it sees.
Fetch me this herb, and be thou here again
Ere the leviathan[16] can swim a league.

PUCK I'll put a girdle round about[17] the earth 175
In forty minutes!   [*Exit*]

Oberon plans to use the flower's juice on Titania, then makes himself invisible as Demetrius and Helena enter, arguing. Demetrius is looking for Hermia, and Helena has followed him.

 剧情简介：欧博让计划将花汁滴入提坦妮娅眼中。这时迪米垂耶和海乐娜上场，欧博让便隐身。迪米垂耶在寻找哈蜜娅，而海乐娜则一路跟着迪米垂耶。

1 Would you rather…

Read lines 180–1 in the script opposite. Would you rather fall in love with a:

- lion
- bear
- wolf
- bull
- monkey
- ape?

What kind of person does each of these animals suggest? Write down your ideas.

2 Oberon's revenge – your view

a Read aloud Oberon's lines 176–85. Write a list of what they reveal about his character. If he were human, is he someone you would like, respect, admire, fear, distrust or something else? What adjective would you use to describe him?

b Write your word on a large sheet of paper. Add a quotation to support your choice, and give some analysis of it. In turn, hold your word up for the class to see and spend a few seconds defending your ideas. Through discussion, come to a class consensus of the best words and quotations.

3 'I am your spaniel' (in pairs)

One person takes the role of Demetrius, the other of Helena. Read lines 188–213 out loud. Discuss what you think of this exchange. (You may want to look at 'Love and marriage', p. 151, and 'Women in Elizabethan England', p. 154.)

1 **render up her page** 交出她的侍童
2 **conference** 谈话
3 **wood** （前一个wood意为"急得发疯"，后一个wood意为"树林"；伊丽莎白时代的人们热衷于文字游戏及双关语）
4 **adamant** （双关，既指坚硬的金刚石，也指有吸引力的磁石）
5 **Leave you** 您只要放弃
6 **entice** 引诱
7 **your spaniel** 您百依百顺的哈巴狗（现代人听起来很反感的比喻）
8 **fawn** 低三下四地讨好乞怜
9 **Use** 对待
10 **spurn** 轻蔑地拒绝，唾弃，踢开
11 **Tempt** 招惹

Stagecraft 导演技巧

The Fairy King and the audience (in small groups)

a Oberon is on the stage alone at first. His soliloquy (独白) tells of his intended revenge. Speculate on the kind of relationship Shakespeare envisaged him having with the audience here. In particular, discuss whether he might speak some or all of his lines directly to the audience.

b 'I am invisible' – easy enough to achieve in a movie, but how could you accomplish this on stage? Discuss this in your group and then write your ideas in your Director's Journal.

OBERON	Having once this juice	
	I'll watch Titania when she is asleep,	
	And drop the liquor of it in her eyes:	
	The next thing then she, waking, looks upon –	
	Be it on lion, bear, or wolf, or bull,	180
	On meddling monkey, or on busy ape –	
	She shall pursue it with the soul of love.	
	And ere I take this charm from off her sight	
	(As I can take it with another herb)	
	I'll make her render up her page[1] to me.	185
	But who comes here? I am invisible,	
	And I will overhear their conference[2].	

Enter DEMETRIUS, HELENA *following him.*

DEMETRIUS	I love thee not, therefore pursue me not.	
	Where is Lysander, and fair Hermia?	
	The one I'll slay, the other slayeth me.	190
	Thou told'st me they were stol'n unto this wood,	
	And here am I, and wood[3] within this wood[3]	
	Because I cannot meet my Hermia.	
	Hence, get thee gone, and follow me no more.	
HELENA	You draw me, you hard-hearted adamant[4]!	195
	But yet you draw not iron, for my heart	
	Is true as steel. Leave you[5] your power to draw,	
	And I shall have no power to follow you.	
DEMETRIUS	Do I entice[6] you? Do I speak you fair?	
	Or rather do I not in plainest truth	200
	Tell you I do not, nor I cannot love you?	
HELENA	And even for that do I love you the more.	
	I am your spaniel[7]; and, Demetrius,	
	The more you beat me I will fawn[8] on you.	
	Use[9] me but as your spaniel: spurn[10] me, strike me,	205
	Neglect me, lose me; only give me leave,	
	Unworthy as I am, to follow you.	
	What worser place can I beg in your love	
	(And yet a place of high respect with me)	
	Than to be usèd as you use your dog?	210
DEMETRIUS	Tempt[11] not too much the hatred of my spirit;	
	For I am sick when I do look on thee.	
HELENA	And I am sick when I look not on you.	

Helena continues to woo Demetrius. He is angry and frustrated at her persistence, and eventually he runs off. She follows him.

 剧情简介：海乐娜继续向迪米垂耶示爱。迪米垂耶被她的执着惹得既恼火又无奈，最后匆忙逃离。海乐娜仍紧追不舍。

Themes 主题分析
Power and control

a **The physical threat** Women often feel more vulnerable at night, especially in isolated places such as a wood. The problem of women's safety at night was as real in Shakespeare's day as it is today. Try speaking Demetrius's lines in a number of ways: menacing, anxious, irritated, frustrated, bored and other ideas of your own. Consider how each reading potentially changes Shakespeare's purpose with this scene.

b **The moral threat** Shakespeare may not have been considering Helena's physical safety as much as the threat to her reputation and respectability. Either way, this scene adds an unpleasantly hard edge (硬棱角，这里指喜剧里的严肃成分) to what is surely a light-hearted play. What other 'hard edges' have you noticed so far in the play?

1	impeach 贬损，损害
2	ill counsel 糟糕建议
3	desert 荒芜
4	trust ... / With ... 把……托付给……
5	brakes 灌木丛
6	Apollo ... chase （莎士比亚时代有名的故事：达芙妮 [Daphne] 逃避阿波罗 [Apollo] 的追求；最终达芙妮被罚变作一棵月桂树）
7	griffin 狮鹫（又称鹰头狮，神话中的狮身鹰首兽）
8	hind 母鹿
9	stay thy questions 忍着听你说
10	do thee mischief 跟你斗，伤害你
11	Fie 呸
12	Your ... sex! 您的不义行为的确让我们女性丢脸！（她被迫做出一些损害女性名誉之事）
13	upon 凭借，通过

Characters 人物分析
Demetrius

Demetrius is a problem character. His language is unpleasant and aggressive in this scene and yet he is a lover, implying that he is a character deserving of the audience's sympathy. How would you play him in Acts 1 and 2? Write down some ideas and consider audience reaction. Also note any parallels between Demetrius, Theseus, Oberon and Egeus.

1 Write a couplet (对句；二行连句) for Demetrius

Helena's final couplet (the two rhyming lines 243–4) sums up her feelings. Write a couplet for Demetrius to say to Helena just before he leaves to sum up his own feelings.

DEMETRIUS	You do impeach[1] your modesty too much,	
	To leave the city and commit yourself	215
	Into the hands of one that loves you not;	
	To trust the opportunity of night,	
	And the ill counsel[2] of a desert[3] place,	
	With[4] the rich worth of your virginity.	
HELENA	Your virtue is my privilege: for that	220
	It is not night when I do see your face,	
	Therefore I think I am not in the night;	
	Nor doth this wood lack worlds of company,	
	For you, in my respect, are all the world.	
	Then how can it be said I am alone	225
	When all the world is here to look on me?	
DEMETRIUS	I'll run from thee and hide me in the brakes[5],	
	And leave thee to the mercy of wild beasts.	
HELENA	The wildest hath not such a heart as you.	
	Run when you will: the story shall be changed;	230
	Apollo flies, and Daphne holds the chase[6],	
	The dove pursues the griffin[7], the mild hind[8]	
	Makes speed to catch the tiger – bootless speed,	
	When cowardice pursues, and valour flies!	
DEMETRIUS	I will not stay thy questions[9]. Let me go;	235
	Or if thou follow me, do not believe	
	But I shall do thee mischief[10] in the wood.	
HELENA	Ay, in the temple, in the town, the field,	
	You do me mischief. Fie[11], Demetrius,	
	Your wrongs do set a scandal on my sex![12]	240
	We cannot fight for love, as men may do;	
	We should be wooed, and were not made to woo.	
	[*Exit Demetrius*]	
	I'll follow thee, and make a heaven of hell,	
	To die upon[13] the hand I love so well.	*Exit*

Oberon vows to help Helena. Puck returns with the flower. Oberon will use it on Titania when she is asleep. He tells Puck to drop the juice of it in Demetrius's eyes when Helena is near.

 剧情简介：欧博让发誓帮助海乐娜。捣蛋精带着魔法花返回。欧博让将趁提坦妮娅熟睡时，把花汁用在她身上。欧博让吩咐捣蛋精在海乐娜靠近时给迪米垂耶的眼睑也抹上花汁。

Themes 主题分析

Power and control

This scene ends with Oberon's decision to use the magic 'love-in-idleness' flower (line 168) to dominate his wife and fill her mind with 'hateful fantasies'. In Act 1 Scene 1 we see Theseus, after subduing Hippolyta through war and courtship, making a decisive judgement on Hermia's future by siding with her father. Make a list of other ways in which Shakespeare mirrors the mortal world with that of the fairies.

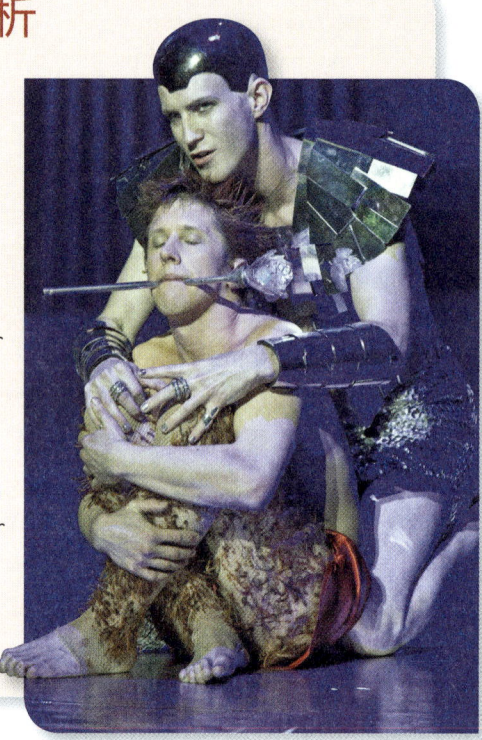

1. nymph 仙女
2. oxlip 牛涎草（高报春，报春花科）
3. overcanopied 树荫覆盖的
4. luscious 芬芳
5. woodbine 忍冬
6. musk-roses 麝香蔷薇
7. eglantine 野蔷薇
8. sometime of = during
9. Lulled 被催眠
10. enamelled 色彩斑斓
11. Weed 外皮（指蛇皮）
12. anoint 涂抹
13. espies 看到

Stagecraft 导演技巧

Out of this world

Costume designers, hair stylists and make-up artists can have a lot of fun developing ideas for presenting the fairies. Choose Oberon, Titania or Puck and design a concept for their costume, hair and make-up. Either draw it or describe it in your Director's Journal.

A Midsummer Night's Dream Act 2 Scene 1
仲夏夜之梦

OBERON	Fare thee well, nymph[1]. Ere he do leave this grove	245
	Thou shalt fly him, and he shall seek thy love.	

Enter Puck.

	Hast thou the flower there? Welcome, wanderer.	
PUCK	Ay, there it is.	
OBERON	I pray thee give it me.	
	I know a bank where the wild thyme blows,	
	Where oxlips[2] and the nodding violet grows,	250
	Quite overcanopied[3] with luscious[4] woodbine[5],	
	With sweet musk-roses[6], and with eglantine[7]:	
	There sleeps Titania sometime of[8] the night,	
	Lulled[9] in these flowers with dances and delight;	
	And there the snake throws her enamelled[10] skin,	255
	Weed[11] wide enough to wrap a fairy in;	
	And with the juice of this I'll streak her eyes,	
	And make her full of hateful fantasies.	
	Take thou some of it, and seek through this grove:	
	A sweet Athenian lady is in love	260
	With a disdainful youth; anoint[12] his eyes,	
	But do it when the next thing he espies[13]	
	May be the lady. Thou shalt know the man	
	By the Athenian garments he hath on.	
	Effect it with some care, that he may prove	265
	More fond on her than she upon her love.	
	And look thou meet me ere the first cock crow.	
PUCK	Fear not, my lord; your servant shall do so.	

Exeunt

Titania orders the fairies to sing her to sleep – and they sing a lullaby. A single fairy is left to guard the sleeping Titania.

剧情简介：提坦妮娅下令众仙子为她唱歌助眠——他们齐唱催眠曲，只留下一位仙子站岗守卫着熟睡的提坦妮娅。

Characters 人物分析
+ - ? (plus, minus, puzzling)

With Titania, Shakespeare has drawn an interesting and complex character (see 'Titania', p. 157). Make notes on what you think of Titania so far, in three columns – positive, negative and puzzling.

- **+** What do you like about her?
- **-** What do you dislike?
- **?** What do you find puzzling?

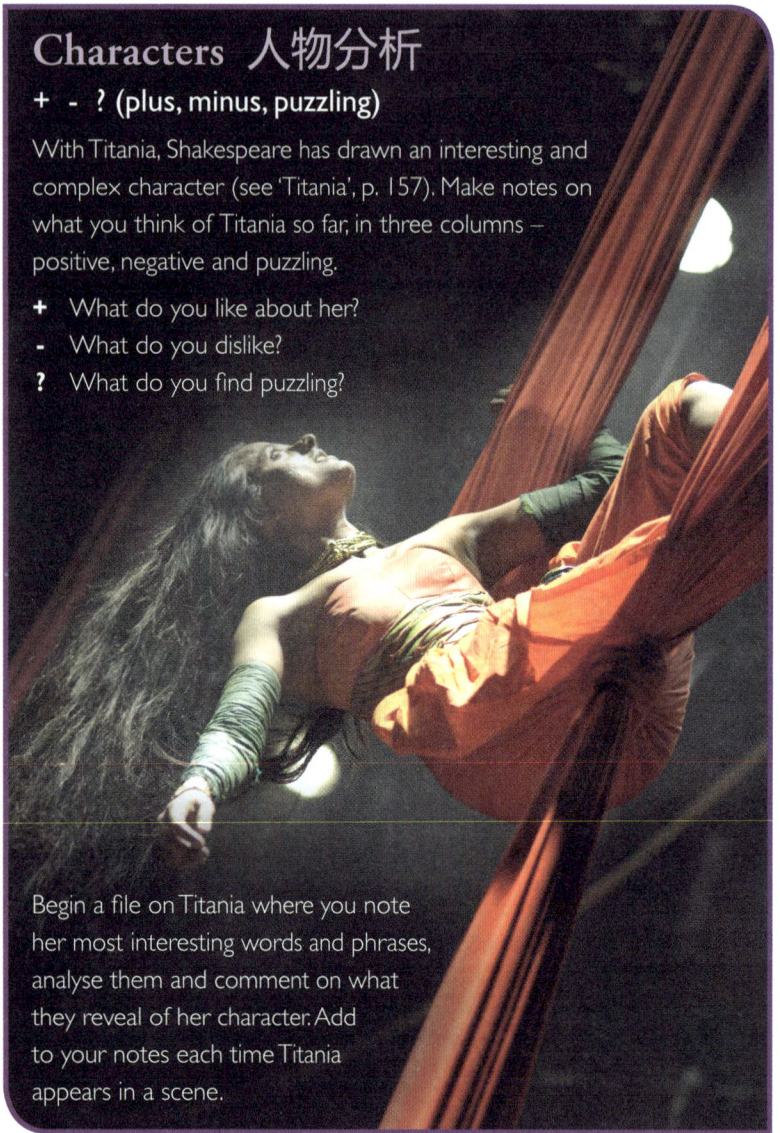

Begin a file on Titania where you note her most interesting words and phrases, analyse them and comment on what they reveal of her character. Add to your notes each time Titania appears in a scene.

1 roundel 圆圈舞
2 third part of a minute 20秒（据说在精灵的世界里，一切皆被缩微，时间也划分得更为细致）
3 cankers 毛毛虫
4 reremice 蝙蝠
5 leathern 皮革般
6 quaint 娇俏精致
7 offices 职责，任务
8 double tongue 分叉的舌头
9 Newts 蝾螈
10 blindworms 蛇蜥
11 Philomel 夜莺
12 nigh = near
13 offence 伤害
14 aloof 在远处
15 sentinel 岗哨，卫兵

Language in the play 剧中语言
Fairy language

The fairies here sing a lullaby for Titania to send her to sleep. Decide your two favourite lines and explore what in particular you like about them. Think about how the fairies' language and imagery paint a picture of the fairy world. Using your quotations and analysis as a starting point, write a paragraph addressing the following question: 'How do Shakespeare's language choices help us understand the fairy world?'

Act 2 Scene 2
The wood

Enter TITANIA, *Queen of Fairies, with her train.*

TITANIA Come, now a roundel[1] and a fairy song,
Then for the third part of a minute[2], hence –
Some to kill cankers[3] in the musk-rose buds,
Some war with reremice[4] for their leathern[5] wings
To make my small elves coats, and some keep back   5
The clamorous owl that nightly hoots and wonders
At our quaint[6] spirits. Sing me now asleep;
Then to your offices[7], and let me rest.
Fairies sing.

[FIRST FAIRY] You spotted snakes with double tongue[8],
    Thorny hedgehogs, be not seen.   10
Newts[9] and blindworms[10], do no wrong,
    Come not near our Fairy Queen.

[CHORUS]   Philomel[11] with melody
    Sing in our sweet lullaby,
Lulla, lulla, lullaby; lulla, lulla, lullaby.   15
    Never harm
    Nor spell nor charm
    Come our lovely lady nigh[12].
    So good night, with lullaby.

FIRST FAIRY Weaving spiders, come not here;   20
    Hence, you longlegged spinners, hence!
Beetles black approach not near;
    Worm nor snail, do no offence[13].

[CHORUS]   Philomel with melody
    Sing in our sweet lullaby,   25
Lulla, lulla, lullaby; lulla, lulla, lullaby.
    Never harm
    Nor spell nor charm
    Come our lovely lady nigh.
    So good night, with lullaby.   30
Titania sleeps.

SECOND FAIRY Hence, away! Now all is well;
One aloof[14] stand sentinel[15]!

[Exeunt Fairies]

Oberon puts the flower's juice on Titania's eyes with a charm that she will wake 'when some vile thing is near!' and fall in love with it. Lysander and Hermia enter, lost. She rejects his advances and they prepare to sleep.

 剧情简介：欧博让将花汁滴在提坦妮娅的眼睑上，并施加咒语，让她"在邪恶之物靠近时"醒来，然后爱上它。理善德和哈蜜娅上场，他俩迷了路。哈蜜娅拒绝与理善德一处共寝，他俩分别准备入睡。

Language in the play 剧中语言

Oberon's spell

Shakespeare fills Oberon's spell (lines 33–40) with animal symbolism. Write a list of the animals that are included and suggest what each might represent. What effect does this have on Oberon's spell? Do you think his final line, 'Wake when some vile thing is near!' is intended to be sinister, amusing, vengeful, evil or something else? Summarise your conclusion in one sentence.

1 Would you rather…

Read through lines 33–40 again. Would you rather be transformed into a:

- cat
- bear
- leopard
- boar?

Explain your choice to the class.

Characters 人物分析

Lysander and Hermia (in pairs)

Shakespeare includes an intimate scene between Lysander and Hermia here, and the audience learns a great deal about them and their relationship. With a partner, choose which lines are the most important in helping us understand the nature of their feelings for each other. Then carry out the following tasks:

a One of you focuses on Hermia's perspective and the other on Lysander's. Write for five minutes describing their feelings as they lie falling asleep under the trees. What are they thinking about: what has happened so far, the difference of opinion they have just had, or their plans and hopes for the future? Use first-person narrative and try to write in **rhyming couplets** (押韵二行连句；对偶句)(two lines of the same length that rhyme), as Shakespeare does here, if you want a challenge.

b Read your responses aloud to each other. Decide if this scene has changed your impressions of these characters. Who do you most empathise with, and why? Report your main ideas back to the class.

1 languish 精神萎靡，憔悴
2 ounce 山猫
3 Pard 豹子
4 troth = truth （实话；诺言）
5 take the sense 要明白
6 Love … conference 爱情的意思在情话里才能明白
7 knit 交织
8 riddles very prettily 巧言善辩
9 much beshrew 我真为……害臊（哈蜜娅显然因说话过头而自责）
10 modesty 节操
11 Becomes 符合

A Midsummer Night's Dream Act 2 Scene 2
仲夏夜之梦

Enter OBERON; [*he squeezes the juice on Titania's eyes*].

OBERON	What thou seest when thou dost wake,
	Do it for thy true love take;
	Love and languish[1] for his sake. 35
	Be it ounce[2] or cat or bear,
	Pard[3], or boar with bristled hair
	In thy eye that shall appear
	When thou wak'st, it is thy dear.
	Wake when some vile thing is near! [*Exit*] 40

Enter LYSANDER *and* HERMIA.

LYSANDER Fair love, you faint with wandering in the wood,
  And, to speak truth, I have forgot our way.
We'll rest us, Hermia, if you think it good,
  And tarry for the comfort of the day.

HERMIA Be it so, Lysander; find you out a bed, 45
For I upon this bank will rest my head.

LYSANDER One turf shall serve as pillow for us both;
One heart, one bed, two bosoms, and one troth[4].

HERMIA Nay, good Lysander, for my sake, my dear,
Lie further off yet; do not lie so near. 50

LYSANDER O take the sense[5], sweet, of my innocence!
Love takes the meaning in love's conference[6];
I mean that my heart unto yours is knit[7],
So that but one heart we can make of it:
Two bosoms interchainèd with an oath, 55
So then two bosoms and a single troth.
Then by your side no bed-room me deny,
For lying so, Hermia, I do not lie.

HERMIA Lysander riddles very prettily[8].
Now much beshrew[9] my manners and my pride 60
If Hermia meant to say Lysander lied.
But, gentle friend, for love and courtesy
Lie further off, in human modesty[10];
Such separation as may well be said
Becomes[11] a virtuous bachelor and a maid, 65
So far be distant, and good night, sweet friend;
Thy love ne'er alter till thy sweet life end!

Hermia and Lysander sleep, and Puck mistakenly puts the juice in Lysander's eyes. Demetrius enters, still chased by Helena. He quickly leaves again, on his own, and goes into the woods.

剧情简介：哈蜜娅和理善德睡着了，捣蛋精误将花汁滴在理善德的眼皮上。迪米垂耶上场，身后仍紧跟着海乐娜。迪米垂耶再次匆忙离开，独自一人进了树林。

Stagecraft 导演技巧

The fairy touch (in pairs)

In this scene, the fairy world – through Puck – directly manipulates the feelings of a mortal. Every new production of the play spends time in rehearsal working out how to present the interactions and the impact they have, because the consequences of such influence could be disturbing, catastrophic (悲惨) or amusing.

How would you want Puck to speak and behave here? In your pair, decide how you think Puck's speech and transformation of Lysander should be performed. Take roles, one person as Puck and the other as director. Act out Puck's speech, focusing on his attitude to the mortal whose life he is changing. Swap roles and direct Puck to display different attitudes – try mischievous, sinister, comic and other ideas of your own. Add notes to your Director's Journal.

▲ *Hermia and Lysander*, by John Simmons (1870).

1 approve 测试，证明
2 Weeds 服装
3 Despisèd = Who despised （前文he的定语；如意义明确，做主语的关系代词在莎剧文本中经常省略）
4 dank 潮湿
5 durst = dares
6 lack-love 薄情（郎）
7 kill-courtesy 无礼（之人）
8 Churl 恶棍
9 owe 拥有
10 charge 命令
11 darkling 在黑暗中
12 on thy peril 后果你自负

Language in the play 剧中语言

Rhyme versus syntax (句法)

There are over 700 rhyming lines in *A Midsummer Night's Dream*. Actors always talk together about whether the rhymes should be emphasised. Some argue they should; others claim that the syntax (word order) is more important, so that the meaning is clearly conveyed to the audience. They say that the lines should 'run on' where appropriate, to bring out the meaning.

Try out the two approaches using Puck's speech in lines 72–89.

A Midsummer Night's Dream Act 2 Scene 2
仲夏夜之梦

LYSANDER	Amen, amen, to that fair prayer say I,	
	And then end life when I end loyalty!	
	Here is my bed; sleep give thee all his rest.	70
HERMIA	With half that wish the wisher's eyes be pressed.	

They sleep.

Enter PUCK.

PUCK Through the forest have I gone,
But Athenian found I none
On whose eyes I might approve[1]
This flower's force in stirring love. 75
Night and silence – Who is here?
Weeds[2] of Athens he doth wear:
This is he my master said
Despisèd[3] the Athenian maid;
And here the maiden, sleeping sound 80
On the dank[4] and dirty ground.
Pretty soul, she durst[5] not lie
Near this lack-love[6], this kill-courtesy[7].
Churl[8], upon thy eyes I throw
All the power this charm doth owe[9]. 85
[*He squeezes the juice on Lysander's eyes.*]
When thou wak'st let love forbid
Sleep his seat on thy eyelid.
So, awake when I am gone;
For I must now to Oberon. *Exit*

Enter DEMETRIUS *and* HELENA, *running*.

HELENA	Stay, though thou kill me, sweet Demetrius!	90
DEMETRIUS	I charge[10] thee, hence, and do not haunt me thus.	
HELENA	O wilt thou darkling[11] leave me? Do not so!	
DEMETRIUS	Stay, on thy peril[12]; I alone will go.	*Exit*

Helena stops to rest and sees Lysander. He wakes up, and immediately falls in love with Helena because of the flower's magic.

剧情简介：海乐娜停下来歇息，看到理善德。理善德在花儿的魔力之下，一醒来便立刻爱上了海乐娜。

Characters 人物分析

Helena

a   Which phrase or line in Helena's speech in the script opposite is the most revealing of her character? Choose one, and write two or three comments on what it suggests about her.

b   Now look back at Helena's speeches in Act 1 and consider how she has developed as a character. The audience has always seen Helena in relation to her suffering at Demetrius's rejection.
In what ways has this been developed by Shakespeare in Act 2? Write a paragraph in which you explain your ideas about Helena and integrate quotations to support them.

1   fond   痴心，愚蠢
2   The … grace   我祈祷得越多，得到的回应却越少
3   dissembling   掩盖真相的
4   glass   镜子
5   sphery eyne   星辰般的双眼
6   Transparent   纯洁天真
7   perish   毁灭
8   touching   达到
9   skill   理智，辨别力
10 Reason … will   理智成为我意志的主宰
11 o'erlook   仔细审阅

1   Lysander – 'raw passion'? (in pairs)

An actor who played Lysander said: 'Lysander gets taken over when he's under the influence of magic; that's where character tends to disappear. It brings out all this raw passion.' Discuss with a partner what the actor means by this. What directions would you give to someone playing the part of Lysander here?

2   The dance of the lovers – who loves whom? (II)

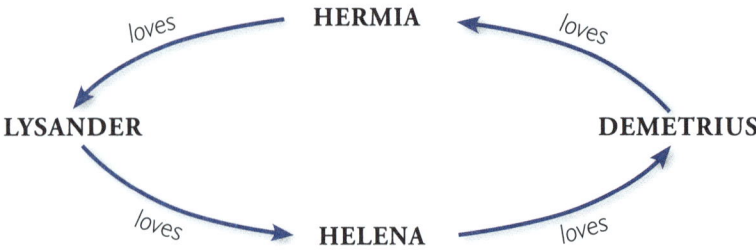

Look back at the diagram on page 10, and discuss the changed relationships shown here.

HELENA	O, I am out of breath in this fond[1] chase!	
	The more my prayer, the lesser is my grace[2].	95
	Happy is Hermia, wheresoe'er she lies,	
	For she hath blessèd and attractive eyes.	
	How came her eyes so bright? Not with salt tears –	
	If so, my eyes are oftener washed than hers.	
	No, no, I am as ugly as a bear,	100
	For beasts that meet me run away for fear.	
	Therefore no marvel though Demetrius	
	Do as a monster fly my presence thus.	
	What wicked and dissembling[3] glass[4] of mine	
	Made me compare with Hermia's sphery eyne[5]?	105
	But who is here? – Lysander, on the ground?	
	Dead, or asleep? I see no blood, no wound.	
	Lysander, if you live, good sir, awake!	
LYSANDER	[*Waking*.]	
	And run through fire I will for thy sweet sake!	
	Transparent[6] Helena, nature shows art	110
	That through thy bosom makes me see thy heart.	
	Where is Demetrius? O, how fit a word	
	Is that vile name to perish[7] on my sword!	
HELENA	Do not say so, Lysander, say not so.	
	What though he love your Hermia? Lord, what though?	115
	Yet Hermia still loves you; then be content.	
LYSANDER	Content with Hermia? No; I do repent	
	The tedious minutes I with her have spent.	
	Not Hermia, but Helena I love.	
	Who will not change a raven for a dove?	120
	The will of man is by his reason swayed,	
	And reason says you are the worthier maid.	
	Things growing are not ripe until their season;	
	So I, being young, till now ripe not to reason.	
	And touching[8] now the point of human skill[9],	125
	Reason becomes the marshal to my will[10]	
	And leads me to your eyes, where I o'erlook[11]	
	Love's stories written in love's richest book.	

Helena thinks Lysander is making fun of her, and leaves. He follows, leaving Hermia behind, still asleep. Hermia wakes from a nightmare, realises she is alone and goes to find Lysander.

剧情简介：海乐娜认为理善德是在拿她寻开心，于是离开了。理善德追了过去，丢下还在睡梦中的哈蜜娅。哈蜜娅从噩梦中醒来，发现自己孤身一人，便去寻找理善德。

1 Three moods, three 'dreams' (in threes)

There are three characters, three moods and three different 'dreams' here. None of the three characters really understands what is going on.

a Each person chooses a character, reads their speech aloud and describes the character's mood – their 'dream' of what is happening.

b Now all concentrate on Hermia's dream. Discuss what it might mean. Share views on whether you agree that dreams sometimes highlight subconscious fears or obsessions. Give examples if you can.

c Together, compare the women's speeches in the script opposite and see if there are any similarities. Then contrast them with Lysander's. If you find differences between the male and female speeches, share them with another group and discuss the implications.

1 **Wherefore** = Why
2 **keen** 尖刻辛辣
3 **flout** 嘲笑，讥讽
4 **insufficiency** 缺乏（吸引迪米垂耶的能力）
5 **Good troth** = In truth（事实上，说实话）
6 **good sooth** 确实
7 **perforce** 有必要
8 **of** = by（用于被动句）
9 **surfeit** 过多，过剩
10 **heresies** 异端邪说
11 **Alack** （感叹词，表示不满或悲哀）
12 **of all loves** 看在爱情的分上
13 **swoon** 晕倒

Language in the play 剧中语言
Disturbing images

Remind yourselves of the 'dance' of the lovers on page 50 – things couldn't get any worse. List as many negative/upsetting images as you can find in lines 94–162. When you have compiled your list, write a few sentences about how the images suggest that the midsummer night's dream is becoming a nightmare.

Themes 主题分析
Dreams and reality (in pairs)

Which is worse – Hermia's dream or her reality? Individually, write your response, justifying your ideas. Then read your partner's work, and underline what you consider to be the best sentence in their response. Read this sentence aloud to the class and explain what you like about it.

HELENA	Wherefore[1] was I to this keen[2] mockery born?	
	When at your hands did I deserve this scorn?	130
	Is't not enough, is't not enough, young man,	
	That I did never, no, nor never can	
	Deserve a sweet look from Demetrius' eye	
	But you must flout[3] my insufficiency[4]?	
	Good troth[5], you do me wrong, good sooth[6], you do,	135
	In such disdainful manner me to woo!	
	But fare you well: perforce[7] I must confess	
	I thought you lord of more true gentleness.	
	O, that a lady of[8] one man refused	
	Should of another therefore be abused! *Exit*	140
LYSANDER	She sees not Hermia. Hermia, sleep thou there,	
	And never mayst thou come Lysander near.	
	For, as a surfeit[9] of the sweetest things	
	The deepest loathing to the stomach brings,	
	Or as the heresies[10] that men do leave	145
	Are hated most of those they did deceive,	
	So thou, my surfeit and my heresy,	
	Of all be hated, but the most of me!	
	And, all my powers, address your love and might	
	To honour Helen, and to be her knight. *Exit*	150
HERMIA	[*Waking.*]	
	Help me, Lysander, help me! Do thy best	
	To pluck this crawling serpent from my breast!	
	Ay me, for pity! What a dream was here!	
	Lysander, look how I do quake with fear –	
	Methought a serpent ate my heart away,	155
	And you sat smiling at his cruel prey.	
	Lysander! What, removed? Lysander, lord!	
	What, out of hearing? Gone? No sound, no word?	
	Alack[11], where are you? Speak and if you hear.	
	Speak, of all loves[12]! I swoon[13] almost with fear.	160
	No? Then I well perceive you are not nigh.	
	Either death or you I'll find immediately. *Exit*	

Looking back at Act 2　第2幕回顾
Activities for groups or individuals

1　Male dominance

In his speeches, Oberon shows his power over the lives of both mortals and fairies. This reinforces the sense that male characters dominate the play (Theseus in Athens, Oberon in the wood). In the production shown on this page, Oberon's power over his surroundings was reflected in dramatic staging and special effects. Perhaps Shakespeare is replicating the realities of his time, or perhaps this reflects the characters' positions of status and power: duke and king.

Discuss whether by depicting the male characters Egeus, Theseus and Demetrius as oppressive and cruel, Shakespeare is encouraging the audience to side with the women.

2　Love and magic: ancient and modern

In Scene 1, lines 155–74, Oberon tells of the flower whose juice on a sleeper's eyelids makes them 'madly dote' on the first person they see when they wake. The idea of love potions is ancient, but even today a connection is often made between love and magic. Songwriters continue to play with this connection.

Find one modern song that uses the language of love and magic, and bring in the lyrics to share with the class.

3 Characters from myth and legend

Indeed your grandams' maids set a bowl of milk out for Robin Goodfellow … the mare, the man in the oak, the puckle, hobgoblin.

This quotation comes from a book Shakespeare probably read, called *The Discovery of Witchcraft*, which was written in 1584. The book describes incidents similar to those the Fairy and Puck talk about at the beginning of Act 2, but, as the quotation implies, hardly anyone believed in Puck (or Robin Goodfellow, as he was often known) any more. Think about what effect is created by using these imaginary characters from myth and superstition in this particular play.

Look carefully at the print of Robin Goodfellow above, which was made in 1639. Describe in detail what you see. Here, Robin appears demonic (有魔力), with his cloven hooves (偶蹄；恶魔的标志) and horns, surrounded by witches. The image suggests that he is more sexually sinister than the character of Puck in *A Midsummer Night's Dream*. What do you think? Consider the character of Puck in the play in light of this contextual information, and be prepared to contribute to a class discussion. (See also 'Fairies and magic', pp. 153–4 for more on Robin Goodfellow). Keep all this in mind as you watch Puck's role develop further in Act 3.

In the wood near the sleeping Titania, the Mechanicals begin their rehearsal. Bottom suggests changes in the play to make it less frightening.

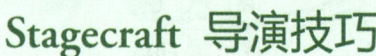
剧情简介：树林里，沉睡的提坦妮娅不远处，工匠们开始排练。包臀提议做些修改，好让剧情不那么吓人。

Stagecraft 导演技巧

'Enter the Clowns (丑角，小丑)'

Shakespeare describes the Mechanicals as 'Clowns' in the stage directions. How might this affect the way a director decides to portray them on stage? What effect do you think Shakespeare hoped this would have on the audience?

a   Imagine that you are the director. What would be your first thoughts on reading this stage direction? Make a few notes on this in your Director's Journal.

b   The stage directions for this scene also specify that 'TITANIA *remains on stage, asleep*'. Again from the director's perspective, comment on where you would position Titania on stage. Sketch a plan. Remember that the audience needs to be aware she is there, but she must not get in the way of the action.

1   **Are we all met?** = Are we all here?
2   **Pat**   正点，准时，正是时候
3   **tiring-house**   （演员的）更衣室，化妆间
4   **bully**   伙计（表示亲昵和关系亲密的友好称谓）
5   **abide**   忍受
6   **By'r lakin**   (by our ladykin 的缩略形式，用于诅咒发誓或恳请；ladykin = little lady)
7   **parlous**   可怕；危险
8   **Not a whit**   完全用不着
9   **prologue**   开场词
10 **eight and six**   "八六体"（一种民谣格律，一行八音节接着一行六音节，如包臀在本场戏中所唱的歌词）
11 **fearful**   （既有"可怕"之意，又有"胆小"之意）
12 **wildfowl**   （诙谐地将狮子喻指为"野禽"，也暗指人）
13 **defect**   （包臀想说effect）
14 **my life for yours**   我用生命向你们担保

1 Who is who? (in pairs)

With a partner, decide who is who in the photograph above, and label the characters. Choose a quotation from the script opposite as an appropriate caption for this photograph of the Mechanicals.

56

Act 3 Scene 1
The wood

Enter the Clowns [, BOTTOM, QUINCE, SNOUT, STARVELING, SNUG *and* FLUTE. TITANIA *remains on stage, asleep*].

BOTTOM   Are we all met?[1]

QUINCE   Pat[2], pat; and here's a marvellous convenient place for our rehearsal. This green plot shall be our stage, this hawthorn brake our tiring-house[3], and we will do it in action as we will do it before the Duke.

BOTTOM   Peter Quince!

QUINCE   What sayest thou, bully[4] Bottom?

BOTTOM   There are things in this comedy of Pyramus and Thisbe that will never please. First, Pyramus must draw a sword to kill himself, which the ladies cannot abide[5]. How answer you that?

SNOUT   By'r lakin[6], a parlous[7] fear!

STARVELING   I believe we must leave the killing out, when all is done.

BOTTOM   Not a whit[8]; I have a device to make all well. Write me a prologue[9], and let the prologue seem to say we will do no harm with our swords, and that Pyramus is not killed indeed; and for the more better assurance, tell them that I, Pyramus, am not Pyramus, but Bottom the weaver: this will put them out of fear.

QUINCE   Well, we will have such a prologue; and it shall be written in eight and six[10].

BOTTOM   No, make it two more: let it be written in eight and eight.

SNOUT   Will not the ladies be afeard of the lion?

STARVELING   I fear it, I promise you.

BOTTOM   Masters, you ought to consider with yourself, to bring in (God shield us!) a lion among ladies is a most dreadful thing; for there is not a more fearful[11] wildfowl[12] than your lion living; and we ought to look to't.

SNOUT   Therefore another prologue must tell he is not a lion.

BOTTOM   Nay, you must name his name, and half his face must be seen through the lion's neck, and he himself must speak through, saying thus, or to the same defect[13]: 'Ladies', or 'Fair ladies, I would wish you', or 'I would request you', or 'I would entreat you, not to fear, not to tremble: my life for yours[14]. If you think I come hither as a lion, it were pity of my life. No, I am no such thing; I am a man,

The Mechanicals discuss how to show moonlight and the wall in the play, and decide they must have an actor represent each.

剧情简介：工匠们商量如何才能展现出戏中的月光和墙，最后决定必须各安排一名演员来扮演。

1 Act it out! (in sevens)

The first half of this scene shows the Mechanicals preparing to rehearse, and Puck's mischievous interference. To gain a first impression of what happens, take parts as the Mechanicals and Puck and read lines 1–98. Don't pause over anything you don't understand – just enjoy the comedy. When you have completed your read-through, the group should split into two and work on some of the activities below.

2 Bottom and the play (in groups of three or four)

In your group, allocate one task to each person from the following list (each task should be written up in around 300 words):

a Pick up as many clues as you can in this scene about the play that Quince has written. Outline the characters and the storyline of the play the Mechanicals propose to perform.

b Complete a character study of Bottom, with quotations.

c Research the original story of Pyramus and Thisbe, two ill-fated lovers, and summarise it.

d Read lines 1–59 of this scene from a director's perspective, and write detailed directions for each character. Record your ideas in your Director's Journal.

Read each others' work and then discuss what you have learnt about Shakespeare's choices in this scene.

▶ What do you think Bottom is saying here?

1 there is two　（此处的主谓不一致是莎士比亚有意为木棍设计的不标准英语）

2 almanac　历书（包含星象学信息的日历）

3 casement　窗扉（带竖铰链的窗框）

4 a bush of thorns　一捆荆棘（传说月亮上有人背负荆棘）

5 disfigure　（木棍想说figure [代表，充当]）

6 chink　裂缝

7 loam　黏土

8 rough-cast　灰泥（石灰和砂石的混合物，用于涂抹外墙）

9 cue　提示语

	as other men are' – and there indeed let him name his name, and tell them plainly he is Snug the joiner.
QUINCE	Well, it shall be so. But there is two[1] hard things: that is, to bring the moonlight into a chamber; for, you know, Pyramus and Thisbe meet by moonlight.
SNUG	Doth the moon shine that night we play our play?
BOTTOM	A calendar, a calendar! Look in the almanac[2] – find out moonshine, find out moonshine!
QUINCE	Yes, it doth shine that night.
BOTTOM	Why, then may you leave a casement[3] of the great chamber window, where we play, open, and the moon may shine in at the casement.
QUINCE	Ay; or else one must come in with a bush of thorns[4] and a lantern, and say he comes to disfigure[5], or to present the person of Moonshine. Then there is another thing: we must have a wall in the great chamber; for Pyramus and Thisbe, says the story, did talk through the chink[6] of a wall.
SNOUT	You can never bring in a wall. What say you, Bottom?
BOTTOM	Some man or other must present Wall; and let him have some plaster, or some loam[7], or some rough-cast[8] about him to signify Wall; or let him hold his fingers thus, and through that cranny shall Pyramus and Thisbe whisper.
QUINCE	If that may be, then all is well. Come, sit down every mother's son, and rehearse your parts. Pyramus, you begin. When you have spoken your speech, enter into the brake, and so everyone according to his cue[9].

Puck enters, and watches as the Mechanicals begin to rehearse, going off with Bottom when he goes off stage. After getting his lines muddled, Flute gives Bottom his cue to reappear.

剧情简介：捣蛋精上场，暗中观察工匠们排练。包臀下台时，捣蛋精与他同下。福笛稀里糊涂说完自己的台词，接着把包臀的返场提示语也读了出来。

Characters 人物分析

'Enter PUCK' (in pairs)

The audience is watching Puck, who is watching the Mechanicals' rehearsal. He asks, 'What hempen homespuns have we swaggering here …?' How does this line help us visualise the characters? Clearly, Puck is amused. But is his amusement born of ridicule, affection or contempt? With a partner, decide how he should say the line.

1. hempen homespuns 土制麻布（喻指土气粗俗的下等人）
2. swaggering 自以为是，大摇大摆
3. cradle 睡椅，休息的地方
4. toward 正在进行
5. odious （包臀把odorous［芳香］说成了odious［讨厌］，急得木棍连连为他纠错）
6. odours 此处应是形容词odorous，包臀说成了名词）
7. hark 听
8. by and by 马上
9. marry （Mary的变体写法，用来表示肯定）
10. lilywhite of hue 如百合花般洁白
11. triumphant 壮丽（用该词来描述野玫瑰，显得荒诞可笑）
12. brisky juvenal 活泼的少年
13. eke = also
14. Jew （可能是福笛对jewel的误读）
15. Ninny's （福笛把希腊神话中的亚述王Ninus错念成Ninny［傻瓜］）
16. cues and all 连同提示语在内（莎士比亚时代的剧场里，演员们并没有完整剧本，只有他们自己的台词部分以及开始说自己台词的提示语）

▲ 'What hempen homespuns have we swaggering here …?'

1 A rehearsal – and bad acting (in threes)

Not only is there a play within a play in *A Midsummer Night's Dream* (in Act 5), there are even rehearsals. Many people think that Shakespeare was mocking groups of actors who travelled around England in the early years of Queen Elizabeth I's reign. Others think he was poking fun at amateur dramatics because he was in one of the first professional theatre companies in England. Whatever the reason, Shakespeare knew how to present bad acting.

First, talk together about the complications of playing characters who are attempting to act well, but failing. Then take parts as Quince, Bottom and Flute, and speak lines 65–84 to show how the timing of the lines helps to reveal the Mechanicals' lack of acting ability.

Enter PUCK.

PUCK What hempen homespuns[1] have we swaggering[2] here 60
       So near the cradle[3] of the Fairy Queen?
       What, a play toward[4]? I'll be an auditor,
       An actor too perhaps, if I see cause.

QUINCE Speak, Pyramus! Thisbe, stand forth!

BOTTOM (*as Pyramus*)
       Thisbe, the flowers of odious[5] savours sweet – 65

QUINCE Odours – 'odorous'!

BOTTOM (*as Pyramus*)
       . . . odours[6] savours sweet.
       So hath thy breath, my dearest Thisbe dear.
       But hark[7], a voice! Stay thou but here awhile,
       And by and by[8] I will to thee appear. *Exit* 70

PUCK A stranger Pyramus than e'er played here. [*Exit*]

FLUTE Must I speak now?

QUINCE Ay, marry[9] must you; for you must understand he goes but to see a noise that he heard, and is to come again.

FLUTE (*as Thisbe*)
       Most radiant Pyramus, most lilywhite of hue[10], 75
       Of colour like the red rose on triumphant[11] briar,
       Most brisky juvenal[12], and eke[13] most lovely Jew[14],
       As true as truest horse that yet would never tire,
       I'll meet thee, Pyramus, at Ninny's[15] tomb –

QUINCE 'Ninus' tomb', man! – Why, you must not speak that yet; that 80
you answer to Pyramus. You speak all your part at once, cues and all[16]. Pyramus, enter – your cue is past. It is 'never tire'.

FLUTE O –
       (*as Thisbe*)
       As true as truest horse, that yet would never tire.

Bottom re-enters with an ass's head (because of Puck's magic), and all his comrades run away. Bottom thinks that they are teasing him to make him frightened. He sings to show he is unafraid.

 剧情简介：包臀重新登场，顶着一个驴脑袋（因为捣蛋精施了魔法），伙计们见状纷纷逃跑。包臀以为大伙儿是在戏弄他，想让他害怕。于是他唱起歌来，以示自己英勇无畏。

1 about a round 绕一圈
2 bog 沼泽
3 knavery 恶作剧
4 translated 变了形，变了样
5 stir 挪动
6 ousel cock 公乌鸫
7 throstle 画眉
8 so true 如此准确
9 wren 鹪鹩
10 little quill 尖细的声音

Stagecraft 导演技巧

'Bottom with the ass head' **(in pairs)**

a   There are only a few moments before Bottom reappears 'with the ass head'. Suggest ways that this might be accomplished by the make-up and costume designers. What effect would they want to achieve with the audience here?

b   List the techniques that Shakespeare uses to highlight the comedy in the script opposite, and explain why this scene is also sad.

A Midsummer Night's Dream Act 3 Scene 1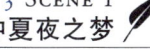
仲夏夜之梦

Enter [Puck], and Bottom with the ass head [on].

BOTTOM (*as Pyramus*)
 If I were fair, fair Thisbe, I were only thine.   85

QUINCE   O monstrous! O strange! We are haunted! Pray, masters, fly, masters! Help!

Exeunt Quince, Snug, Flute, Snout and Starveling

PUCK   I'll follow you: I'll lead you about a round[1],
  Through bog[2], through bush, through brake, through briar;
 Sometime a horse I'll be, sometime a hound,   90
  A hog, a headless bear, sometime a fire,
 And neigh, and bark, and grunt, and roar, and burn,
 Like horse, hound, hog, bear, fire at every turn.   *Exit*

BOTTOM   Why do they run away? This is a knavery[3] of them to make me afeard.   95

Enter Snout.

SNOUT   O Bottom, thou art changed. What do I see on thee?

BOTTOM   What do you see? You see an ass head of your own, do you?
               [*Exit Snout*]

Enter Quince.

QUINCE   Bless thee, Bottom, bless thee! Thou art translated[4]!   *Exit*

BOTTOM   I see their knavery. This is to make an ass of me, to fright me, if they could; but I will not stir[5] from this place, do what they can. I will walk up and down here, and will sing, that they shall hear I am not afraid.   100
 [*Sings.*] The ousel cock[6] so black of hue,
  With orange-tawny bill,
 The throstle[7] with his note so true[8],   105
  The wren[9] with little quill[10] –

Bottom's song wakes Titania who, under the influence of the potion, instantly falls in love with him. She vows to keep him with her.

 剧情简介：包臀的歌声吵醒了提坦妮娅，在魔法花汁的药效下，她立刻爱上了包臀并发誓将他留在身边。

Themes 主题分析
'reason and love keep little company'
The relationship between reason and love is one of the themes of the play, and Bottom's lines 120–1 stress how far they apart. *A Midsummer Night's Dream* shows vividly how love makes people act very irrationally. Make a list of the characters who you think are being reasonable, and another list of those who are dominated by their emotions, particularly love.

1 finch   燕雀
2 plainsong   曲调简单
3 dares not answer nay   （布谷鸟 [cuckoo] 叫让人联想到戴绿帽子 [cuckold]，这里表示没有哪位男士敢确定自己从未遭遇过）
4 set his wit to   与……斗智
5 give a bird the lie   称一只鸟为骗子
6 enthrallèd   被俘获
7 virtue's force   男子美德的力量（virtue在词源上表示男子气概，这里用来描述驴头包臀，尤为讽刺）
8 gleek   打趣
9 of no common rate   非普通级别，非同寻常
10 still doth tend upon   永远侍奉
11 state   王国，朝廷
12 deep   深海，海底
13 purge thy mortal grossness   解除你凡人肉身的体重
14 airy spirit   无影无形的精灵

'What angel wakes me from my flowery bed?' This is one of Shakespeare's most famous lines. It is ironic. Why?

1 Bottom – 'wise' and 'beautiful'? (in small groups)
Titania is clearly talking nonsense about Bottom. On the one hand this creates comedy and is amusing for the audience, but do you think Shakespeare might also be making a point about the way people behave when they are in love? If so, what is this point? Discuss with your group and present your thoughts to the class as a whole.

TITANIA [*Waking.*] What angel wakes me from my flowery bed?
BOTTOM [*Sings.*]
      The finch[1], the sparrow, and the lark,
        The plainsong[2] cuckoo grey,
      Whose note full many a man doth mark 110
        And dares not answer nay[3] –
for indeed, who would set his wit to[4] so foolish a bird? Who would give a bird the lie[5], though he cry 'cuckoo' never so?
TITANIA I pray thee, gentle mortal, sing again;
Mine ear is much enamoured of thy note. 115
So is mine eye enthrallèd[6] to thy shape,
And thy fair virtue's force[7] perforce doth move me
On the first view to say, to swear, I love thee.
BOTTOM Methinks, mistress, you should have little reason for that. And yet, to say the truth, reason and love keep little company together 120 nowadays; the more the pity that some honest neighbours will not make them friends. Nay, I can gleek[8] upon occasion.
TITANIA Thou art as wise as thou art beautiful.
BOTTOM Not so neither; but if I had wit enough to get out of this wood, I have enough to serve mine own turn. 125
TITANIA Out of this wood do not desire to go:
Thou shalt remain here, whether thou wilt or no.
I am a spirit of no common rate[9];
The summer still doth tend upon[10] my state[11],
And I do love thee. Therefore go with me. 130
I'll give thee fairies to attend on thee,
And they shall fetch thee jewels from the deep[12],
And sing, while thou on pressèd flowers dost sleep;
And I will purge thy mortal grossness[13] so
That thou shalt like an airy spirit[14] go. 135
Peaseblossom, Cobweb, Moth, and Mustardseed!

Enter four Fairies.

PEASEBLOSSOM Ready.
COBWEB And I.
MOTH And I.
MUSTARDSEED And I. 140

Titania asks her fairies to look after Bottom. He learns their names. Bottom is then led to Titania's bower.
剧情简介：提坦妮娅要她的仙子们照顾包臀。包臀逐一问了仙子们的名字，然后被带到提坦妮娅的闺房。

Language in the play 剧中语言
Titania's love

Look carefully at Titania's speech (lines 174–8). What does the language and imagery reveal about the nature of her love for Bottom? What could be happening on stage as she speaks these lines? Write down your ideas in the form of notes, stage directions or extended commentary.

1 **gambol** 跳跃
2 **apricocks** = apricots（杏）
3 **dewberries** 露莓（一种浆果，有些像蓝莓）
4 **humble-bees** 蜜蜂；大黄蜂（现在写作bumble-bee）
5 **do him courtesies** 对他以礼相待
6 **cry your worships mercy** （一般意思是"请求阁下见谅"，此处有法语的感谢[merci]之意）
7 **I ... acquaintance** 我希望进一步了解您
8 **if I cut my finger** （蜘蛛网在旧时被用来止血）
9 **Squash** 未成熟的豌豆荚
10 **Peascod** 成熟的豌豆荚
11 **patience** 好脾气
12 **made my eyes water** （芥末微辣，会使人流泪）
13 **bower** （诗歌中）闺房
14 **enforcèd** 被暴力强夺的

Characters 人物分析
Bottom (in small groups)

Bottom is the only character from the mortal world to see and talk to the fairies. Bottom and Titania have both been transformed.

a Discuss what sort of relationship these two characters have. Use the photograph above as part of your discussions.

b Which lines in the script opposite reveal most about each character? Choose one line for Titania and one for Bottom, and think about what each shows about the character. Explain your findings to the rest of the group. Compare your choices.

ALL	Where shall we go?	
TITANIA	Be kind and courteous to this gentleman:	
	Hop in his walks and gambol¹ in his eyes;	
	Feed him with apricocks² and dewberries³,	
	With purple grapes, green figs, and mulberries;	145
	The honey-bags steal from the humble-bees⁴,	
	And for night-tapers crop their waxen thighs,	
	And light them at the fiery glow-worms' eyes	
	To have my love to bed, and to arise;	
	And pluck the wings from painted butterflies	150
	To fan the moonbeams from his sleeping eyes.	
	Nod to him, elves, and do him courtesies⁵.	
PEASEBLOSSOM	Hail, mortal!	
COBWEB	Hail!	
MOTH	Hail!	155
MUSTARDSEED	Hail!	
BOTTOM	I cry your worships mercy⁶, heartily. I beseech your worship's name.	
COBWEB	Cobweb.	
BOTTOM	I shall desire you of more acquaintance⁷, good Master Cobweb; if I cut my finger⁸ I shall make bold with you. Your name, honest gentleman?	160
PEASEBLOSSOM	Peaseblossom.	
BOTTOM	I pray you commend me to Mistress Squash⁹, your mother, and to Master Peascod¹⁰, your father. Good Master Peaseblossom, I shall desire you of more acquaintance, too. – Your name, I beseech you, sir?	165
MUSTARDSEED	Mustardseed.	
BOTTOM	Good Master Mustardseed, I know your patience¹¹ well. That same cowardly, giant-like ox-beef hath devoured many a gentleman of your house. I promise you, your kindred hath made my eyes water¹² ere now. I desire you of more acquaintance, good Master Mustardseed.	170
TITANIA	Come, wait upon him. Lead him to my bower¹³.	
	The moon methinks looks with a watery eye,	175
	And when she weeps, weeps every little flower,	
	Lamenting some enforcèd¹⁴ chastity.	
	Tie up my lover's tongue; bring him silently.	

Exeunt

Oberon wonders who or what Titania now loves. Puck says she loves a 'monster' and explains what he has done to Bottom and the other Mechanicals.

剧情简介：欧博让好奇提坦妮娅现在会爱上谁，或者会爱上什么东西。捣蛋精说她爱上个"怪物"，接着讲述了他给包臀和其他工匠施魔法的经过。

1 Speak it – act it! (in small groups)

Puck tells how he took a hand in the Mechanicals' rehearsal, with hilarious results. Lines 6–34 invite acting out. As one person slowly speaks the lines, the others in the group enact them.

1	night-rule	晚间例行活动
2	consecrated	圣洁
3	patches	小丑们
4	rude	粗俗
5	that barren sort	那帮无脑的家伙
6	Forsook	离开（forsake的过去式）
7	nole	头
8	mimic	演员
9	spy	看见
10	fowler	捕野禽者
11	russet-pated choughs	红头山鸦
12	cawing	鸣叫
13	gun's report	枪声
14	Sever themselves	纷纷逃散
15	apparel	衣服
16	yielders	投降者

◀ What kind of statement is being made about Oberon and Puck in this production? Look carefully at the use of colours, the styling and the body language. Share your ideas with a partner.

Stagecraft 导演技巧

Retelling the tale

In this scene, Shakespeare chooses to retell the story of Bottom's transformation and Titania's waking in detail. The audience has just seen this on stage. Consider why Shakespeare decides to pause here for this extended narration. What effect does it have on the audience? Note down some suggestions in your Director's Journal.

A Midsummer Night's Dream Act 3 Scene 2
仲夏夜之梦

Act 3 Scene 2
The wood

Enter OBERON, *King of Fairies.*

OBERON I wonder if Titania be awaked;
Then what it was that next came in her eye,
Which she must dote on, in extremity.

Enter PUCK.

Here comes my messenger. How now, mad spirit?
What night-rule[1] now about this haunted grove?　　　　5

PUCK My mistress with a monster is in love.
Near to her close and consecrated[2] bower,
While she was in her dull and sleeping hour,
A crew of patches[3], rude[4] mechanicals,
That work for bread upon Athenian stalls,　　　　10
Were met together to rehearse a play
Intended for great Theseus' nuptial day.
The shallowest thick-skin of that barren sort[5],
Who Pyramus presented, in their sport
Forsook[6] his scene and entered in a brake,　　　　15
When I did him at this advantage take:
An ass's nole[7] I fixèd on his head.
Anon his Thisbe must be answerèd,
And forth my mimic[8] comes. When they him spy[9] –
As wild geese that the creeping fowler[10] eye,　　　　20
Or russet-pated choughs[11], many in sort,
Rising and cawing[12] at the gun's report[13],
Sever themselves[14] and madly sweep the sky –
So at his sight away his fellows fly,
And at our stamp here o'er and o'er one falls;　　　　25
He 'Murder!' cries, and help from Athens calls.
Their sense thus weak, lost with their fears thus strong,
Made senseless things begin to do them wrong,
For briars and thorns at their apparel[15] snatch,
Some sleeves, some hats; from yielders[16] all things catch.　　　　30

Oberon is pleased to hear that Titania has fallen in love with Bottom. Puck says he has also dealt with the 'Athenian'. Demetrius finds Hermia and tries to court her. She accuses him of having murdered Lysander.

剧情简介：欧博让得知提坦妮娅爱上了包臀，心里很满意。捣蛋精说他还办妥了那个"雅典人"的事情。迪米垂耶找到哈蜜娅，向她求爱。哈蜜娅指控迪米垂耶谋杀了理善德。

Write about it 写作练习
Darkness and confusion

Shakespeare uses language to create emotional atmosphere.

a Identify words and images in lines 43–81 that best bring out Hermia's and Demetrius's feelings. Group them in any way that appeals to you or is helpful. For example, you could consider language that is violent. Choose the three or four most interesting words, phrases or images.

b Write for ten minutes in response to the title: 'Explain how Shakespeare portrays love in this scene.'

▼ This photograph is from a 2012 production that used modern dress. Discuss how successful you think this is. What are the advantages of setting Shakespeare in different time periods rather than remaining faithful to traditional costumes? Talk through your ideas with a partner.

1 latched   滴上
2 of ... eyed   他必定看见她
3 Stand close   躲起来
4 rebuke   斥责，训斥
5 chide   责骂
6 Being o'er shoes in blood   已经到了这个地步，不如做得更甚（血已没过鞋子，那就让它没得更深些）
7 be bored   被刺穿
8 Her brother's   （月亮女神狄阿娜 [Diana] 的哥哥是太阳神阿波罗 [Apollo]）
9 noontide   正午时分
10 th'Antipodes   地球另一面的居民
11 dead   面如死灰
12 grim   冷酷残忍
13 yonder   = over there; that
14 Venus   金星（也指罗马神话中的爱神维纳斯）
15 carcass   遗骸，尸体

A Midsummer Night's Dream Act 3 Scene 2
仲夏夜之梦

	I led them on in this distracted fear,	
	And left sweet Pyramus translated there;	
	When in that moment, so it came to pass,	
	Titania waked, and straightway loved an ass.	
OBERON	This falls out better than I could devise.	35
	But hast thou yet latched¹ the Athenian's eyes	
	With the love juice, as I did bid thee do?	
PUCK	I took him sleeping – that is finished too –	
	And the Athenian woman by his side,	
	That when he waked, of force she must be eyed².	40

Enter DEMETRIUS *and* HERMIA.

OBERON	Stand close³: this is the same Athenian.	
PUCK	This is the woman, but not this the man.	
DEMETRIUS	O, why rebuke⁴ you him that loves you so?	
	Lay breath so bitter on your bitter foe.	
HERMIA	Now I but chide⁵; but I should use thee worse,	45
	For thou, I fear, hast given me cause to curse.	
	If thou hast slain Lysander in his sleep,	
	Being o'er shoes in blood⁶, plunge in the deep,	
	And kill me too.	
	The sun was not so true unto the day	50
	As he to me. Would he have stol'n away	
	From sleeping Hermia? I'll believe as soon	
	This whole earth may be bored⁷, and that the moon	
	May through the centre creep, and so displease	
	Her brother's⁸ noontide⁹ with th'Antipodes¹⁰.	55
	It cannot be but thou hast murdered him:	
	So should a murderer look; so dead¹¹, so grim¹².	
DEMETRIUS	So should the murdered look, and so should I,	
	Pierced through the heart with your stern cruelty;	
	Yet you, the murderer, look as bright, as clear,	60
	As yonder¹³ Venus¹⁴ in her glimmering sphere.	
HERMIA	What's this to my Lysander? Where is he?	
	Ah, good Demetrius, wilt thou give him me?	
DEMETRIUS	I had rather give his carcass¹⁵ to my hounds.	

Hermia storms off, after accusing Demetrius of murder. Demetrius, too tired to follow, goes to sleep. Oberon tells Puck to find Helena in order to correct his mistake.

 剧情简介：哈蜜娅指控完迪米垂耶谋杀后，气冲冲离开。迪米垂耶此时已筋疲力尽，无力追赶，倒头便睡。欧博让叫捣蛋精去把海乐娜找来，他要纠正捣蛋精犯的错。

1 Getting to know the lovers (in pairs)

Shakespeare presents distinct views of the world through the different groups in the play (such as the lovers and fairies). Each character in these groups also has their own opinions, such as Hermia and Demetrius here.

a Go through lines 43–81 in your pair. One person makes notes on what Hermia thinks is going on here, the other on what Demetrius thinks.

b Share your ideas and compare the thoughts of the two lovers. Suggest similarities to and differences from the encounter between Lysander and Hermia in Act 2 Scene 2, lines 41–71.

Characters 人物分析
Oberon – different intentions?

a Read Oberon's two speeches in the script opposite. Write a paragraph on what the lines tell you about this character and his motives in dealing with the mortals.

b Compare these speeches with those of Oberon in Act 2, particularly between lines 146–87 in Scene 1.

c Write a further paragraph comparing Oberon's motives with his treatment of his wife. Think about his words here in Act 3 Scene 2, lines 96–7: 'All fancy-sick she is and pale of cheer / With sighs of love, that costs the fresh blood dear.' Consider also his threat in Act 2 Scene 1, lines 146–7: 'Well, go thy way. Thou shalt not from this grove / Til I torment thee for this injury.'

2 Are men fickle (易变)? (in pairs)

Puck says 'one man holding troth, / A million fail' (see note in glossary on this page). Debate whether men are fickle in love, and, if so, whether they are more fickle than women. Make notes to prepare for a group discussion.

Stagecraft 导演技巧
'look how I go!'

> I go, I go, look how I go!
> Swifter than arrow from the Tartar's bow.

Suggest how the actor playing Puck should leave the stage here.

---

1 cur 狗东西
2 Henceforth 从今以后
3 Durst = Dare
4 worm 蛇
5 adder 蝰蛇（毒蛇）
6 doubler tongue 分叉更多的舌头
7 misprised = mistaken
8 heaviness 抑郁
9 For … owe = For debt that sorrow doth owe bankrupt sleep（亏欠太多的睡眠）
10 tender 还债（即他欠自己一些睡眠）
11 misprision = mistake
12 perforce ensue 必定接踵而来
13 Then … oath 那么命运就会成为主宰，如果有一个对爱忠诚的男人，就有百万个一次次背叛誓言的男人
14 look thou find 你务必要找到
15 fancy-sick 害相思病
16 cheer 容颜
17 against = when
18 Tartar 鞑靼人

A Midsummer Night's Dream Act 3 Scene 2
仲夏夜之梦

HERMIA	Out, dog! Out, cur[1]! Thou driv'st me past the bounds	65
	Of maiden's patience. Hast thou slain him then?	
	Henceforth[2] be never numbered among men.	
	O, once tell true; tell true, even for my sake:	
	Durst[3] thou have looked upon him being awake?	
	And hast thou killed him sleeping? O, brave touch!	70
	Could not a worm[4], an adder[5] do so much?	
	An adder did it; for with doubler tongue[6]	
	Than thine, thou serpent, never adder stung.	
DEMETRIUS	You spend your passion on a misprised[7] mood.	
	I am not guilty of Lysander's blood,	75
	Nor is he dead, for aught that I can tell.	
HERMIA	I pray thee, tell me then that he is well.	
DEMETRIUS	And if I could, what should I get therefor?	
HERMIA	A privilege, never to see me more;	
	And from thy hated presence part I so.	80
	See me no more, whether he be dead or no. *Exit*	
DEMETRIUS	There is no following her in this fierce vein;	
	Here therefore for a while I will remain.	
	So sorrow's heaviness[8] doth heavier grow	
	For debt that bankrupt sleep doth sorrow owe[9],	85
	Which now in some slight measure it will pay,	
	If for his tender[10] here I make some stay.	
	[*He*] *lies down* [*and sleeps*].	
OBERON	What hast thou done? Thou hast mistaken quite,	
	And laid the love juice on some true love's sight.	
	Of thy misprision[11] must perforce ensue[12]	90
	Some true love turned, and not a false turned true.	
PUCK	Then fate o'errules, that, one man holding troth,	
	A million fail, confounding oath on oath[13].	
OBERON	About the wood go swifter than the wind,	
	And Helena of Athens look thou find[14].	95
	All fancy-sick[15] she is and pale of cheer[16]	
	With sighs of love, that costs the fresh blood dear.	
	By some illusion see thou bring her here;	
	I'll charm his eyes against[17] she do appear.	
PUCK	I go, I go, look how I go!	100
	Swifter than arrow from the Tartar's[18] bow. *Exit*	

73

Oberon puts the magic juice on Demetrius's eyes, and Lysander enters with Helena. He is still trying to convince Helena that he loves her. She thinks he's lying.

剧情简介： 欧博让将魔法汁滴在迪米垂耶的眼睑上，接着理善德随海乐娜上场。他仍在努力说服海乐娜相信他爱她。海乐娜认为他在说谎。

1 Puck – a child?

Today, Puck is usually played by an adult. But folklore about Puck, or Robin Goodfellow, portrays him as very young. Does he seem childlike? List the ways in which Puck behaves and thinks like a child. Find quotations and events that suggest he might be pleased at the mayhem (混乱) and be insensitive to the feelings of the lovers.

1 dye 颜色
2 apple 瞳孔
3 espy 看见
4 fee 回报
5 fond pageant 愚蠢的表演
6 befall prepost'rously 结果荒诞，违反常理
7 derision 愚弄，嘲笑
8 vow 发誓许诺
9 nativity 产生之时
10 badge of faith 象征忠诚的徽章（这里指眼泪）
11 advance 显示出
12 truth kills … fray 当您对我的真诚誓言违背了您对哈蜜娅的真诚誓言，那就是恶魔般的神圣对决
13 light as tales 和编造的故事一样轻（没有分量）

Themes 主题分析

'Lord, what fools these mortals be!' (in small groups)

Here, the audience laughs along with Puck at 'mortals' like the lovers. Are human beings fools? In what ways?

Place a large sheet of paper in the centre of your group. Together, suggest moments so far in the play where mortals have been shown behaving or speaking foolishly, and write them on the paper. Everyone should contribute. Each group decides on the best ideas and shares them with the class.

2 Class direction (whole class)

You need three volunteers – one to play Puck, one to play Oberon and one the sleeping Demetrius. The class directs the actors through lines 88–121. Take all suggestions seriously, try them and evaluate them. Think about:

• showing relationships • movement • gestures • tone of voice
• use of silence • emphasis on particular words • creating dramatic effect

See if you can reach a unanimous decision about what works best as a vision of the characters in this episode. To work, this exercise needs imagination, confidence and, most importantly, respectful listening skills.

A Midsummer Night's Dream Act 3 Scene 2
仲夏夜之梦

OBERON   [*Squeezing the juice on Demetrius's eyes.*]
          Flower of this purple dye¹,
          Hit with Cupid's archery,
          Sink in apple² of his eye.
          When his love he doth espy³,   105
          Let her shine as gloriously
          As the Venus of the sky.
          When thou wak'st, if she be by,
          Beg of her for remedy.

                    Enter Puck.

PUCK   Captain of our fairy band,   110
          Helena is here at hand,
          And the youth mistook by me,
          Pleading for a lover's fee⁴.
          Shall we their fond pageant⁵ see?
          Lord, what fools these mortals be!   115

OBERON   Stand aside. The noise they make
          Will cause Demetrius to awake.

PUCK   Then will two at once woo one –
          That must needs be sport alone;
          And those things do best please me   120
          That befall prepost'rously⁶.

            Enter LYSANDER *and* HELENA.

LYSANDER Why should you think that I should woo in scorn?
              Scorn and derision⁷ never come in tears.
          Look when I vow⁸, I weep; and vows so born,
              In their nativity⁹ all truth appears.   125
          How can these things in me seem scorn to you,
          Bearing the badge of faith¹⁰ to prove them true?

HELENA   You do advance¹¹ your cunning more and more.
              When truth kills truth, O devilish-holy fray¹²!
          These vows are Hermia's. Will you give her o'er?   130
              Weigh oath with oath, and you will nothing weigh;
          Your vows to her and me, put in two scales,
          Will even weigh, and both as light as tales¹³.

LYSANDER I had no judgement when to her I swore.

Demetrius wakes, and tells Helena in very exaggerated language how much he loves her. She thinks that he is part of the plot to mock her.

剧情简介：迪米垂耶一觉醒来，用极尽夸张的语言向海乐娜讲述他是多么爱她。海乐娜认为迪米垂耶也一起谋划来戏弄她。

Characters 人物分析

Demetrius's transformation

Remind yourself of Demetrius's language and behaviour towards Helena so far in the play.

a Find three quotations that sum up his character and his feelings for Helena prior to waking under the influence of the potion.

b Now choose three quotations that show his transformation upon waking.

If you would like to reflect more on this, see 'Demetrius', page 160.

1 Taurus   托罗斯山脉（在土耳其境内，泛指高山）
2 courtesy   礼貌举止
3 join in souls   串通一气
4 parts   天赋，品质
5 trim exploit   卓越的功绩（反讽）
6 noble sort   良好的品格
7 extort   折磨，压迫
8 sport   乐趣

◀ Notice Puck's and Oberon's expressions. What might they be thinking as they watch Helena, Demetrius and Lysander?

Write about it 写作练习

Helena's changing emotions

Read Helena's speech in the script opposite carefully. Reveal Helena's changing emotions and her developing character by writing down her thoughts and feelings in modern prose using the first person.

1 The dance of the lovers – who loves whom? (III)

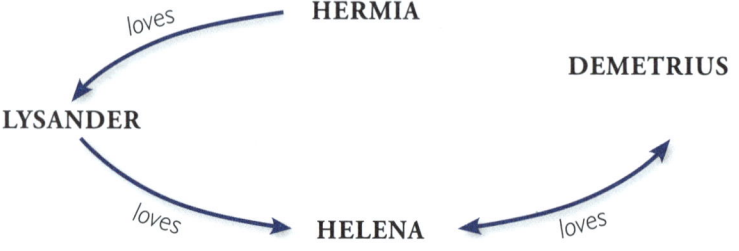

HELENA	Nor none, in my mind, now you give her o'er.	135
LYSANDER	Demetrius loves her, and he loves not you.	
DEMETRIUS	(*Waking*.)	
	O Helen, goddess, nymph, perfect, divine!	
	To what, my love, shall I compare thine eyne?	
	Crystal is muddy! O, how ripe in show	
	Thy lips, those kissing cherries, tempting grow!	140
	That pure congealèd white, high Taurus'[1] snow,	
	Fanned with the eastern wind, turns to a crow	
	When thou hold'st up thy hand. O, let me kiss	
	This princess of pure white, this seal of bliss!	
HELENA	O spite! O Hell! I see you all are bent	145
	To set against me for your merriment.	
	If you were civil, and knew courtesy[2],	
	You would not do me thus much injury.	
	Can you not hate me, as I know you do,	
	But you must join in souls[3] to mock me too?	150
	If you were men, as men you are in show,	
	You would not use a gentle lady so,	
	To vow, and swear, and superpraise my parts[4],	
	When I am sure you hate me with your hearts.	
	You both are rivals, and love Hermia;	155
	And now both rivals to mock Helena.	
	A trim exploit[5], a manly enterprise,	
	To conjure tears up in a poor maid's eyes	
	With your derision! None of noble sort[6]	
	Would so offend a virgin, and extort[7]	160
	A poor soul's patience, all to make you sport[8].	

Lysander and Demetrius argue over Helena. Hermia enters and asks Lysander why he left her. Lysander replies it is because he hates her.

 剧情简介：理善德和迪米垂耶为了海乐娜争论不休。哈蜜娅上场，质问理善德为何离她而去。理善德回答这是因为他讨厌她。

1 The lovers at war

Remember that the two men are under the influence of the flower's magic, but the two women do not suffer the same enchantment; they are bewildered by what's going on.

a Keep this difference between the state of the men and that of the women in mind as you read or act out the rest of the scene.

b Look carefully at the photos on this and the previous page, and consider how the actors in the two productions are revealing their state of mind.

Stagecraft 导演技巧

Onlookers – or voyeurs (偷窥狂)? (in small groups)

When you read the lovers' developing quarrels it is easy to forget that Puck and Oberon are also on stage watching, although when you see a performance their presence is always obvious. This kind of voyeurism – watching the pain and confusion of others – does not reflect well on them. But are Puck and Oberon simply voyeurs?

a Explore the involvement and responses of Puck and Oberon. Should they move or stay still? Should they exchange glances with each other and/or with the audience? Draw up a list of suggestions and try them out in your group.

b How can you make it clear to an audience who is visible and who is invisible? In the production pictured below, Puck and Oberon are positioned high out of the lovers' sightline. In another, the colour of their costumes allowed them to melt into the background. In a third, Oberon and Puck wore luminous cloaks to indicate their magic invisibility. What would you do? Discuss this in your groups, and sketch some of your ideas.

1 **yield you up my part** 舍弃我这部分给您
2 **bequeath** 转让
3 **idle breath** 废话
4 **guest-wise sojourned** 过客般短暂停留
5 **Disparage** 低估，贬低
6 **Lest** 否则
7 **aby** 付出代价
8 **apprehension** 理解力
9 **recompense** 补偿
10 **press to go** 敦促离开
11 **bide** 停留；忍受
12 **engilds the night** 给黑夜镀上金光
13 **oes and eyes** 繁星（oes是o的复数形式，指小亮片；eyes与i的复数谐音双关）
14 **bare** （旧时bear的过去式）

LYSANDER	You are unkind, Demetrius: be not so,	
	For you love Hermia – this you know I know –	
	And here with all good will, with all my heart,	
	In Hermia's love I yield you up my part[1];	165
	And yours of Helena to me bequeath[2],	
	Whom I do love, and will do till my death.	
HELENA	Never did mockers waste more idle breath[3].	
DEMETRIUS	Lysander, keep thy Hermia; I will none.	
	If e'er I loved her, all that love is gone.	170
	My heart to her but as guest-wise sojourned[4],	
	And now to Helen is it home returned,	
	There to remain.	
LYSANDER	Helen, it is not so.	
DEMETRIUS	Disparage[5] not the faith thou dost not know,	
	Lest[6] to thy peril thou aby[7] it dear.	175
	Look where thy love comes: yonder is thy dear.	

Enter Hermia.

HERMIA	Dark night, that from the eye his function takes,	
	The ear more quick of apprehension[8] makes;	
	Wherein it doth impair the seeing sense	
	It pays the hearing double recompense[9].	180
	Thou art not by mine eye, Lysander, found;	
	Mine ear, I thank it, brought me to thy sound.	
	But why unkindly didst thou leave me so?	
LYSANDER	Why should he stay whom love doth press to go[10]?	
HERMIA	What love could press Lysander from my side?	185
LYSANDER	Lysander's love, that would not let him bide[11],	
	Fair Helena – who more engilds the night[12]	
	Than all yon fiery oes and eyes[13] of light.	
	[*To Hermia*] Why seek'st thou me? Could not this make thee know	
	The hate I bare[14] thee made me leave thee so?	190
HERMIA	You speak not as you think; it cannot be.	

Helena now thinks everyone is mocking her, and complains that Hermia should behave better as they have been such close friends for so long.

剧情简介：海乐娜此时觉得每个人都在戏弄她，于是抱怨说哈蜜娅应该表现得更好，因为她们是这么久的好朋友。

▲ The lovers, watched intently by Puck and Oberon. Which line do you think is being spoken at this moment?

1 Lo　（表惊讶）瞧
2 confederacy　同谋
3 conjoined　串通
4 in spite of me　为了欺侮我
5 Injurious　欺负人的，无礼的
6 contrived　合谋
7 bait　折磨
8 foul derision　恶意的嘲弄
9 chid　责备
10 artificial　技艺精湛
11 sampler　刺绣图样
12 warbling　歌唱
13 in one key　音调和谐
14 incorporate　融为一体
15 But … partition　分开的部分连接在一起
16 coats in heraldry　族徽上的图案（一般由盾形图案、头盔、顶饰等构成）
17 crest　盾形上方的饰章，顶饰
18 rent　撕碎
19 asunder　碎，散

1 Helena's speech (in pairs)

a One of you reads Helena's speech aloud. During this, the other person notes down the words and phrases that dominate and/or resonate most strongly with them.

b Swap roles and repeat the activity.

c Now compare what you have written down. Prioritise the most important ideas for you both. Together, construct one sentence describing the most important ideas communicated by this speech.

2 Sisterhood under pressure (in small groups)

Helena's speech raises the issue of loyalty between women. Discuss whether you think falling in love always puts a strain on female friendships. Share your ideas on what emotions you think the female characters feel here. Then consider if those same feelings are present in female relationships today – and whether it is the same for men.

HELENA	Lo[1], she is one of this confederacy[2]!	
	Now I perceive they have conjoined[3] all three	
	To fashion this false sport in spite of me[4].	
	Injurious[5] Hermia, most ungrateful maid,	195
	Have you conspired, have you with these contrived[6]	
	To bait[7] me with this foul derision[8]?	
	Is all the counsel that we two have shared,	
	The sisters' vows, the hours that we have spent	
	When we have chid[9] the hasty-footed time	200
	For parting us – O, is all forgot?	
	All schooldays' friendship, childhood innocence?	
	We, Hermia, like two artificial[10] gods	
	Have with our needles created both one flower,	
	Both on one sampler[11], sitting on one cushion,	205
	Both warbling[12] of one song, both in one key[13],	
	As if our hands, our sides, voices, and minds	
	Had been incorporate[14]. So we grew together	
	Like to a double cherry, seeming parted,	
	But yet an union in partition[15],	210
	Two lovely berries moulded on one stem;	
	So with two seeming bodies but one heart,	
	Two of the first, like coats in heraldry[16],	
	Due but to one, and crownèd with one crest[17].	
	And will you rent[18] our ancient love asunder[19],	215
	To join with men in scorning your poor friend?	
	It is not friendly, 'tis not maidenly.	
	Our sex, as well as I, may chide you for it,	
	Though I alone do feel the injury.	
HERMIA	I am amazèd at your passionate words.	220
	I scorn you not; it seems that you scorn me.	

Helena asks Hermia to have pity on her, and starts to leave because she's sure they are mocking her. Lysander offers to fight Demetrius for Helena.

 剧情简介：海乐娜求哈蜜娅同情她，然后她准备离开，因为她确信这三个人都在戏弄自己。理善德提出要为了海乐娜而与迪米垂耶决斗。

1 Helena's bewilderment (困惑) and distress (in pairs)

Helena, thoroughly confused by what is going on, makes three long speeches.

a Her first speech, lines 192–219, stresses the great friendship she and Hermia have always enjoyed. Work through it, identifying all the images of positive relationships and childhood. Which image strikes you as most powerfully conveying close friendship? Explain why.

b In her second speech, lines 222–35, she accuses Hermia of encouraging the two men to mock her, and appeals for pity. Take turns to speak the lines, bringing out Helena's accusatory tone as strongly as you can by stressing the words that most express her feelings.

c Her third speech, lines 237–44, is spoken to all three of the other characters. She accuses them all of laughing at her, condemns them for making her the subject of their 'sport', and prepares to leave, blaming herself. By this time Helena is probably very emotional and may accompany all she says with gestures and facial expressions. Speak the lines, using actions to illustrate their meaning.

1 even but now 就在刚才
2 celestial 天上，非凡
3 tender me 给予我
4 setting on 唆使
5 What though = What if
6 in grace 得到宠爱
7 hung upon with 依赖
8 Persever = Persevere（接着［装下去］）
9 counterfeit 假装
10 sad 凝重
11 Make mouths 扮鬼脸
12 chronicled 载入史册
13 make me 强加给我
14 argument 争执
15 ye 你们
16 compel 用武力强迫
17 withdraw 拔剑

Themes 主题分析

Men fighting over women (in pairs)

In lines 248–56, the men begin to quarrel and they resort to threats of violence – 'withdraw, and prove it too'. The lines suggest a rather conventional response and clearly mirror other scenes of male domination and aggression. The language seems to indicate that things are getting out of control. Before you read on, briefly predict some of the ways in which this conflict could end.

HELENA	Have you not set Lysander, as in scorn,
	To follow me, and praise my eyes and face?
	And made your other love, Demetrius,
	Who even but now[1] did spurn me with his foot,
	To call me goddess, nymph, divine and rare,
	Precious, celestial[2]? Wherefore speaks he this
	To her he hates? And wherefore doth Lysander
	Deny your love, so rich within his soul,
	And tender me[3], forsooth, affection,
	But by your setting on[4], by your consent?
	What though[5] I be not so in grace[6] as you,
	So hung upon with[7] love, so fortunate,
	But miserable most, to love unloved:
	This you should pity rather than despise.
HERMIA	I understand not what you mean by this.
HELENA	Ay, do! Persever[8], counterfeit[9] sad[10] looks,
	Make mouths[11] upon me when I turn my back,
	Wink each at other, hold the sweet jest up.
	This sport, well carried, shall be chronicled[12].
	If you have any pity, grace, or manners,
	You would not make me[13] such an argument[14].
	But fare ye[15] well. 'Tis partly my own fault,
	Which death or absence soon shall remedy.
LYSANDER	Stay, gentle Helena: hear my excuse,
	My love, my life, my soul, fair Helena!
HELENA	O, excellent!
HERMIA	[*To Lysander*] Sweet, do not scorn her so.
DEMETRIUS	If she cannot entreat, I can compel[16].
LYSANDER	Thou canst compel no more than she entreat;
	Thy threats have no more strength than her weak prayers.
	Helen, I love thee, by my life, I do:
	I swear by that which I will lose for thee
	To prove him false that says I love thee not.
DEMETRIUS	I say I love thee more than he can do.
LYSANDER	If thou say so, withdraw[17], and prove it too.
DEMETRIUS	Quick, come.

Hermia clings on to Lysander as he insults her and tells her that he hates her and loves Helena.
剧情简介：哈蜜娅对理善德恋恋不舍，哪怕理善德对她几番羞辱，并说讨厌她而爱海乐娜。

1 The quarrel – a read-through (in fours)

The quarrel between the lovers really heats up here. The episode provides wonderful entertainment in the theatre because, although it might seem serious, it usually comes over as very funny with lots of physical humour. **Dramatic irony** (戏剧反讽) (when the audience knows something the characters do not) also plays a big part of the audience's amused response, as we are the only ones who know what is truly going on. To gain a first impression of what happens, take parts and read lines 256–344.

Write about it 写作练习

Lysander's insults

Lysander's insults – 'Ethiop' and 'tawny Tartar' (references to Hermia's dark hair and complexion) – sound uncomfortable to modern ears. We are now sensitive to racist abuse in a way that the Elizabethans were not. In addition, in Shakespeare's time a tan was considered to be unladylike and to look weather-beaten. Ladies didn't walk much in the open air – it was the working people who had to be out in all weathers.

If you were directing a production, would you omit these insults? Write a few sentences giving the reasons for your decision.

2 Hermia's puzzlement – all questions (in pairs)

Now it is Hermia's turn to be bewildered by what is happening. She simply cannot understand why Lysander rejects and insults her. Most of what she says in the script opposite is in the form of questions.

Count the number of questions and analyse each one. Discuss why Shakespeare gives Hermia so many questions here. Suggest how you might answer her.

1 whereto tends all this　这到底都是怎么回事
2 Ethiop　埃塞俄比人（即今天的埃塞俄比亚人，在古希腊文里，这个词的意思是"黑脸"；这里暗指哈蜜娅皮肤黑）
3 break loose　挣开，摆脱
4 take on　装腔作势
5 tame man　没骨气的懦夫，胆小鬼
6 cat　（比喻哈蜜娅像猫一样黏人）
7 burr　刺儿果（容易黏附在人的衣服或动物的皮毛上）
8 let loose　松开
9 tawny　棕色（指皮肤黝黑）
10 bond　书面保证
11 bond　约束（两方面意思：理善德对海乐娜的爱；哈蜜娅纠缠着理善德，造成对他的约束）
12 erewhile　之前，刚才
13 In earnest　当真

A Midsummer Night's Dream Act 3 Scene 2
仲夏夜之梦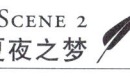

HERMIA	Lysander, whereto tends all this[1]?
LYSANDER	Away, you Ethiop[2]!
DEMETRIUS	No, no, sir,
	Seem to break loose[3], take on[4] as you would follow,
	But yet come not. You are a tame man[5], go.
LYSANDER	Hang off, thou cat[6], thou burr[7]! Vile thing, let loose[8],
	Or I will shake thee from me like a serpent.
HERMIA	Why are you grown so rude? What change is this,
	Sweet love?
LYSANDER	Thy love? – out, tawny[9] Tartar, out;
	Out, loathed medicine! O hated potion, hence!
HERMIA	Do you not jest?
HELENA	Yes, sooth, and so do you.
LYSANDER	Demetrius, I will keep my word with thee.
DEMETRIUS	I would I had your bond[10], for I perceive
	A weak bond[11] holds you. I'll not trust your word.
LYSANDER	What? Should I hurt her, strike her, kill her dead?
	Although I hate her, I'll not harm her so.
HERMIA	What? Can you do me greater harm than hate?
	Hate me? Wherefore? O me, what news, my love?
	Am not I Hermia? Are not you Lysander?
	I am as fair now as I was erewhile[12].
	Since night you loved me; yet since night you left me.
	Why then, you left me – O, the gods forbid! –
	In earnest[13], shall I say?
LYSANDER	Ay, by my life;
	And never did desire to see thee more.
	Therefore be out of hope, of question, of doubt;
	Be certain, nothing truer – 'tis no jest
	That I do hate thee and love Helena.

Hermia turns on Helena and threatens to fight her, thinking Helena has stolen Lysander's love. Helena says she will return to Athens.

 剧情简介：哈蜜娅认定是海乐娜偷走了理善德的爱，于是转而责骂海乐娜，并扬言要与之开战。海乐娜表示她要回雅典。

Stagecraft 导演技巧

Quarrels, insults and fights (in fours)

Hermia's puzzlement now turns to anger and she directs her rage at Helena, accusing her of having stolen Lysander's love. Hermia's accusations arouse Helena's indignation (愤慨), and she responds with similar passion (notice again how Shakespeare shows that 'reason and love keep little company'). Anger leads to insults and insults to violence.

The two women seem very close to fighting, and in line 303 Helena says 'Let her not strike me'. Most directors create a very physical scene here. How would you stage this? In your group, come up with some ideas and try them out. Look at the images on this page and on page 88 to get you started. Record your ideas in your Director's Journal.

1 **juggler** 变戏法的（哈蜜娅以为海乐娜用魔法吸引了理善德）
2 **canker-blossom** 勾引虫子的花
3 **i'faith** 确实
4 **bashfulness** 腼腆
5 **counterfeit** 骗子
6 **personage** 身段，身材
7 **prevailed with him** 征服了他（理善德）
8 **painted maypole** 五月节彩柱（人们在五月节围着跳舞的细高花柱；哈蜜娅借此挖苦海乐娜高瘦的身材）
9 **curst** 恶毒
10 **shrewishness** 撒泼
11 **maid for my cowardice** 胆怯的淑女
12 **evermore** 向来，一直
13 **Save that** 除……外；只是……
14 **stealth unto** 秘密潜入
15 **so** 如果
16 **simple** 单纯

▼ Demetrius and Lysander holding back Hermia.

Characters 人物分析

Love conceals, anger reveals

In previous scenes, we have witnessed a strong friendship between Hermia and Helena. Here, their characters and their relationship appear more complex. Write down evidence of how their relationship has changed. Use your ideas to construct a paragraph that explores this scene and what it reveals about the characters of both women.

A Midsummer Night's Dream Act 3 Scene 2
仲夏夜之梦

HERMIA [*To Helena*]
O me, you juggler[1], you canker-blossom[2],
You thief of love! What, have you come by night
And stol'n my love's heart from him?

HELENA   Fine, i'faith[3]!
Have you no modesty, no maiden shame,   285
No touch of bashfulness[4]? What, will you tear
Impatient answers from my gentle tongue?
Fie, fie, you counterfeit[5], you puppet, you!

HERMIA 'Puppet'? Why so? – Ay, that way goes the game.
Now I perceive that she hath made compare   290
Between our statures; she hath urged her height,
And with her personage[6], her tall personage,
Her height, forsooth, she hath prevailed with him[7].
And are you grown so high in his esteem
Because I am so dwarfish and so low?   295
How low am I, thou painted maypole[8]? Speak!
How low am I? I am not yet so low
But that my nails can reach unto thine eyes.

HELENA I pray you, though you mock me, gentlemen,
Let her not hurt me. I was never curst[9];   300
I have no gift at all in shrewishness[10].
I am a right maid for my cowardice[11];
Let her not strike me. You perhaps may think
Because she is something lower than myself
That I can match her.

HERMIA   Lower? Hark, again!   305

HELENA Good Hermia, do not be so bitter with me.
I evermore[12] did love you, Hermia,
Did ever keep your counsels, never wronged you,
Save that[13] in love unto Demetrius
I told him of your stealth unto[14] this wood.   310
He followed you; for love I followed him,
But he hath chid me hence, and threatened me
To strike me, spurn me, nay, to kill me too.
And now, so[15] you will let me quiet go,
To Athens will I bear my folly back,   315
And follow you no further. Let me go;
You see how simple[16] and how fond I am.

Helena explains her fear of 'little' Hermia. Lysander and Demetrius leave to fight. Helena runs away and Hermia follows.

 剧情简介：海乐娜述说着她如何惧怕"小个子"哈蜜娅。理善德与迪米垂耶下场去决斗。海乐娜跑开，哈蜜娅追下。

Language in the play 剧中语言

Insults – 'You bead, you acorn' (in small groups)

a In your group, make a list of all the insults in the script opposite. Each person should then choose their two favourites. Take turns to shout them at each other. Add gestures and facial expressions to increase their impact.

b These insults now sound old-fashioned, but are there any that you would recommend bringing back? Why?

1 keen 尖刻，恶毒
2 shrewd 凶悍
3 vixen 雌狐狸（泼妇，母夜叉）
4 flout 欺侮；嘲笑
5 minimus 卑微
6 knot-grass 扁蓄草，两耳草（被认为会阻碍生长发育）
7 too officious 过分殷勤
8 cheek by jowl 面对面
9 coil 吵闹，混乱
10 'long of 因为
11 curst company 可怕的同伴
12 fray 打架

1 Storyboard (故事板)

Act 3 Scene 2 is a long and complex scene, and it is easy to lose track of the order of events. Create a six-frame storyboard of the action in the lovers' story in this scene, up to the point of Hermia's exit. Place a caption or quotation in each frame that you feel best summarises the key moment in the scene.

A Midsummer Night's Dream Act 3 Scene 2
仲夏夜之梦

HERMIA	Why, get you gone! Who is't that hinders you?
HELENA	A foolish heart that I leave here behind.
HERMIA	What, with Lysander?
HELENA	With Demetrius. 320
LYSANDER	Be not afraid; she shall not harm thee, Helena.
DEMETRIUS	No, sir. She shall not, though you take her part.
HELENA	O, when she is angry she is keen[1] and shrewd[2];
	She was a vixen[3] when she went to school,
	And though she be but little, she is fierce. 325
HERMIA	Little again? Nothing but low and little?
	Why will you suffer her to flout[4] me thus?
	Let me come to her.
LYSANDER	Get you gone, you dwarf,
	You minimus[5] of hindering knot-grass[6] made,
	You bead, you acorn.
DEMETRIUS	You are too officious[7] 330
	In her behalf that scorns your services.
	Let her alone: speak not of Helena,
	Take not her part; for if thou dost intend
	Never so little show of love to her,
	Thou shalt aby it.
LYSANDER	Now she holds me not – 335
	Now follow, if thou dur'st, to try whose right,
	Of thine or mine, is most in Helena.
DEMETRIUS	Follow? Nay, I'll go with thee, cheek by jowl[8].
	Exeunt Lysander and Demetrius
HERMIA	You, mistress, all this coil[9] is 'long of[10] you.
	Nay, go not back.
HELENA	I will not trust you, I, 340
	Nor longer stay in your curst company[11].
	Your hands than mine are quicker for a fray[12];
	My legs are longer, though, to run away! *[Exit]*
HERMIA	I am amazed, and know not what to say. *Exit*

89

Puck explains his mistake. Oberon orders him to lead Lysander and Demetrius astray by imitating their voices. He will 'beg' the boy from Titania, then release her from the charm and put all things right.

剧情简介：捣蛋精解释为何自己会认错人。欧博让命令他去模仿理善德和迪米垂耶俩人的嗓音，把他俩引入歧途。欧博让则要去跟提坦妮娅"讨要"那个男孩，然后解除对她施的魔法，让一切回归正常。

Stagecraft 导演技巧

Master and servant (in pairs)

a Talk together about how, in performance, you would show the relationship between Oberon and Puck here.

b During a long speech, the other actor on stage has the problem of reacting but saying nothing. Take turns to speak Oberon's lines in the script opposite while the other responds as Puck. His responses can be as subtle or as physical as you wish. Choose your favourite reaction and share it with the class.

1 Oberon the peacemaker

a Consider the photograph below and the one on page 92. What do they suggest about Oberon's qualities and whether he really wishes to bring about love and harmony? Use evidence from the script opposite to support your views.

b Oberon's power over others is clear in his speech here. Sum up in your own words exactly how he intends to put things right.

1 enterprise 承担的工作
2 sort 结果
3 jangling 吵闹，斗嘴
4 Hie 快走
5 welkin 天空，天穹
6 Acheron 传说中地狱的冥河
7 testy 好争斗，一触即跳
8 Like … tongue 你时而模仿理善德的声音
9 bitter wrong 尖刻的责骂，臭骂
10 rail 辱骂
11 death-counterfeiting sleep 死一般的沉睡
12 leaden 铅一般沉重
13 wonted 平常，惯常
14 fruitless 无用
15 wend 继续，延续
16 league 爱的誓约，联姻
17 date 持续期，有效期

Themes 主题分析

Waking from a dream

Oberon suggests that when the lovers wake, 'all this derision / Shall seem a dream and fruitless vision'.

How might the audience react to the suggestion that everything that has happened is just a dream, a kind of surreal (离奇，怪诞) parallel universe?

A Midsummer Night's Dream Act 3 Scene 2
仲夏夜之梦

Oberon and Puck come forward.

OBERON This is thy negligence. Still thou mistak'st, 345
Or else committ'st thy knaveries wilfully.

PUCK Believe me, King of Shadows, I mistook.
Did not you tell me I should know the man
By the Athenian garments he had on?
And so far blameless proves my enterprise[1] 350
That I have 'nointed an Athenian's eyes;
And so far am I glad it so did sort[2],
As this their jangling[3] I esteem a sport.

OBERON Thou seest these lovers seek a place to fight:
Hie[4] therefore, Robin, overcast the night; 355
The starry welkin[5] cover thou anon
With drooping fog as black as Acheron[6],
And lead these testy[7] rivals so astray
As one come not within another's way.
Like to Lysander sometime frame thy tongue[8], 360
Then stir Demetrius up with bitter wrong[9],
And sometime rail[10] thou like Demetrius;
And from each other look thou lead them thus,
Till o'er their brows death-counterfeiting sleep[11]
With leaden[12] legs and batty wings doth creep. 365
Then crush this herb into Lysander's eye,
Whose liquor hath this virtuous property,
To take from thence all error with his might,
And make his eyeballs roll with wonted[13] sight.
When they next wake, all this derision 370
Shall seem a dream and fruitless[14] vision,
And back to Athens shall the lovers wend[15]
With league[16] whose date[17] till death shall never end.
Whiles I in this affair do thee employ
I'll to my Queen and beg her Indian boy; 375
And then I will her charmèd eye release
From monster's view, and all things shall be peace.

Day approaches, and though the fairies (unlike other spirits) can exist in the day, Oberon urges haste. Puck looks forward to misleading the lovers. Lysander returns and Puck deceives him.

✒ 剧情简介：天将破晓，尽管这群仙子并非见光即消失的那类精灵，但欧博让还是催促捣蛋精赶紧去办。捣蛋精已迫不及待地要去误导这两位情敌了。理善德返场，捣蛋精骗他。

▼ Why do you think the director of this production has chosen to portray Oberon and Puck in this way?

1 dragons （希腊神话中月亮女神辛西娅［Cynthia］驾着飞龙拉的车驶过天空）
2 full 非常（用来加强语气）
3 Aurora's harbinger 奥婼菈的先驱（即启明星、晨星，宣告黎明女神的到来；奥婼菈是罗马神话中的黎明女神）
4 consort 与……为伴
5 forester 林官（保护野物，防备偷猎者；诗歌中也指猎人）
6 groves may tread 可以在树林中游走
7 notwithstanding 尽管如此
8 effect 完成
9 Goblin 小妖精
10 drawn 剑已出鞘
11 plainer 更为开阔

Language in the play 剧中语言

Puck's and Oberon's language (in pairs)

a With your partner, focus on either Puck's or Oberon's speech and explore what you find interesting and powerful in their imagery and diction. What picture of each character and of the fairy world is being painted here, and to what effect?

b Move to sit with someone who has considered the other character. In turn, talk through your ideas. Ask questions if there is anything you don't understand about your partner's ideas.

Write about it 写作练习

Images of the fairy world (by yourself)

Spend fifteen minutes writing a response to the following statement: 'The language of the fairy world is full of intense and memorable imagery.' Use quotations from this scene to support your ideas and opinions.

PUCK	My fairy lord, this must be done with haste,
	For night's swift dragons[1] cut the clouds full[2] fast,
	And yonder shines Aurora's harbinger[3], 380
	At whose approach ghosts wandering here and there
	Troop home to churchyards. Damnèd spirits all,
	That in crossways and floods have burial,
	Already to their wormy beds are gone.
	For fear lest day should look their shames upon, 385
	They wilfully themselves exile from light,
	And must for aye consort[4] with black-browed night.
OBERON	But we are spirits of another sort.
	I with the morning's love have oft made sport,
	And like a forester[5] the groves may tread[6] 390
	Even till the eastern gate, all fiery-red,
	Opening on Neptune with fair blessèd beams,
	Turns into yellow gold his salt green streams.
	But notwithstanding[7], haste, make no delay;
	We may effect[8] this business yet ere day. [*Exit*] 395
PUCK	Up and down, up and down,
	I will lead them up and down;
	I am feared in field and town.
	Goblin[9], lead them up and down.
	Here comes one. 400

Enter Lysander.

LYSANDER	Where art thou, proud Demetrius? Speak thou now.
PUCK	Here, villain, drawn[10] and ready! Where art thou?
LYSANDER	I will be with thee straight.
PUCK	Follow me then
	To plainer[11] ground.
	[*Exit Lysander*]

Puck misleads both Demetrius and Lysander by imitating their voices. Both men finally have had enough and fall asleep.

剧情简介：捣蛋精模仿迪米垂耶和理善德的声音，把他俩骗得团团转。两个人终于疲惫不堪，睡着了。

1 recreant 懦夫；恶棍
2 defiled 玷污名誉，侮辱
3 manhood 男子气概（通常指力量与勇气）
4 dares me on 挑衅我
5 lighter-heeled 腿脚更轻快
6 Abide 面对
7 wot 知道
8 stand 站住；迎战
9 buy this dear 为此付出沉痛代价
10 faintness constraineth me 疲乏困住了我
11 measure out my length 卧倒，躺下

Stagecraft 导演技巧

Four practical problems to resolve (in small groups)

a Consider how Puck should imitate Lysander's voice well enough to fool Demetrius (and, a little later, imitate Demetrius's own voice). Discuss the different dramatic effects of using good imitation and deliberately inaccurate imitation.

b It is meant to be as dark as 'black-browed night', so Lysander and Demetrius cannot see each other and become confused. How could this effect be achieved and yet still allow the audience to see the action clearly?

c Work out how to position the lovers near to one another. Remember that Lysander must sleep near Hermia, so that he falls back in love with her when he wakes. The stage direction simply reads '*Sleeps*', but in many productions Puck takes a direct (and often very funny) part in getting the lovers to sleep near their intended partners.

d The characters in this play sleep a lot and this could cause practical problems on stage. If you were directing, would you want actors to lie on the bare stage floor, or would you want a set that offered more comfortable options such as mossy banks or grassy glades? Talk together about the problems and the solutions, and then sketch or write in your Director's Journal your ideas for a set that accommodates the sleeping lovers.

Enter Demetrius.

DEMETRIUS Lysander, speak again.
Thou runaway, thou coward, art thou fled?   405
Speak! In some bush? Where dost thou hide thy head?
PUCK Thou coward, art thou bragging to the stars,
Telling the bushes that thou look'st for wars,
And wilt not come? Come, recreant¹, come, thou child,
I'll whip thee with a rod. He is defiled²   410
That draws a sword on thee.
DEMETRIUS   Yea, art thou there?
PUCK Follow my voice. We'll try no manhood³ here.

Exeunt

[*Enter Lysander.*]

LYSANDER He goes before me, and still dares me on⁴;
When I come where he calls, then he is gone.
The villain is much lighter-heeled⁵ than I;   415
I followed fast, but faster he did fly,
That fallen am I in dark uneven way,
And here will rest me. (*Lies down.*) Come, thou gentle day,
For if but once thou show me thy grey light
I'll find Demetrius and revenge this spite. [*Sleeps.*] 420

Enter Puck and Demetrius.

PUCK Ho, ho, ho! Coward, why com'st thou not?
DEMETRIUS Abide⁶ me if thou dar'st, for well I wot⁷
Thou runn'st before me, shifting every place,
And dar'st not stand⁸ nor look me in the face.
Where art thou now?
PUCK   Come hither; I am here.   425
DEMETRIUS Nay then, thou mock'st me. Thou shalt buy this dear⁹
If ever I thy face by daylight see.
Now, go thy way; faintness constraineth me¹⁰
To measure out my length¹¹ on this cold bed.
By day's approach look to be visited. [*Sleeps.*]   430

Helena and Hermia enter separately, exhausted, and fall asleep. Puck puts the magic juice on Lysander's eyes to make him love Hermia again.

剧情简介： 海乐娜与哈蜜娅分别上场，精疲力竭，也睡着了。捣蛋精将魔药汁滴在理善德的眼上，让他重新爱上哈蜜娅。

Language in the play 剧中语言

Rhymes – mortals and fairies (in threes)

The final two episodes of this scene (from line 350) are in rhyming verse (韵文；诗体). The rhymes are particularly obvious in the script opposite. In Shakespeare's day, 'east' could rhyme with 'detest'.

Take parts and read aloud the script opposite, emphasising the rhymes. Then talk together about whether Puck (a fairy) can more convincingly stress the rhymes than Hermia and Helena (mortals). What would be your advice to the actors?

Write about it 写作练习

Sleep and dreams

At the end of the scene, the lovers are asleep. Write down the thoughts and feelings of each as they drift into sleep. Use rhyming couplets if you dare! Alternatively, write about their dreams.

1 Improvise an awakening
(in fours)

Improvise a scene immediately following this one, in which the lovers wake up and discover that they are now neatly sorted out into couples. How confused or amazed are they? What do they remember? How do they decipher the 'dream' from reality? You will find out how Shakespeare dramatises the wakening in the next act.

1 Abate 缩短
2 From … detest 离开这些厌恶与我为伍的人
3 Steal 躲开
4 curst 脾气暴躁
5 Bedabbled 沾湿，玷污
6 Naught = Nothing
7 Jack … again （此处混合了三个莎士比亚时代的谚语：Let every man have his own，All shall be well and Jack shall have Jill以及All is well and the man has his mare again，意思都是"男人最终都能得到适合自己的女人"）

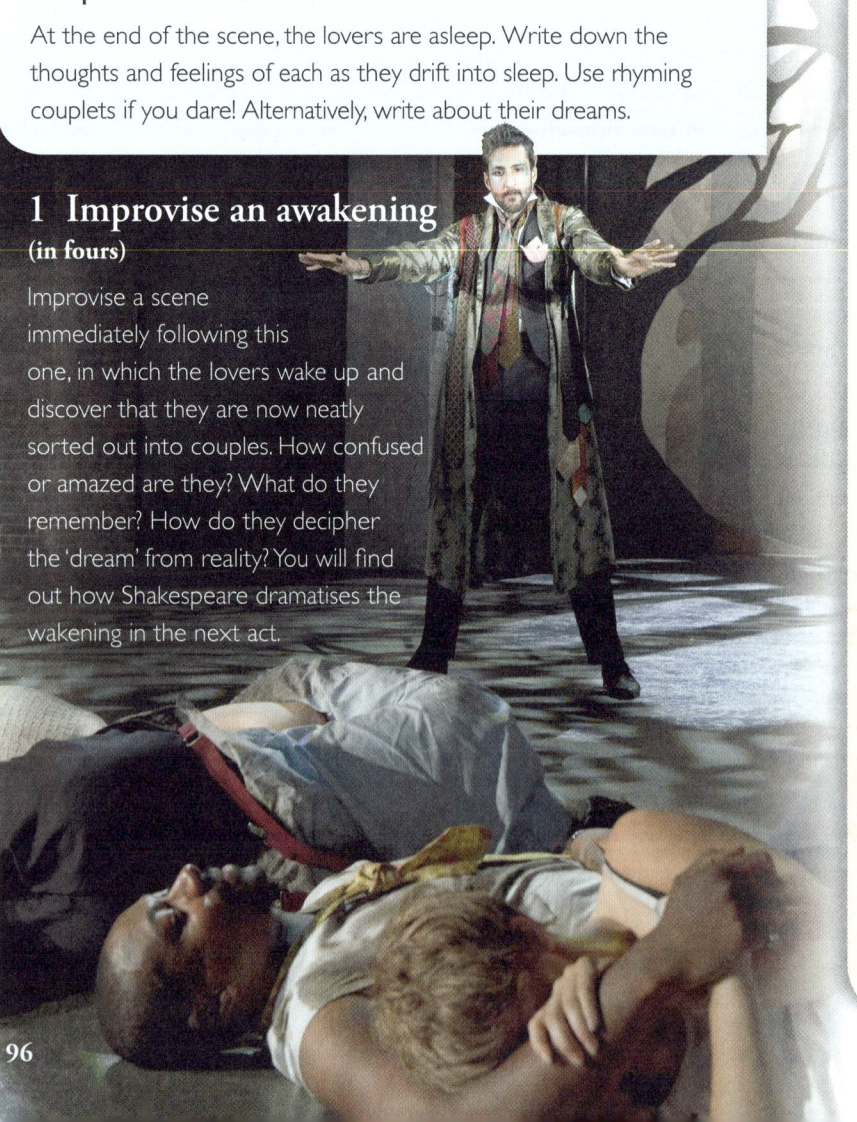

A Midsummer Night's Dream Act 3 Scene 2
仲夏夜之梦

Enter Helena.

HELENA O weary night, O long and tedious night,
　　Abate¹ thy hours, shine comforts from the east,
That I may back to Athens by daylight
　　From these that my poor company detest²;
And sleep, that sometimes shuts up sorrow's eye, 435
Steal³ me awhile from mine own company. (*Sleeps.*)

PUCK　　Yet but three? Come one more,
　　Two of both kinds makes up four.
　　Here she comes, curst⁴ and sad.
　　Cupid is a knavish lad 440
　　Thus to make poor females mad.

Enter Hermia.

HERMIA Never so weary, never so in woe,
　　Bedabbled⁵ with the dew, and torn with briars –
I can no further crawl, no further go;
　　My legs can keep no pace with my desires. 445
Here will I rest me till the break of day.
Heavens shield Lysander, if they mean a fray. [*Sleeps.*]

PUCK　　　　On the ground
　　　　Sleep sound.
　　　　I'll apply 450
　　　　To your eye,
　　Gentle lover, remedy.
　　[*Squeezes the juice on Lysander's eyes.*]
　　　　When thou wak'st,
　　　　Thou tak'st
　　　　True delight 455
　　　　In the sight
　　　　Of thy former lady's eye;
　　And the country proverb known,
　　That every man should take his own,
　　In your waking shall be shown. 460
　　　　Jack shall have Jill,
　　　　Naught⁶ shall go ill:
The man shall have his mare again⁷, and all shall be well.
　　　　[*Exit Puck*;] *the lovers remain on stage, asleep*

97

A Midsummer Night's Dream 仲夏夜之梦

Looking back at Act 3 第3幕回顾
Activities for groups or individuals

1 Transformation

There are many myths about people being transformed into animals, including asses (you may want to research this in both mythology and literature). Bottom is something of an ass (fool) already. Some people have seen a darker side to his transformation into a real ass, associating the ass with sexual prowess. Others see it as a mockery of romance and of both men and women's behaviour when in love.

Discuss with a partner the effect on the audience of including this transformation in the play. Share your ideas with the class.

2 The world of the wood

Creating a magical woodland on stage, where so much complex action and change occurs, is a significant undertaking for a set designer. Use one or more of the following activities to help you visualise the importance and impact of setting in the play.

a **Map** Devise a map of Athens and the wood. The play hints at locations, but think about Titania's bower in relation to the Mechanicals' rehearsal space. Also insert where the various lovers' scenes might take place. (Remember that the Mechanicals don't meet the lovers.)

b **Website** Design a website for 'a wood near Athens'. Your aim is to attract tourists.

c **Mood board** Create a mood board (a poster that uses colours, images, textures and samples to present a design) to show how you think the world of the woods should look on stage. You could use drawings, photographs, paints, images from magazines or other productions, fabric samples and so on.

d **Board game** Develop a board game based on *A Midsummer Night's Dream*.

e **Stage set** For professional stage productions, designers always make a detailed model set before proceeding to the full-sized version. Sketch or describe in writing your own stage set for the woodland scenes.

f **Costume design** Design costumes for the fairy world. In the play's imagery, fairies are connected with the natural world and the woodland. Use this connection to help your thinking about costume and colour. As you design costumes for the fairy world, think of contrasting dress for the Mechanicals, the lovers and the court.

3 Binary oppositions (二元对立)

A **binary opposition** is a pair of opposites commonly used in literature to compare ideas, values and language. Literature is full of comparisons and juxtapositions between ideas such as youth and age, innocence and experience and good and evil. A good example is the opposition of day and night, where night represents menace, danger and the unconscious, and is juxtaposed with day – a time of clarity, light and consciousness. Interesting binary oppositions in *A Midsummer Night's Dream* are the contrasting of the rational versus the emotional, and dreams versus reality.

In a group, make a list of as many binary opposites in the play as you can find. Which characters would you attach each of these to in particular? Try to find evidence in the script that supports your understanding of each of your opposites.

4 Stage directions

There is a lot of movement and action in Act 3, making it complex for actors to enter, exit, respond appropriately and position themselves on stage. Pick a part of this act that interests you, and rewrite the stage directions to give the actors more information and thus try to improve their performance.

▲ *The Nightmare* by John Henry Fuseli, 1781.

5 Midsummer dream – or nightmare?

There are many nightmarish things about this play – including Bottom being turned into an ass, and Hermia's nightmare of the snake.

Describe, paint or draw a memorable dream you have had. Then, in groups, relate your dreams and nightmares, and see if you can find meaning in them. Discuss whether you believe dreams have any significance to our lives, if they reveal our fears and if they can inform or influence reality.

Titania speaks lovingly to Bottom. He gives instructions to her fairies to scratch him and find him food.
剧情简介：提坦妮娅对包臀亲热地说着情话。包臀差遣提坦妮娅的仙子们为他挠痒、觅食。

Characters 人物分析

Bottom (in sixes)

a With your group, discuss how you would portray Bottom here. During your discussion, consider the following questions:

- How aware is Bottom of what is happening? Is he puzzled or can he not believe his good fortune?
- Look again at the requests he makes of the fairies. What do you find interesting and amusing?
- What do we learn about Bottom's character? How does he view himself?
- What do you notice about his language (for example, note his **malapropisms** (近音词误用) – the mistaken use of words that sound similar)? What do you think his tone would be as he talks to the fairies?

b Now practise acting out the scene up to line 99. Afterwards, perform your version to the class.

1 coy 抚摸，爱抚
2 Mounsieur = Monsieur（先生；包臀的法语很糟糕）
3 thistle 蓟
4 fret 烦躁
5 overflown 被淹死
6 signior 先生（意大利语）
7 neaf 拳头
8 leave your courtesy 不必多礼
9 Cavalery 骑士（包臀对cavalier的误用）
10 tender 娇嫩
11 the tongs and the bones 火钳和骨板（旧时很简陋的乐器）
12 a peck of provender 一堆干草料（peck是容量单位）
13 munch 大声咀嚼
14 bottle 捆
15 fellow 可比物，同等物

▲ Bottom, Titania and the fairies. Talk with a partner about the mood that you think this production has created of the fairy world.

Act 4 Scene 1
The wood

Enter TITANIA, *Queen of Fairies, and* BOTTOM, *and fairies [including* PEASEBLOSSOM, COBWEB *and* MUSTARDSEED;] *and the King* OBERON *behind them.*

TITANIA   Come, sit thee down upon this flowery bed
While I thy amiable cheeks do coy[1],
And stick musk-roses in thy sleek smooth head,
And kiss thy fair large ears, my gentle joy.

BOTTOM   Where's Peaseblossom?

PEASEBLOSSOM   Ready.

BOTTOM   Scratch my head, Peaseblossom. Where's Mounsieur[2] Cobweb?

COBWEB   Ready.

BOTTOM   Mounsieur Cobweb, good Mounsieur, get you your weapons in your hand, and kill me a red-hipped humble-bee on the top of a thistle[3]; and, good Mounsieur, bring me the honey-bag. Do not fret[4] yourself too much in the action, Mounsieur; and, good Mounsieur, have a care the honey-bag break not; I would be loath to have you overflown[5] with a honey-bag, signior[6]. Where's Mounsieur Mustardseed?

MUSTARDSEED   Ready.

BOTTOM   Give me your neaf[7], Mounsieur Mustardseed. Pray you, leave your courtesy[8], good Mounsieur.

MUSTARDSEED   What's your will?

BOTTOM   Nothing, good Mounsieur, but to help Cavalery[9] Peaseblossom to scratch. I must to the barber's, Mounsieur, for methinks I am marvellous hairy about the face. And I am such a tender[10] ass, if my hair do but tickle me, I must scratch.

TITANIA   What, wilt thou hear some music, my sweet love?

BOTTOM   I have a reasonable good ear in music. Let's have the tongs and the bones[11].

TITANIA   Or say, sweet love, what thou desir'st to eat.

BOTTOM   Truly, a peck of provender[12], I could munch[13] your good dry oats. Methinks I have a great desire to a bottle[14] of hay. Good hay, sweet hay hath no fellow[15].

Bottom and Titania sleep. Oberon talks to Puck about his pity for Titania, and how she has handed over the changeling boy. He removes the spell from her.

剧情简介：包臀和提坦妮娅睡着了。欧博让向捣蛋精诉说起他对提坦妮娅的怜悯，还说起提坦妮娅是如何把调包孩儿交给他的。欧博让解除了对提坦妮娅施的魔咒。

Language in the play 剧中语言

'O, how I love thee! How I dote on thee!'

a How do you respond to Titania's language in the script opposite? Decide what you think this scene reveals about her character and consider how an audience might react to her words. Describe this reaction in one word.

b Oberon says about Titania, 'Her dotage now I do begin to pity' (line 44). Do you think his words cause a change in the audience's feeling towards Titania at this point in the play? What single word would you choose now to describe the audience's reaction?

Write about it 写作练习

Titania and Bottom

a The picture below is powerful and amusing, but also rather disturbing. What type of relationship is being presented in this production? Compare it to the image on page 100. Consider the effects of the two pictures on a live audience. What aspects of each character and their situations are emphasised in each image?

b Write for ten minutes, analysing the detail in these two photographs. Begin with costume and staging.

1 venturous 胆大，爱冒险
2 stir 打扰
3 exposition （包臀想说的词是disposition [意向，倾向]）
4 wind thee in my arms 把你搂进我的臂弯
5 be all ways away 分头散去
6 woodbine … entwist 旋花如此温柔地缠绕着可爱的忍冬（两种都是蔓类攀缘植物）
7 female ivy 常春藤（藤类植物因依附在树上而被认为具有女性特征）
8 dotage 愚蠢；痴恋
9 upbraid 责骂，指责
10 orient 东方（常见于诗歌中，用来描述东方出产的明亮珍珠）
11 bewail 悲叹，哀伤
12 taunted 讥讽
13 scalp 头皮
14 swain 村夫
15 repair = return（返回）
16 fierce vexation of a dream 一场令人心烦的噩梦

TITANIA	I have a venturous[1] fairy that shall seek	
	The squirrel's hoard, and fetch thee new nuts.	
BOTTOM	I had rather have a handful or two of dried peas. But, I pray	
	you, let none of your people stir[2] me; I have an exposition[3] of sleep	35
	come upon me.	
TITANIA	Sleep thou, and I will wind thee in my arms[4].	
	Fairies be gone, and be all ways away[5].	

[*Exeunt Fairies*]

So doth the woodbine the sweet honeysuckle
Gently entwist[6]; the female ivy[7] so   40
Enrings the barky fingers of the elm.
O, how I love thee! How I dote on thee!

[*They sleep.*]

Enter PUCK.

OBERON [*Coming forward.*]
Welcome, good Robin. Seest thou this sweet sight?
Her dotage[8] now I do begin to pity;
For, meeting her of late behind the wood   45
Seeking sweet favours for this hateful fool,
I did upbraid[9] her and fall out with her,
For she his hairy temples then had rounded
With coronet of fresh and fragrant flowers;
And that same dew, which sometime on the buds   50
Was wont to swell like round and orient[10] pearls,
Stood now within the pretty flowerets' eyes
Like tears that did their own disgrace bewail[11].
When I had at my pleasure taunted[12] her,
And she in mild terms begged my patience,   55
I then did ask of her her changeling child,
Which straight she gave me, and her fairy sent
To bear him to my bower in Fairyland.
And now I have the boy, I will undo
This hateful imperfection of her eyes.   60
And, gentle Puck, take this transformèd scalp[13]
From off the head of this Athenian swain[14],
That, he awaking when the other do,
May all to Athens back again repair[15],
And think no more of this night's accidents   65
But as the fierce vexation of a dream[16].
But first I will release the Fairy Queen.

[*Squeezing a herb on Titania's eyes.*]

Titania wakes, and she and Oberon are reconciled. Puck removes the ass's head from Bottom. All leave except the 'mortals' (the lovers and Bottom).

 剧情简介：提坦妮娅醒来，与欧博让重归于好。捣蛋精把驴头从包臀身上变走了。仙灵悉数离场，只剩几位"凡人"（两对情侣和包臀）。

1 Music and dance = harmony (in pairs)

The resolution of the conflict between Titania and Oberon is marked by both dance and music. In Elizabethan times, the harmony of music was often taken as a symbol of human harmony. The music and dance in modern productions vary widely. Sometimes they are formal and dignified, sometimes wildly extravagant.

What kind of music and dance do you think is suitable for this moment in the play? Develop a short dance for Titania and Oberon, perhaps to some appropriate music you have found or have created yourselves.

1	**wast wont** 惯于，惯常
2	**Dian's bud** 荻安（即荻阿娜，罗马神话中的贞洁女神）的花苞（可能是丘比特之花[三色堇]的解药）
3	**Methought** = I thought
4	**enamoured of** 迷恋上，痴恋于
5	**pass** 发生
6	**music call** = call music（吩咐奏乐）
7	**strike … sleep**（欧博让要求安静和轻柔的音乐，好让那两对恋人和包臀不会醒来）
8	**strike … sense** = strike the sense more dead / Than common sleep of all these five
9	**charmeth sleep** 催眠
10	**amity** 和睦
11	**fair prosperity** 前景繁荣
12	**jollity** 欢乐
13	**attend** 听
14	**mark** 注意
15	**compass** 环绕

Themes 主题分析

Gender and power

Up to this point in the play, Oberon's language has been consistently assertive (坚定自信). But between lines 82 and 95 in the script opposite, it is markedly different in style and tone from his first speeches in Act 2 Scene 1 (lines 60–80). There, his diction and syntax are commanding ('Am I not thy lord?', line 63). However, there are still elements of this attempted dominance here: 'Titania, music call'. His language is abrupt and he clearly still expects to be obeyed.

Make a list of the similarities and differences in Oberon's language here compared with his earlier appearances, and suggest possible reasons for this change. Remember, the quarrel is resolved and he and Titania are now in harmony; however, Oberon is very much in control and has achieved his aims.

	Be as thou wast wont[1] to be;	
	See as thou wast wont to see.	
	Dian's bud[2] o'er Cupid's flower	70
	Hath such force and blessèd power.	
	Now, my Titania, wake you, my sweet Queen!	
TITANIA	[*Starting up*.]	
	My Oberon, what visions have I seen!	
	Methought[3] I was enamoured of[4] an ass.	
OBERON	There lies your love.	
TITANIA	How came these things to pass[5]?	75
	O, how mine eyes do loathe his visage now!	
OBERON	Silence awhile: Robin, take off this head.	
	Titania, music call[6], and strike more dead	
	Than common sleep[7] of all these five the sense[8].	
TITANIA	Music, ho, music such as charmeth sleep[9]!	80
	[*Soft music plays*.]	
PUCK	[*To Bottom, removing the ass's head*]	
	Now when thou wak'st, with thine own fool's eyes peep.	
OBERON	Sound, music! Come, my Queen, take hands with me,	
	And rock the ground whereon these sleepers be.	
	[*They dance*.]	
	Now thou and I are new in amity[10],	
	And will tomorrow midnight solemnly	85
	Dance in Duke Theseus' house triumphantly,	
	And bless it to all fair prosperity[11].	
	There shall the pairs of faithful lovers be	
	Wedded, with Theseus, all in jollity[12].	
PUCK	Fairy King, attend[13], and mark[14]:	90
	I do hear the morning lark.	
OBERON	Then, my Queen, in silence sad,	
	Trip we after night's shade;	
	We the globe can compass[15] soon,	
	Swifter than the wandering moon.	95
TITANIA	Come, my lord, and in our flight	
	Tell me how it came this night	
	That I sleeping here was found	
	With these mortals on the ground.	
	Exeunt Oberon, Titania and Puck	

Theseus, Hippolyta and the others enter, on an early morning hunting expedition. After praising the barking of the hounds, they find the sleeping lovers.

 剧情简介：提修、希炮丽塔及其他人上场，进行清晨狩猎。他们正夸赞着猎犬的吠声，突然发现睡梦中的两对恋人。

Write about it 写作练习

From night to day

The transition between the exit of the fairies at line 99 and the entrance of the court moves the action from the fairy world of moonlight to the daylight world of the mortals.

Write a paragraph describing how you would signal this change on stage in a dramatically effective way.

Stagecraft 导演技巧

In praise of hunting dogs (in pairs)

a Theseus's and Hippolyta's speeches about the hounds may be difficult for a modern audience to understand. Take parts and speak lines 100–23, then discuss how you think the lines could be delivered on stage to engage the imagination and interest of the audience.

b Would you cut some of these lines for a modern production? What argument would you use to convince a director to cut or to keep? Record your ideas in your Director's Journal.

1 Theseus – a joke? And a warning? (in pairs)

a 'The rite of May' (line 130) connects with the festivals of Elizabethan England (as does the title of the play itself). In some of these festivals, ordinary behaviour and laws were dispensed with (摒弃). Such festivals celebrated disorder and allowed people to behave in a way that was free of ordinary constraints. In performance, Theseus's words 'No doubt they rose up early to observe / The rite of May' (lines 129–30) often provoke audience laughter. Talk together about whether you think that is an appropriate response – and why.

b In lines 132–3, Theseus says:

> But speak, Egeus; is this not the day
> That Hermia should give the answer of her choice?

Is this a menacing (险恶) moment? Remember the threat to put Hermia in a convent or execute her. Consider how Theseus might speak these lines. How might the lovers react to both? Make suggestions for all the actors.

1 *Wind horns* 吹奏号角
2 **observation is performed** （五月节的）庆典仪式已经礼毕
3 **vaward** 早晨
4 **Uncouple** 解开链锁（猎狗常一对一对拴在一起）
5 **Dispatch** 快派人去
6 **Cadmus** 卡德摩（希腊神话中忒拜 [Thebes，又译作"底比斯"] 的创建者）
7 **Crete** 克里特（希腊第一大岛，位于地中海）
8 **bayed the bear** 围捕那头熊
9 **Sparta** 斯巴达（以猎犬闻名）
10 **chiding** 呵斥声
11 **So flewed, so sanded** （猎犬的）上唇就这样下垂，颜色也这样沙黄
12 **dewlapped** 颈部垂着肉
13 **Thessalian bulls** （斗野公牛是古代色萨利 [Thessaly，希腊中北部的一个地区] 的一项运动）
14 **matched in mouth like bells** 狗吠声配合和谐得似铃铛
15 **tuneable** 悦耳
16 **hallooed** 吆喝
17 **cheered** 加油
18 **rite of May** 五月节庆典（以感恩春天的丰收）
19 **in grace of our solemnity** 庆祝我们的结婚典礼

A Midsummer Night's Dream Act 4 Scene 1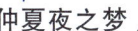
仲夏夜之梦

Wind horns¹. Enter THESEUS *with* HIPPOLYTA, EGEUS, *and all his train.*

THESEUS Go, one of you, find out the forester; 100
For now our observation is performed²,
And since we have the vaward³ of the day,
My love shall hear the music of my hounds.
Uncouple⁴ in the western valley; let them go:
Dispatch⁵, I say, and find the forester. 105

[*Exit an Attendant*]

We will, fair Queen, up to the mountain's top,
And mark the musical confusion
Of hounds and echo in conjunction.

HIPPOLYTA I was with Hercules and Cadmus⁶ once,
When in a wood of Crete⁷ they bayed the bear⁸ 110
With hounds of Sparta⁹: never did I hear
Such gallant chiding¹⁰; for besides the groves,
The skies, the fountains, every region near
Seemed all one mutual cry. I never heard
So musical a discord, such sweet thunder. 115

THESEUS My hounds are bred out of the Spartan kind,
So flewed, so sanded¹¹; and their heads are hung
With ears that sweep away the morning dew;
Crook-kneed, and dewlapped¹² like Thessalian bulls¹³;
Slow in pursuit, but matched in mouth like bells¹⁴, 120
Each under each. A cry more tuneable¹⁵
Was never hallooed¹⁶ to nor cheered¹⁷ with horn
In Crete, in Sparta, nor in Thessaly.
Judge when you hear. But soft, what nymphs are these?

EGEUS My lord, this is my daughter here asleep, 125
And this Lysander; this Demetrius is,
This Helena, old Nedar's Helena.
I wonder of their being here together.

THESEUS No doubt they rose up early to observe
The rite of May¹⁸, and hearing our intent 130
Came here in grace of our solemnity¹⁹.
But speak, Egeus; is not this the day
That Hermia should give answer of her choice?

EGEUS It is, my lord.

107

The lovers are woken by shouts and blasts on horns. Lysander tries to explain what has happened. Egeus urges Theseus to punish Lysander for attempting to elope with Hermia.

剧情简介：恋人们被呼喊声和号角声吵醒。理善德试图解释出了什么事。伊杰敦促提修惩处理善德，因为他企图带哈蜜娅私奔。

1 The dance of the lovers – who loves whom? (IV)

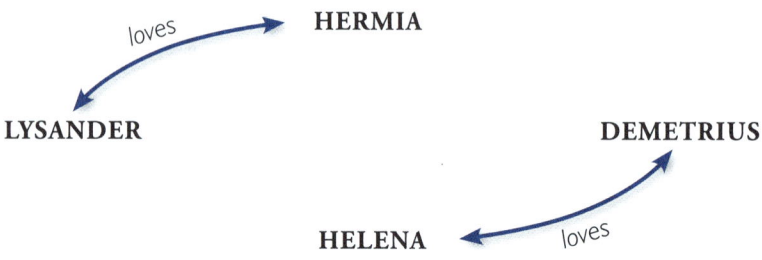

This is the final arrangement of the lovers. Look back at how the 'dance' of the lovers has progressed through the play, on pages 10, 50 and 76. Compare all the dances and identify what patterns emerge.

Stagecraft 导演技巧

Just how do they awake? (in small groups)

The lovers 'all start up'. But how? Puck has ensured that when each awakes they will first see the person they love. Put the stage direction into action by performing their awakening. Remember, each character first sees his or her lover, then Theseus and his court – with Egeus.

Characters 人物分析

Egeus – still an angry father

Egeus, having not experienced the night's 'dreams', persists in viewing the world as one in conflict. He continues to demand his legal rights as an Athenian father. For him, the 'dream' has had no effect on the real world.

This is the last time Egeus speaks in the play. What are your final thoughts on him? Write a brief character sketch as a guide for an actor preparing to play this part.

1 Good morrow = Good morning
2 Saint Valentine 情人节（据传说，罗马帝国的皇帝曾禁止所有单身男性邦民结婚，强迫他们从军。有一位名叫瓦伦泰 [Valentine] 的教士不顾这一禁令，秘密替人证婚，因此于269年2月14日被绞死。教宗于496年追认瓦伦泰为圣人，并将其遇难日定为纪念日。1969年这一纪念日被教廷废除。人们传统上相信鸟儿也在这一天求偶）
3 woodbirds 林鸟（双关，也可理解为wooden birds [木鸟]）
4 couple 配对
5 concord 和睦
6 jealousy 猜疑
7 enmity 敌对
8 amazedly 惊诧；困惑不解
9 as yet 至今
10 bethink me 记得
11 Our intent 我们的计划或意图
12 Without … law 远离被雅典法律制裁的危险
13 defeated 欺骗，蒙蔽

A Midsummer Night's Dream Act 4 Scene 1
仲夏夜之梦

THESEUS	Go, bid the huntsmen wake them with their horns. 135
	Shout within; wind horns; [the lovers] all start up.
	Good morrow¹, friends. Saint Valentine² is past;
	Begin these woodbirds³ but to couple⁴ now?
	[The lovers kneel.]
LYSANDER	Pardon, my lord.
THESEUS	I pray you all, stand up.
	I know you two are rival enemies:
	How comes this gentle concord⁵ in the world, 140
	That hatred is so far from jealousy⁶
	To sleep by hate, and fear no enmity⁷?
LYSANDER	My lord, I shall reply amazedly⁸,
	Half sleep, half waking; but as yet⁹, I swear,
	I cannot truly say how I came here. 145
	But as I think (for truly would I speak)
	And now I do bethink me¹⁰, so it is –
	I came with Hermia hither. Our intent¹¹
	Was to be gone from Athens, where we might
	Without the peril of the Athenian law¹² – 150
EGEUS	Enough, enough, my lord; you have enough –
	I beg the law, the law upon his head!
	They would have stol'n away, they would, Demetrius,
	Thereby to have defeated¹³ you and me,
	You of your wife, and me of my consent, 155
	Of my consent that she should be your wife.

Demetrius explains his love for Hermia has melted and he loves Helena, now and evermore. Theseus instructs the lovers to come with him to be married. All leave except the lovers.

 剧情简介：迪米垂耶澄清说他对哈蜜娅的爱已消失殆尽，从现在起直到永远，他爱的都是海乐娜。提修授意恋人们与他一道举行婚礼。众人离开，只剩两对恋人。

Language in the play 剧中语言
Romantic and heartfelt

a Demetrius's lines 172–3 are very emotional:

> Now I do wish it, love it, long for it,
> And will for evermore be true to it.

Will speeches such as this make all Helena's suffering and humiliation worthwhile for her? Write a paragraph in the form of a diary entry, describing how she feels on hearing these words.

b Demetrius's speech is a heartfelt exploration of the nature of love. He uses evocative imagery – toys and trinkets (小玩意儿), sickness and health and taste and food – to describe his feelings. Analyse the language of love in Demetrius's speech and then write a paragraph responding to this question: 'How does Shakespeare present love through Demetrius's language?'

c Theseus made a joke about St Valentine's Day at line 136. *A Midsummer Night's Dream* is a romantic comedy full of beautiful verse. Which lines in the play would make appropriate verses for a Valentine's Day card? Design your card with a dream theme, using a quotation from the play.

1	stealth	秘密行动
2	in fancy	因为爱
3	remembrance	回忆
4	idle gaud	一文不值的玩物
5	virtue	本质
6	betrothed	已有婚约
7	discourse	讲述
8	overbear your will	不顾您的愿望
9	eternally be knit	永结良缘
10	something worn	差不多消磨完了

Themes 主题分析
Dominant men? (in small groups)

At this moment, Theseus is the dominant character.

a In your group, take turns to read aloud all Theseus's speeches in Scene 1, then speak Oberon's lines from earlier in the scene. Talk together about the similarities and differences between the two characters, list your ideas and then use them to create a Venn diagram (文氏图) like the one below.

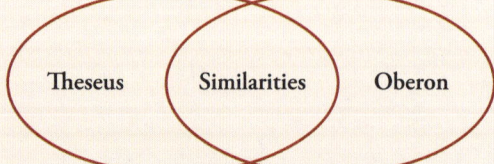

b Discuss these statements:
- Both the fairy and mortal worlds are totally dominated by men.
- Shakespeare presents clear limitations to male power in this play.

DEMETRIUS	My lord, fair Helen told me of their stealth[1],
	Of this their purpose hither to this wood;
	And I in fury hither followed them,
	Fair Helena in fancy[2] following me. 160
	But, my good lord, I wot not by what power
	(But by some power it is), my love to Hermia,
	Melted as the snow, seems to me now
	As the remembrance[3] of an idle gaud[4]
	Which in my childhood I did dote upon; 165
	And all the faith, the virtue[5] of my heart,
	The object and the pleasure of mine eye,
	Is only Helena. To her, my lord,
	Was I betrothed[6] ere I saw Hermia;
	But like a sickness did I loathe this food. 170
	But, as in health come to my natural taste,
	Now I do wish it, love it, long for it,
	And will for evermore be true to it.
THESEUS	Fair lovers, you are fortunately met.
	Of this discourse[7] we more will hear anon. 175
	Egeus, I will overbear your will[8];
	For in the temple, by and by, with us
	These couples shall eternally be knit[9].
	And, for the morning now is something worn[10],
	Our purposed hunting shall be set aside. 180
	Away with us to Athens. Three and three,
	We'll hold a feast in great solemnity.
	Come, Hippolyta.

Exit Theseus with Hippolyta, Egeus, and his train

The lovers wonder if they are dreaming, agree they are awake, and follow the duke. Bottom wakes, and wonders at his 'dream'.

 剧情简介：恋人们怀疑自己是否仍在睡梦中，一致确认大家都是清醒的之后，也随着大公下场。包臀醒了过来，对自己的"梦"迷惑不已。

1 Reflections on dreaming – the lovers (in fours)

a Take the parts of the lovers, and read aloud their short moment of reflection here (lines 184–96). Then talk together about the different ways in which the lovers describe their experiences. Consider each speech in turn and suggest how it could be delivered on stage.

b Demetrius says 'let us recount our dreams' as they walk back to Athens. In role, do just that. Each character tells not only what they think happened, but also what they have learned about their behaviour, their relationships and about love.

Language in the play 剧中语言
Similes and metaphors

Each of the four lovers tries to describe their thoughts using a variety of similes and metaphors. Pick the one you like the most and analyse it in as much detail as you can.

2 Reflections on dreaming – Bottom (in pairs)

a Individually, read and make notes on Bottom's reflections, which he speaks alone on stage.

b Identify the lines in Bottom's speech that have similarities with this passage in the Bible:

> But as it is written, Eye hath not seen, nor ear heard, neither have entered into the heart of man, the things which God hath prepared for them that love him.
>
> 1 Corinthians 2.9

Speculate on the purpose of this connection.

c Bottom says he will get Peter Quince to write a ballad called 'Bottom's Dream'. Write and perform your own version of the ballad.

Write about it 写作练习
Bottom the philosopher

Bottom appears to be at his most philosophical here. What might he have learned about love, life and himself? Choose the most revealing words and phrases to describe his experience. Write about 100 words on how the events of the previous night have changed his character. Use your chosen quotations to support your ideas.

---

1 undistinguishable 难以觉察，几乎看不见
2 parted eye 有重影的眼睛
3 by the way 路上
4 Heigh ho! （模仿驴叫声，也可能是在打哈欠）
5 God's my life! = God save my life!
6 patched fool 身穿碎布戏服的俳优
7 ballad 民谣，歌谣
8 hath no bottom 没有结论；难以理解；没有坚实的基础；虚假的幻觉
9 Peradventure 也许
10 gracious 讨喜，吸引人
11 her （指工匠们排演的剧中角色提兹碧）

A Midsummer Night's Dream Act 4 Scene 1
仲夏夜之梦

DEMETRIUS These things seem small and undistinguishable¹,
Like far-off mountains turnèd into clouds. 185
HERMIA Methinks I see these things with parted eye²,
When everything seems double.
HELENA So methinks;
And I have found Demetrius, like a jewel,
Mine own, and not mine own.
DEMETRIUS Are you sure
That we are awake? It seems to me 190
That yet we sleep, we dream. Do not you think
The Duke was here, and bid us follow him?
HERMIA Yea, and my father.
HELENA And Hippolyta.
LYSANDER And he did bid us follow to the temple.
DEMETRIUS Why, then, we are awake. Let's follow him, 195
And by the way³ let us recount our dreams.

Exeunt lovers

Bottom wakes.

BOTTOM When my cue comes, call me, and I will answer. My next is 'Most fair Pyramus'. Heigh ho!⁴ Peter Quince? Flute the bellows-mender? Snout the tinker? Starveling? God's my life!⁵ Stolen hence and left me asleep! I have had a most rare vision. I have had a dream, 200 past the wit of man to say what dream it was. Man is but an ass if he go about to expound this dream. Methought I was – there is no man can tell what. Methought I was – and methought I had – but man is but a patched fool⁶ if he will offer to say what methought I had. The eye of man hath not heard, the ear of man hath not seen, 205 man's hand is not able to taste, his tongue to conceive, nor his heart to report what my dream was! I will get Peter Quince to write a ballad⁷ of this dream; it shall be called 'Bottom's Dream', because it hath no bottom⁸; and I will sing it in the latter end of a play, before the Duke. Peradventure⁹, to make it the more gracious¹⁰, I shall sing 210 it at her¹¹ death. *Exit*

The Mechanicals, without Bottom, despair (they had been looking forward to a regular salary from the duke for their performance). But Bottom suddenly arrives with the news that their play has been chosen.

 剧情简介：工匠们没了包臀，陷入绝望（他们一直盼着能靠这次演出从大公那儿谋个稳定差事）。然而包臀又突然带着好消息回来：他们的戏入选了。

1 The Mechanicals: a team? (in fives)

Throughout the play, the audience has been witness to formal justice, magic, love, conflict – and here we have a moment of real friendship.

a Take parts and read the whole scene opposite.

b Talk together about what sort of relationship the Mechanicals seem to have at this moment. Consider, in particular, how the group feels about Bottom. Where would you find evidence in the rest of the play for your conclusions?

c Compare your impression with the picture below and with the images on pages 18, 22 and 56.

1	Out of doubt	无疑
2	transported	被掳到另一个世界（委婉表示被杀；W. Aldis Wright认为，根据麻秆的说话习惯，此处意为"变形"）
3	marred	被毁了
4	discharge	扮演，表演
5	handicraft man	手艺人
6	the best person	形象最佳
7	A paramour … naught	（福笛认为paramour[情人]是不体面、不光彩的；木棍的本意为paragon[典范]）
8	we … men	我们就都发财了（按后文的说法，如果他们演出，一天能赚6便士）
9	And = If	
10	hearts	好友们
11	courageous day	令人振奋的好日子
12	fell out	发生
13	good strings to your beards	系好你们的假胡须（舞台表演的假胡须要么是粘上的，要么是用带子系上的）
14	pumps	轻便鞋
15	presently	立即
16	preferred	上报（有待批准）
17	linen	内衣
18	pare	剪掉

2 Prediction

The audience now knows that the Mechanicals are to perform their play for Duke Theseus, and has already seen them in rehearsal. Make some predictions on how you think the performance will go. Consider in detail each character, the part they are to play and the impression of the whole performance so far.

Act 4 Scene 2
Athens

Enter QUINCE, FLUTE, SNOUT *and* STARVELING.

QUINCE   Have you sent to Bottom's house? Is he come home yet?

STARVELING   He cannot be heard of. Out of doubt[1] he is transported[2].

FLUTE   If he come not, then the play is marred[3]. It goes not forward. Doth it?

QUINCE   It is not possible. You have not a man in all Athens able to discharge[4] Pyramus but he.

FLUTE   No, he hath simply the best wit of any handicraft man[5] in Athens.

QUINCE   Yea, and the best person[6], too; and he is a very paramour for a sweet voice.

FLUTE   You must say 'paragon'. A paramour is (God bless us!) a thing of naught[7]. *Enter* SNUG *the joiner.*

SNUG   Masters, the Duke is coming from the temple, and there is two or three lords and ladies more married. If our sport had gone forward, we had all been made men[8].

FLUTE   O, sweet bully Bottom! Thus hath he lost sixpence a day during his life: he could not have 'scaped sixpence a day. And[9] the Duke had not given him sixpence a day for playing Pyramus, I'll be hanged. He would have deserved it. Sixpence a day in Pyramus, or nothing. *Enter* BOTTOM.

BOTTOM   Where are these lads? Where are these hearts[10]?

QUINCE   Bottom! O most courageous day[11]! O most happy hour!

BOTTOM   Masters, I am to discourse wonders – but ask me not what; for if I tell you, I am not true Athenian. I will tell you everything, right as it fell out[12].

QUINCE   Let us hear, sweet Bottom.

BOTTOM   Not a word of me. All that I will tell you is – that the Duke hath dined. Get your apparel together, good strings to your beards[13], new ribbons to your pumps[14]: meet presently[15] at the palace, every man look o'er his part. For the short and the long is, our play is preferred[16]. In any case, let Thisbe have clean linen[17]; and let not him that plays the lion pare[18] his nails, for they shall hang out for the lion's claws. And, most dear actors, eat no onions nor garlic; for we are to utter sweet breath, and I do not doubt but to hear them say it is a sweet comedy. No more words. Away! Go, away! *Exeunt*

A Midsummer Night's Dream
仲夏夜之梦

Looking back at Act 4 第4幕回顾
Activities for groups or individuals

1 All conflict ended

In most plays, conflicts are not resolved until the final scene. But *A Midsummer Night's Dream* is different. Only Egeus remains unsatisfied, and he does not appear again. The play's conflicts are ended, but there is still one more act to come. This is a good moment to list the conflicts that the play has explored. Write them down and then consider:

- the themes and ideas that Shakespeare explores though each conflict
- the language used to describe each theme/idea (you may want to refer back to the binary oppositions explored on page 98 and consider submission versus defiance, duty versus honour and dreams versus reality)
- how each conflict is resolved.

Now write a paragraph in which you analyse each point of conflict. Justify your ideas with evidence from the text.

2 Titania and Hippolyta: power and context

You could think of both Titania and Hippolyta as 'vanquished' (被征服) women who have to learn their 'duty' to their lord. But many productions use all types of stage business (戏台动作) to show that these characters are not without power and influence.

a Remind yourself of all Titania's and Hippolyta's appearances in the play so far. Then write notes on how the language Shakespeare gives them, and the non-verbal techniques an actor can use, show them to have independence of spirit and action.

▼ Titania and Oberon's conflict comes to an end, and the couple dance together.

LOOKING BACK AT ACT 4

b What aspects of Titania and Hippolyta's behaviour might a twenty-first-century audience find difficult to understand or sympathise with? If you could alter the script, what changes to the lines of these two characters would you suggest?

c What ideas do you have for how Hippolyta and Titania should be played? Write suggestions for the director of a modern production of the play.

d Discuss as a group the similarities and differences in the issues that the female characters in the play face with those that women face in the twenty-first century.

3 Exploring Shakespeare's imagination

Shakespeare has presented a complex 'dream world' that raises many questions. Here are some to start you thinking:

- What does each group of characters believe about this dream world?
- What do you make of it?
- Whose imagination is at work here: the characters', Shakespeare's, the audience's?

In groups of three, each take responsibility for one of the following:

- Bottom
- Titania
- the lovers.

Research, reflect and make notes on their particular experiences or dreams, how the 'dreams' were presented to the audience, how the experience was described, and the consequences of and changes wrought by the experience.

In turn, share your ideas. Then together discuss the play in relation to imagination, individual psychology and the worlds of dream and reality.

4 Celebrity stories

Complete one of the following tasks:

a Today, gossip columns and celebrity magazines would be having a field day with the prospect of so many high-profile weddings to come. Write two or three magazine or newspaper gossip stories based on the events of the play up to the end of Act 4. What sort of background details would journalists be interested in? Who would they want to quote? Have they found out about the strange night in the woods?

b Compose a tabloid newspaper (通俗小报) or gossip magazine 'scoop' on the upcoming weddings. Speculate on the scandal, headlines, expense, dress designers and so on. Think carefully about your writing style and target audience.

5 Fairies – an assignment

An actor who played a fairy in *A Midsummer Night's Dream* once said, 'The minute you say "fairy" to people, they think they know exactly what it is.' People have preconceived ideas about what fairies look like and how they behave. Modern audiences may well perceive fairies as comical, whereas the Elizabethans' belief in the supernatural may have made for a more serious approach.

Prepare an assignment on fairies. It can include notes, different types of illustrations, extracts from the play and so on. To get started, look at the many images of fairies in this edition. Also consider the fairies' names, and what they do in the play. Then reflect on these possibilities:

- non-human spirits and their capacity for good and evil
- fairies at the bottom of the garden
- the fairies' function of bringing on stage the world of fantasy and imagination
- fairies as representatives of magical and spiritual forces in human lives.

You may also want to read 'Fairies and magic', page 153.

6 A fifty-word summary

Write an account of what happens in Act 4 in exactly fifty words.

Theseus and Hippolyta talk about the lovers' story, and the power of imagination in poet, lover and madman – who all see things that are not there.

剧情简介：提修和希袍丽塔谈论着情侣们的经历，还有诗人、恋人和疯子共有的想象力——他们都看见了不存在的东西。

Stagecraft 导演技巧

Return to Athens (in pairs)

In Act 5, Shakespeare returns the action to Theseus's palace in Athens. As set designers, you and a partner need to decide if the set should remain identical to the one at the start of the play, or if you should focus on revealing parallels, echoes and developments that have taken place. Think about what has happened in the time since the audience last saw Athens. Draw up a proposal for the director to consider.

Write about it 写作练习

Shakespeare's poetry (in pairs)

Shakespeare was a poet as well as a playwright. The speeches of Theseus (and also those of Titania) are considered to be among the finest examples of Shakespeare's dramatic poetry. Sometimes actors playing Theseus are criticised for speaking the lines opposite simply as poetry, rather than as part of the dramatic script of a play.

a Talk together about what you consider to be the differences between 'poetry' and 'dramatic poetry'. Pool your ideas on how the actors could deliver the lines to ensure that the audience experiences both 'poetry' and 'drama'. Put your ideas into practice by performing the lines.

b It is interesting that Theseus does not believe the lovers' story. Analyse his speech (lines 2–22) in detail. He begins sceptically and then explores the power of the imagination, which creates madmen but also inspires the poet.

c On your own, write a paragraph in which you respond to the ideas that Theseus expresses in the script opposite. Do you think his views on literature have any relevance to this play?

1 antique 古老
2 toys 童话，传说；玩意儿
3 seething 热血沸腾，骚动不安
4 apprehend 抓住；明白
5 lunatic 疯子
6 compact = composed （构成）
7 frantic 疯狂
8 Helen 特洛伊的海伦（神话传说中的美女）
9 a brow of Egypt 一个吉卜赛人的脸庞（吉卜赛人通常皮肤黝黑；Gipsy这个词来源于Egyptian，因此吉卜赛人当时被叫作Egypt）
10 in a fine frenzy rolling 滴溜溜狂转
11 bodies forth 体现出
12 tricks 伎俩
13 transfigured 变了模样
14 constancy 永恒；坚贞
15 admirable 不可思议，离奇

Act 5 Scene 1
Athens Theseus' palace

Enter THESEUS, HIPPOLYTA, PHILOSTRATE, *Lords and Attendants.*

HIPPOLYTA	'Tis strange, my Theseus, that these lovers speak of.	
THESEUS	More strange than true. I never may believe	
	These antique[1] fables, nor these fairy toys[2].	
	Lovers and madmen have such seething[3] brains,	
	Such shaping fantasies, that apprehend[4]	5
	More than cool reason ever comprehends.	
	The lunatic[5], the lover, and the poet	
	Are of imagination all compact[6]:	
	One sees more devils than vast hell can hold;	
	That is the madman. The lover, all as frantic[7],	10
	Sees Helen's[8] beauty in a brow of Egypt[9].	
	The poet's eye, in a fine frenzy rolling[10],	
	Doth glance from heaven to earth, from earth to heaven;	
	And as imagination bodies forth[11]	
	The forms of things unknown, the poet's pen	15
	Turns them to shapes, and gives to airy nothing	
	A local habitation and a name.	
	Such tricks[12] hath strong imagination	
	That if it would but apprehend some joy,	
	It comprehends some bringer of that joy;	20
	Or in the night, imagining some fear,	
	How easy is a bush supposed a bear?	
HIPPOLYTA	But all the story of the night told over,	
	And all their minds transfigured[13] so together,	
	More witnesseth than fancy's images,	25
	And grows to something of great constancy[14];	
	But howsoever, strange and admirable[15].	

The lovers enter, and Theseus looks through the list of performances ready for the evening's entertainment. He rejects the first three, but is attracted by the play *Pyramus and Thisbe*.

 剧情简介：恋人们上场，提修浏览着为晚会准备的节目单。他筛掉了前三个节目，但《丕若莫和提兹碧》这出戏倒是引起了他的兴趣。

Stagecraft 导演技巧

Staging the play within a play

Look carefully at the photograph below, which shows how this important scene was set in a recent production. Make a list of the decisions that have been made about the set and the positioning of the actors. Consider the practical and dramatic implications of those decisions. Suggest three improvements you would make.

1 **More than to us** 愿伴随您多过伴随我们
2 **board** 餐桌
3 **masques** 假面舞会
4 **after-supper** 晚餐后的甜点
5 **manager of mirth** 娱乐长（娱乐活动的组织者和挑选者）
6 **anguish** 苦恼
7 **abridgement** 消遣
8 **beguile** 打发
9 **brief** 节目单
10 **ripe** = ready
11 **Centaurs** 半人马（又译作"人头马"，希腊神话里中的一种怪物，腰部以上是人，以下是马）
12 **eunuch** 阉人（嗓音高似女声的男性）
13 **tipsy Bacchanals** 头重脚轻的酒神节参加者
14 **Thracian singer** 色雷斯歌手（即歌手奥菲乌[Orpheus，又译作"俄耳甫斯"]，希腊神话中的音乐家、诗人、预言家，在酒神节上被撕成碎片）
15 **device** 把戏；节目
16 **Thebes** 忒拜（又译作"底比斯"，古希腊的一个城邦。在希腊神话里，提修曾款待过流浪四方的忒拜国王俄狄浦斯[Oedipus]，还帮助过攻打忒拜的阿尔戈斯国王阿爪斯托[Adrastos]，埋葬了他战死疆场的六位战友）
17 **Muses** 缪斯（希腊神话中司文艺、美术、音乐、舞蹈等的九位女神）
18 **Of ... beggary** （当时诗人和学者常在贫困中离世；莎士比亚可能受到斯宾塞[Edmund Spenser]《缪斯的眼泪》的影响）
19 **satire keen** 尖刻的讽刺
20 **Not sorting with** 不适合
21 **tragical mirth** 悲惨的欢乐（矛盾语[oxymoron]，一种矛盾修辞法；工匠们的戏不可能既悲惨又欢乐）
22 **concord** 和谐，协调

A MIDSUMMER NIGHT'S DREAM ACT 5 SCENE 1
仲夏夜之梦

Enter the lovers: LYSANDER, DEMETRIUS, HERMIA *and* HELENA.

THESEUS	Here come the lovers, full of joy and mirth.
	Joy, gentle friends, joy and fresh days of love
	Accompany your hearts!
LYSANDER	More than to us[1]
	Wait in your royal walks, your board[2], your bed!
THESEUS	Come now: what masques[3], what dances shall we have
	To wear away this long age of three hours
	Between our after-supper[4] and bedtime?
	Where is our usual manager of mirth[5]?
	What revels are in hand? Is there no play
	To ease the anguish[6] of a torturing hour?
	Call Philostrate.
PHILOSTRATE	Here, mighty Theseus.
THESEUS	Say, what abridgement[7] have you for this evening?
	What masque, what music? How shall we beguile[8]
	The lazy time if not with some delight?
PHILOSTRATE	[*Giving him a paper.*]
	There is a brief[9] how many sports are ripe[10].
	Make choice of which your highness will see first.
THESEUS	[*Reading.*]
	'The battle with the Centaurs[11], to be sung
	By an Athenian eunuch[12] to the harp' –
	We'll none of that; that have I told my love
	In glory of my kinsman, Hercules.
	[*Reading.*] 'The riot of the tipsy Bacchanals[13],
	Tearing the Thracian singer[14] in their rage' –
	That is an old device[15], and it was played
	When I from Thebes[16] came last a conqueror.
	[*Reading.*] 'The thrice three Muses[17] mourning for the death
	Of learning, late deceased in beggary[18]' –
	That is some satire keen[19] and critical,
	Not sorting with[20] a nuptial ceremony.
	[*Reading.*] 'A tedious brief scene of young Pyramus
	And his love Thisbe, very tragical mirth[21]' –
	Merry and tragical? Tedious and brief?
	That is hot ice and wondrous strange snow!
	How shall we find the concord[22] of this discord?

Theseus decides on the Mechanicals' play despite the objections of Philostrate, who says the rehearsal was laughably bad.

 剧情简介：不顾菲勒斯垂反对，提修决定就看工匠们的这出戏。菲勒斯垂说这出戏排得实在是烂到可笑。

1 Philostrate – a snob? (in pairs)

Philostrate picks out the key words from the Mechanicals' description of their play and uses these words to convince Theseus that the play is not worth seeing. Take turns to catch his superior tone of voice. Afterwards, discuss whether he is being fair to the Mechanicals. Do you think he might be concerned as much with their social class as by the quality of their performance?

Stagecraft 导演技巧

Two audiences – two responses (in pairs)

The Mechanicals will perform to two audiences: the court characters on stage, and the real theatre audience. So the theatre audience is able to witness the characters' responses to the Mechanicals' play as well as watching the play itself. This is quite demanding on the audience, as it demands focus on two areas of the stage at once, but it also allows more opportunity for humour: the play and the response. The theatre audience also gets an outsider's view of the Mechanicals' play through Philostrate's description.

a Suggest reasons why Shakespeare included Philostrate's description of the play (after all, both audiences are about to see it). Discuss whether you think that both audiences will react in the same way (you will soon discover the views of the onstage audience).

b Think of other plays, movies and books that 'layer' your responses (that is, you respond to the performance and to the onstage audience's response). Examples are *Hamlet*, the movie *The Truman Show* and 'The Tale of the Three Brothers' in *Harry Potter and the Deathly Hallows*. Discuss the dramatic effect of such layering.

Characters 人物分析

Hippolyta's response: 'I love not to see …'

Like Philostrate, Hippolyta is also worried about seeing the performance, but her motivation appears to be different.

a Summarise her argument in a couple of sentences.

b How might Hippolyta speak lines 85–6? Suggest what they reveal about her. As you read on, compare her words to the men's responses.

1 apt 贴切
2 'merry' tears "快乐的" 泪花
3 Hard-handed men 手艺人
4 toiled 绞尽
5 unbreathed memories 没有用过的脑汁
6 sport 娱乐，乐趣
7 intents = purpose
8 Extremely stretched 竭尽全力
9 conned 记住
10 simpleness 纯朴，真诚
11 duty 敬畏
12 tender it 呈现
13 wretchedness o'ercharged 无能的人做超过自身能力的事
14 perishing 毁灭

PHILOSTRATE	A play there is, my lord, some ten words long,	
	Which is as 'brief' as I have known a play,	
	But by ten words, my lord, it is too long,	
	Which makes it 'tedious'. For in all the play	
	There is not one word apt[1], one player fitted.	65
	And 'tragical', my noble lord, it is,	
	For Pyramus therein doth kill himself,	
	Which when I saw rehearsed, I must confess,	
	Made mine eyes water; but more 'merry' tears[2]	
	The passion of loud laughter never shed.	70
THESEUS	What are they that do play it?	
PHILOSTRATE	Hard-handed men[3] that work in Athens here,	
	Which never laboured in their minds till now;	
	And now have toiled[4] their unbreathed memories[5]	
	With this same play against your nuptial.	75
THESEUS	And we will hear it.	
PHILOSTRATE	No, my noble lord,	
	It is not for you. I have heard it over,	
	And it is nothing, nothing in the world,	
	Unless you can find sport[6] in their intents[7],	
	Extremely stretched[8], and conned[9] with cruel pain,	80
	To do you service.	
THESEUS	I will hear that play;	
	For never anything can be amiss	
	When simpleness[10] and duty[11] tender it[12].	
	Go bring them in; and take your places, ladies.	
	[*Exit Philostrate*]	
HIPPOLYTA	I love not to see wretchedness o'ercharged[13],	85
	And duty in his service perishing[14].	
THESEUS	Why, gentle sweet, you shall see no such thing.	
HIPPOLYTA	He says they can do nothing in this kind.	

Theseus explains his choice of the Mechanicals' play: it is the thought that counts among simple people. Quince then enters and begins the play, rather strangely.

 剧情简介：提修解释他选中工匠之戏的理由：纯朴之人的可贵在于其思想。接着木棍上场开始演出，演得莫名其妙。

1 On show – does it make you tongue-tied?
(in pairs)

We are all on show to others every time we are in public. But great occasions can stop us speaking altogether. In lines 93–105, Theseus talks about learned people such as 'great clerks' being unable to talk during official welcomes. He also criticises the 'audacious eloquence', or insincerity, of those who speak a little too well in public. Theseus prefers 'love' (in the sense of sincere affection) and 'tongue-tied simplicity': those who speak little ('least') communicate a great deal ('speak most'). Theseus feels that it is important to understand the speaker's intentions even when the language and delivery is mismanaged and poorly performed.

With a partner, talk about the prospect of speaking in public. What are the three elements that would help ensure a confident and successful speech? Make notes and then compare your ideas with another pair.

1	noble respect	高贵的崇敬
2	in might, not merit	根据演员的能力，而不是成就来判断（看重是否尽力，而非是否优秀）
3	clerks	学者
4	purposèd	准备要
5	premeditated welcomes	预先想好的欢迎词
6	periods	停顿
7	midst	中间
8	Throttle	磕磕巴巴
9	dumbly	一言不发，哑口无言
10	rattling tongue	巧舌
11	saucy	放肆无礼
12	audacious eloquence	胆大妄为的口才
13	to my capacity	据我看来
14	addressed	准备好了
15	in despite	带着恶意
16	stand upon points	注意标点或细节（木棍不顾句读，开场词说得莫名其妙，模棱两可）
17	rid	信马由缰，信口开河
18	rough colt	未驯化的小野马
19	stop	（既可指句号 [full stop]，也可指马术用语"勒马"）
20	moral	教训；评论
21	recorder	笛子
22	in government	在控制之中

Language in the play 剧中语言
Watch your punctuation! (in pairs)

Quince's Prologue (lines 108–17) has much of its punctuation in the wrong place (that's why the court jokes about his 'points' and 'stops' – the punctuation).

a One person delivers his speech as it is written. The other improves the punctuation to make better sense, and then reads this version. Which one works best dramatically? Why?

b Look at the word choices and repetitions in the Prologue, and together come up with one observation on what it reveals about Quince. Share this with the class.

Stagecraft 导演技巧
Asides (旁白): does Quince hear? (in fours)

a Discuss whether Quince hears the comments of the court (lines 118–23), or whether they are **asides** (heard only by the audience).

b Try acting it out both ways: if Quince hears, he will react; if he doesn't, he simply carries on. Remember, 'dramatic effect' is your guide: what the audience most enjoys.

Keep this 'overhearing' notion in mind for the rest of the Mechanicals' play.

| THESEUS | The kinder we, to give them thanks for nothing. |
| | Our sport shall be to take what they mistake; | 90
	And what poor duty cannot do, noble respect[1]
	Takes it in might, not merit[2].
	Where I have come, great clerks[3] have purposèd[4]
	To greet me with premeditated welcomes[5],
	Where I have seen them shiver and look pale,	95
	Make periods[6] in the midst[7] of sentences,
	Throttle[8] their practised accent in their fears,
	And in conclusion dumbly[9] have broke off,
	Not paying me a welcome. Trust me, sweet,
	Out of this silence yet I picked a welcome,	100
	And in the modesty of fearful duty
	I read as much as from the rattling tongue[10]
	Of saucy[11] and audacious eloquence[12].
	Love, therefore, and tongue-tied simplicity
	In least speak most, to my capacity[13].	105

[Enter Philostrate.]

| PHILOSTRATE | So please your grace, the Prologue is addressed[14]. |
| THESEUS | Let him approach. |

Flourish of trumpets.

Enter QUINCE *as Prologue.*

| QUINCE | If we offend, it is with our good will. |
| | That you should think, we come not to offend, |
| | But with good will. To show our simple skill, | 110
	That is the true beginning of our end.
	Consider then, we come but in despite[15].
	We do not come as minding to content you,
	Our true intent is. All for your delight,
	We are not here. That you should here repent you,	115
	The actors are at hand; and by their show
	You shall know all that you are like to know.
THESEUS	This fellow doth not stand upon points[16].
LYSANDER	He hath rid[17] his prologue like a rough colt[18]; he knows not the stop[19]. A good moral[20], my lord; it is not enough to speak, but to speak true.	120
HIPPOLYTA	Indeed, he hath played on this prologue like a child on a recorder[21] – a sound, but not in government[22].

Theseus comments on how mixed up Quince's introduction was. Quince continues with the Prologue, which explains the play, and introduces the characters.

剧情简介：提修点评木棍的介绍词说得实在太乱。木棍接着念开场词，说明剧情，介绍剧中角色。

1 The Prologue – an outline of the play (in sixes)

Quince's description of the play the Mechanicals are about to perform usually generates a lot of laughter among the audience in the theatre. This is your chance to work on the lines to create a very funny performance. Take parts and work on the following activities.

a **Entrances and exits** At the beginning of the Prologue, all the Mechanicals come on to the stage and all but Snout exit at the end of it. How would you have them do this? For example, it might be a noisy and messy entrance and exit, with the Mechanicals nervous and excited; or perhaps more subdued – overawed by the occasion. Try out a few different ideas.

b **Mime to the Prologue** As Quince speaks the Prologue, each of the Mechanicals comes forward to mime the character or object they are portraying. Experiment with different ways of presenting your mimes. You may want to act over the top, or stumbling and muddling, or in any other way that you think might work. Is it possible to be funny, foolish and endearing at once? It is important that the audience laughs but also empathises. Try out ways to achieve that response.

c **The play itself** Talk together about what the Prologue suggests about the sort of play the Mechanicals will present. Also discuss the likely dramatic impact of such a description, and what this tells you about the Mechanicals and their ideas of what a play should be.

1 certain 当然，肯定
2 This … rough-cast （壶嘴的扮相为一堵墙，衣服上涂着粗灰浆）
3 sunder 分隔
4 lanthorn = lantern （灯笼）
5 did … scorn 没有感到羞耻
6 grisly 可怕
7 hight 被称作
8 affright 受到惊吓
9 mantle 斗篷
10 fall 遗落
11 Whereat 于是
12 broached 刺穿
13 tarrying 等候
14 in mulberry shade 在桑树的树荫里
15 twain 两位，一双
16 At large 尽情

A Midsummer Night's Dream Act 5 Scene 1
仲夏夜之梦

THESEUS His speech was like a tangled chain, nothing impaired, but all disordered. Who is next? 125

Enter with a Trumpeter before them [BOTTOM *as*] *Pyramus,* [FLUTE *as*] *Thisbe,* [SNOUT *as*] *Wall,* [STARVELING *as*] *Moonshine and* [SNUG *as*] *Lion.*

QUINCE (*as Prologue*)
    Gentles, perchance you wonder at this show,
        But wonder on, till truth make all things plain.
    This man is Pyramus, if you would know;
        This beauteous lady Thisbe is, certain[1].
    This man with lime and rough-cast[2] doth present 130
        Wall, that vile wall which did these lovers sunder[3];
    And through Wall's chink, poor souls, they are content
        To whisper – at the which let no man wonder.
    This man with lanthorn[4], dog, and bush of thorn,
        Presenteth Moonshine; for, if you will know, 135
    By moonshine did these lovers think no scorn[5]
        To meet at Ninus' tomb, there, there to woo.
    This grisly[6] beast, which Lion hight[7] by name,
        The trusty Thisbe, coming first by night,
    Did scare away, or rather did affright[8]; 140
    And as she fled, her mantle[9] she did fall[10],
        Which Lion vile with bloody mouth did stain.
    Anon comes Pyramus, sweet youth and tall,
        And finds his trusty Thisbe's mantle slain;
    Whereat[11] with blade, with bloody, blameful blade, 145
        He bravely broached[12] his boiling bloody breast;
    And Thisbe, tarrying[13] in mulberry shade[14],
        His dagger drew, and died. For all the rest,
    Let Lion, Moonshine, Wall, and lovers twain[15]
    At large[16] discourse, while here they do remain. 150
        Exeunt Quince, Bottom, Flute, Snug and Starveling

Snout, as the Wall, explains his role. Bottom, as Pyramus, enters and begins the play's action.
剧情简介：壶嘴，饰墙，介绍自己所扮角色。包臀，饰丕若莫，上场开始表演。

1 Snout's opportunity – Wall! (in pairs)

Snout gets his great opportunity to speak as Wall. After his speech in the script opposite, he has only two more lines in the play, so he will surely make the most of lines 153–62.

Take turns to step into role and deliver his speech. Make the most of the rhymes and the stage directions that are built in to the language.

Stagecraft 导演技巧

Character comments (in small groups)

Discuss, come to a consensus and write detailed answers to these two questions:

- How would you want the onstage audience to respond to Theseus's and Demetrius's sarcastic and patronising comments?
- How would you direct the onstage audience to create that response?

Language in the play 剧中语言

Bottom's up! (in pairs)

At last Bottom gets his chance to show what he can do. In every production of the play, he seizes it wholeheartedly and throws himself into the role of tragic hero.

Take turns to act out Bottom's first speech as Pyramus – the other person can be Wall. Bottom's speech is full of repetition of words, sounds and ideas, so use them to increase the comedy. Here are some hints:

- **'O'** Bottom's notion of a tragic hero is that he uses 'O' whenever he can – so make the most of those exclamations.
- **Rhymes** There are all kinds of rhymes in the speech, not simply at the ends of lines. Exploit them for comic effect.
- **Rhythms** The lines are very rhythmical: phrases or sentences echo each other. Bottom thinks he must do full justice to those rhythms, making sure his audience really hears them.
- **Words** Bottom wants to convince his audience that it is 'night', that he speaks to 'Wall' and that he's sad ('alack'). Emphasise!

1 interlude 短戏
2 befall = happen
3 sinister 左边
4 lime and hair （用来涂墙的）石灰和毛发
5 partition 隔离墙（也可指学术书中的一个章节，迪米垂耶暗讽即使是壶嘴的台词，也比学术书更有智慧）
6 blink 眨眼睛
7 Jove （即Jupiter，罗马神话中的主神，在希腊神话中对应的是宙斯）
8 sensible 有感知力（即是个活物）
9 curse again （既然是个活物，应该回骂）
10 fall （既有"发生"之意，也可指墙倒塌）
11 pat = exactly

A Midsummer Night's Dream Act 5 Scene 1
仲夏夜之梦

THESEUS I wonder if the lion be to speak?
DEMETRIUS No wonder, my lord; one lion may, when many asses do.
SNOUT (*as Wall*)
  In this same interlude¹ it doth befall²
  That I, one Snout by name, present a wall;
  And such a wall as I would have you think   155
  That had in it a crannied hole or chink,
  Through which the lovers, Pyramus and Thisbe,
  Did whisper often, very secretly.
  This loam, this rough-cast, and this stone doth show
  That I am that same wall; the truth is so.   160
  And this the cranny is, right and sinister³,
  Through which the fearful lovers are to whisper.
THESEUS Would you desire lime and hair⁴ to speak better?
DEMETRIUS It is the wittiest partition⁵ that ever I heard discourse, my lord.   165

Enter [Bottom as] Pyramus.

THESEUS Pyramus draws near the wall; silence!
BOTTOM (*as Pyramus*)
  O grim-looked night, O night with hue so black,
   O night which ever art when day is not!
  O night, O night, alack, alack, alack,
   I fear my Thisbe's promise is forgot!   170
  And thou, O wall, O sweet, O lovely wall,
   That stand'st between her father's ground and mine,
  Thou wall, O wall, O sweet and lovely wall,
   Show me thy chink, to blink⁶ through with mine eyne.
    [*Wall parts his fingers.*]
  Thanks, courteous wall; Jove⁷ shield thee well for this!   175
   But what see I? No Thisbe do I see.
  O wicked wall, through whom I see no bliss,
   Cursed be thy stones for thus deceiving me!
THESEUS The wall, methinks, being sensible⁸, should curse again⁹.
BOTTOM No, in truth sir, he should not. 'Deceiving me' is Thisbe's cue. She is to enter now, and I am to spy her through the wall. You shall see it will fall¹⁰ pat¹¹ as I told you. Yonder she comes.   180

Thisbe and Pyramus declare their love for each other through the chink in the wall, and agree to meet at 'Ninny's tomb'.

剧情简介：提兹碧和丕若莫透过墙缝互诉爱心，最后约定在"傻瓜的坟地"相会。

1 Mistakes (in small groups)

Keep a running tally of everything the Mechanicals get wrong in the performance. The audience watching on stage is of a higher social status than the Mechanicals, and would be better and more classically educated. Discuss how they would react to each mistake.

2 Third wheel (in threes)

Snout, as Wall, is listening in to the love talk, so his reactions to what he hears and sees are important. Talk together about his possible responses. Then discuss Flute's adopted 'female' voice and actions, and Bottom's over-the-top acting and mispronunciations. Remember that the aim is to make the 'real' (not onstage) audience laugh. Get up and act the lines in different ways.

Compare how the two productions shown on this page have chosen to present this moment. Think about the decisions regarding costumes, set, hair and make-up, and the impact those decisions might have had on an audience.

1 full = very
2 and = if / whether
3 Think what thou wilt 不论你怎么想
4 thy lover's grace 情人大人
5 Limander / Helen （应为Leander和Hero，即忠贞恋人的典范；出自马洛［Christopher Marlowe］的诗作 Hero and Leander）
6 trusty 忠诚
7 Fates 神话中的命运三女神（Clotho、Lachesis、Atropos）
8 Shafalus to Procrus （福笛又说错，实为神话中另一对忠贞恋人 Cephalus 与 Procris）
9 Ninny's tomb （包臀重犯了第三幕排演时福笛所犯的错误，应为 Ninus' tomb）
10 straightway 径直；立刻
11 Tide life, tide death 无论死活

Enter [Flute as] Thisbe.

FLUTE (*as Thisbe*)
    O wall, full[1] often hast thou heard my moans,
     For parting my fair Pyramus and me.
    My cherry lips have often kissed thy stones,   185
     Thy stones with lime and hair knit up in thee.

BOTTOM (*as Pyramus*)
    I see a voice; now will I to the chink,
     To spy and[2] I can hear my Thisbe's face.
    Thisbe!

FLUTE (*as Thisbe*)
      My love! Thou art my love, I think?

BOTTOM (*as Pyramus*)
    Think what thou wilt[3], I am thy lover's grace[4],   190
    And like Limander[5] am I trusty[6] still.

FLUTE (*as Thisbe*)
    And I like Helen[5], till the Fates[7] me kill.

BOTTOM (*as Pyramus*)
    Not Shafalus to Procrus[8] was so true.

FLUTE (*as Thisbe*)
    As Shafalus to Procrus, I to you.

BOTTOM (*as Pyramus*)
    O, kiss me through the hole of this vile wall!   195

FLUTE (*as Thisbe*)
    I kiss the wall's hole, not your lips at all.

BOTTOM (*as Pyramus*)
    Wilt thou at Ninny's tomb[9] meet me straightway[10]?

FLUTE (*as Thisbe*)
    Tide life, tide death[11], I come without delay.
      [*Exeunt Bottom and Flute in different directions*]

The onstage audience comments on the play, and Snug (as Lion) enters, explaining he is not really a lion.
剧情简介：台上的观众对这出戏议论纷纷，榫卯（饰狮子）上场，解释说他并不是一头真狮子。

Write about it 写作练习

A silly, ridiculous play? (in small groups)

Hippolyta says, 'This is the silliest stuff that ever I heard.' Her comment is echoed by Samuel Pepys, the famous diarist, who said when he saw the play in 1662: 'We saw *Midsummer Night's Dreame*, which I have never seen before, nor shall ever again, for it is the most insipid (枯燥乏味) ridiculous play that I ever saw in my life.' Theseus replies to Hippolyta, 'The best in this kind are but shadows'.

a Talk together and note down your ideas in response to the following three questions:

- How do you feel about Hippolyta's and Pepys's views?
- What are some possible meanings of Theseus's remark?
- What might Shakespeare have replied to Pepys if he had had the chance?

b On your own, write a letter from Pepys to Shakespeare criticising the play. Swap your letter with the person sitting next to you. Write Shakespeare's response to that person's letter.

1 dischargèd 演完了
2 mural 墙
3 wilful 乐意
4 shadows 幻影（对现实的反映或模仿）
5 pass for 作为……混过去
6 fell 凶残
7 dam 母兽
8 in strife 气势汹汹
9 gentle （作为兽中之王）高贵；（由于照顾到女士）温和
10 fox … goose （狐狸以谨慎狡猾闻名，此处暗示这只狮子很胆怯；鹅在英文里象征愚笨，提修的意思是：这头狮子既不威猛，又呆头呆脑）
11 discretion 谨慎

Stagecraft 导演技巧

Snug the lion

Design a costume for Snug. Remember that the Mechanicals are amateurs who have never put on a play before. How professional do you think the costume should be? Look at the costumes in the images on this and previous pages as a starting point.

SNOUT (*as Wall*)
>Thus have I, Wall, my part dischargèd[1] so;
>And being done, thus Wall away doth go. *Exit* 200

THESEUS Now is the mural[2] down between the two neighbours.

DEMETRIUS No remedy, my lord, when walls are so wilful[3] to hear without warning.

HIPPOLYTA This is the silliest stuff that ever I heard.

THESEUS The best in this kind are but shadows[4]; and the worst are no worse, if imagination amend them. 205

HIPPOLYTA It must be your imagination then, and not theirs.

THESEUS If we imagine no worse of them than they of themselves, they may pass for[5] excellent men. Here come two noble beasts in, a man and a lion. 210

Enter [Snug as] Lion and [Starveling as] Moonshine.

SNUG (*as Lion*)
>You ladies, you whose gentle hearts do fear
>>The smallest monstrous mouse that creeps on floor,
>May now, perchance, both quake and tremble here,
>>When Lion rough in wildest rage doth roar.
>Then know that I as Snug the joiner am 215
>A lion fell[6], nor else no lion's dam[7];
>For if I should as lion come in strife[8]
>Into this place, 'twere pity on my life.

THESEUS A very gentle[9] beast, and of a good conscience.

DEMETRIUS The very best at a beast, my lord, that e'er I saw. 220

LYSANDER This lion is a very fox for his valour.

THESEUS True; and a goose[10] for his discretion[11].

DEMETRIUS Not so, my lord; for his valour cannot carry his discretion; and the fox carries the goose.

THESEUS His discretion, I am sure, cannot carry his valour; for the goose carries not the fox. It is well: leave it to his discretion, and let us listen to the moon. 225

Starveling, Moonshine, manages to explain his role, despite the comments of the onstage audience. Thisbe arrives, only to be frightened away by the lion.

 剧情简介：尽管台上的观众议论纷纷，饰演月光的麻秆尽力诠释着自己的角色。提兹碧一上场，就被狮子给吓跑了。

1 An unruly – and snobbish – audience? (in sevens)

The onstage audience seems to be getting out of hand. Starveling finds his performance is not appreciated. Take parts and read through lines 228–55 several times. Consider how Starveling says his lines 242–4. Is he irritated by the audience, intimidated by them or bored with the whole thing?

1 hornèd moon　两头尖尖的月亮
2 horns on his head　头上长角（意同"戴绿帽子"）
3 crescent　新月
4 already in snuff　都快熄灭了
5 aweary　厌倦
6 Would = I wish
7 wane　月亏；即将退场
8 stay the time　等到演出结束
9 Well moused　(提修嘲笑狮子撕咬那件斗篷像猫咬老鼠)
10 worries　撕咬

Language in the play 剧中语言
Imagining the moon (in pairs)

The image of the moon is common throughout *A Midsummer Night's Dream*.

a With a partner, choose five references to the moon in the play and analyse them in detail. Start with the two quotations below, and find three more by revisiting Acts 1 to 4.

Another moon – but O, methinks, how slow
This old moon wanes! She lingers my desires (Act 1 Scene 1, lines 3–4)

Ill met by moonlight, proud Titania! (Act 2 Scene 1, line 60)

b Write a short paragraph on what you think the moon might represent in this play. Why is it such an important image?

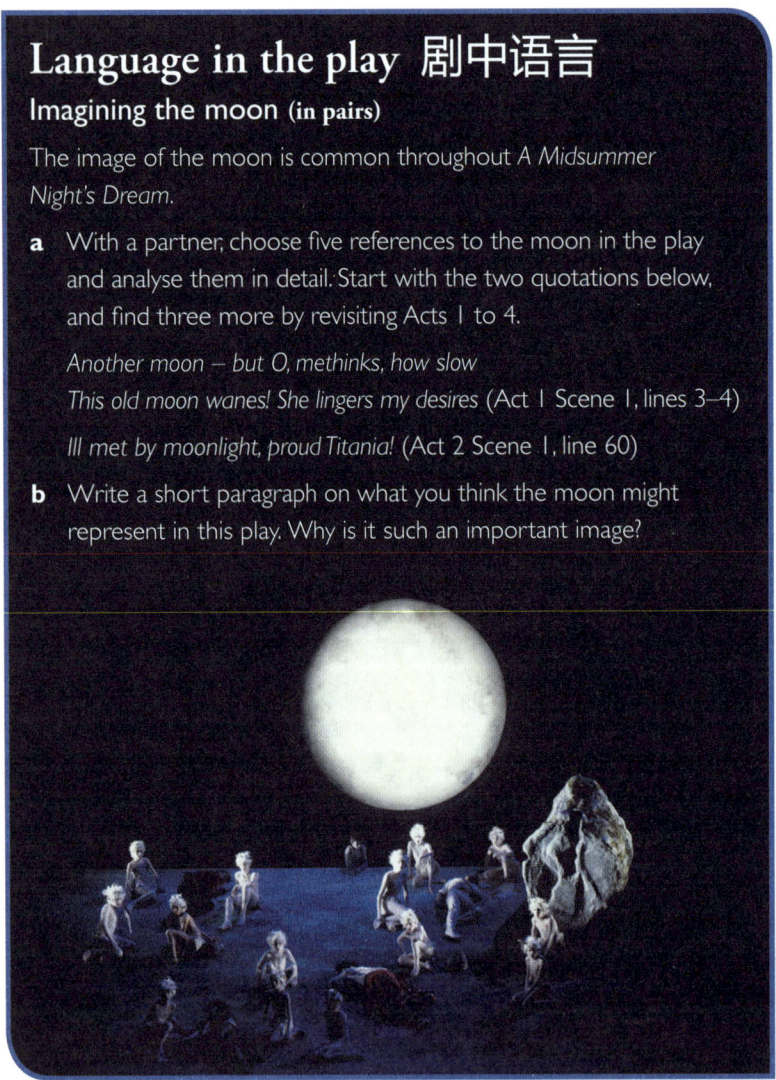

2 From imagining to creating

Because of the recurrent use of moon imagery, and because much of the action takes place at night, the moon is frequently used as a key element of set design and lighting effects in Acts 2, 3 and 4. Using the photograph above as a starting point, develop an idea of your own for physically integrating the moon into the play. The use of the moon in set design could present an amusing contrast with Starveling's lantern in this scene.

STARVELING (*as Moonshine*)
    This lanthorn doth the hornèd moon[1] present –

DEMETRIUS   He should have worn the horns on his head[2].

THESEUS   He is no crescent[3], and his horns are invisible within the circumference.

STARVELING (*as Moonshine*)
    This lanthorn doth the hornèd moon present;
    Myself the man i'th'moon do seem to be –

THESEUS   This is the greatest error of all the rest; the man should be put into the lantern. How is it else the man i'th'moon?

DEMETRIUS   He dares not come there, for the candle; for you see it is already in snuff[4].

HIPPOLYTA   I am aweary[5] of this moon. Would[6] he would change!

THESEUS   It appears by his small light of discretion that he is in the wane[7]; but yet in courtesy, in all reason, we must stay the time[8].

LYSANDER   Proceed, Moon.

STARVELING   All that I have to say is to tell you that the lanthorn is the moon, I the man i'th'moon, this thorn bush my thorn bush, and this dog my dog.

DEMETRIUS   Why, all these should be in the lantern, for all these are in the moon. But silence: here comes Thisbe.

Enter [Flute as] Thisbe.

FLUTE (*as Thisbe*)
    This is old Ninny's tomb. Where is my love?

SNUG (*as Lion*)   O!

Lion roars. Thisbe runs off [dropping her mantle]

DEMETRIUS   Well roared, Lion!

THESEUS   Well run, Thisbe!

HIPPOLYTA   Well shone, Moon! Truly, the moon shines with a good grace.

THESEUS   Well moused[9], Lion!

DEMETRIUS   And then came Pyramus –

LYSANDER   And so the lion vanished.

[Lion worries[10] Thisbe's mantle, and exit]

Pyramus enters full of expectation. He then sees Thisbe's blood-stained mantle, and calls for his own death.
剧情简介：丕若莫满怀期待地上场。他于是看到了提兹碧血染的斗篷，呼号着要为爱殉情。

1 Bottom struts his stuff (卖弄一番，露一手) (in small groups)

Now Bottom really gets the chance to display his acting skills. His speech in the script opposite and his lines 275–90 later in the scene are all part of the same sequence. First, get some experience of his whole performance by taking turns to speak as Bottom from line 256 to 290. Use the suggestions in the 'Language' box on page 128 and below to help you make the episode as funny as possible.

- **Humour** Shakespeare makes Bottom's attempts at acting humorous partly through his overuse of alliteration*: 'gracious, golden, glittering gleams'. Make sure he emphasises all those hard 'g's.
- **Iambic pentameter (抑扬五音步)** (see p.164) Bottom begins with four lines in the traditional style of tragic heroes: lines with five beats. He will make sure that his audience appreciates that he knows his classics. Ensure that five emphatic stresses come over in each line. You will find he does just the same in his next speech, in lines 275–90.
- **Doggerel (打油诗)** Bottom does not keep up the 'high style' of his beginning. He changes to the very simple rhythms of two or three beats to a line. Again, take every opportunity to bring out those rhythms.

2 Romeo and Juliet – a parody?

As you work on the Mechanicals' play, keep thinking about whether Shakespeare is mocking romantic narratives, such as his own *Romeo and Juliet* perhaps, which he wrote around the same time as *A Midsummer Night's Dream*. Watch for romantic clichés in the remainder of the Mechanicals' play.

▼ The deaths of Romeo and Juliet.

1	**dole** 悲伤
2	**dainty duck** 可爱的鸭子（亲切的昵称）
3	**Furies** 复仇三女神（通常被描述成惩罚罪恶的三姐妹；复仇女神和命运女神都关系到宿命、命运及神灵或超自然力量对现实生活的干预）
4	**Fates … thrum** 命运女神纺出人类的生命线，将其剪断即终结生命（thread and thrum反映出包臀的职业是织工）
5	**Quail** 毁灭
6	**conclude** 终结
7	**quell** 杀害
8	**passion** 悲痛，哀恸
9	**Beshrew my heart** 让我的心死了吧（较文雅的诅咒语）
*	**alliteration** 头韵，指诗句里两个或多个词的第一个辅音相同，如 sing a song of sixpence，类似中文的双声。

A Midsummer Night's Dream Act 5 Scene 1
仲夏夜之梦

Enter [Bottom as] Pyramus.

BOTTOM (*as Pyramus*)
    Sweet moon, I thank thee for thy sunny beams;
     I thank thee, moon, for shining now so bright;
    For by thy gracious, golden, glittering gleams
     I trust to take of truest Thisbe sight.
      But stay – O spite!   260
      But mark, poor Knight,
    What dreadful dole[1] is here?
      Eyes, do you see?
      How can it be?
    O dainty duck[2], O dear!   265
      Thy mantle good –
      What, stained with blood?
    Approach, ye Furies[3] fell!
      O Fates, come, come,
      Cut thread and thrum[4],   270
    Quail[5], crush, conclude[6], and quell[7].

THESEUS This passion[8], and the death of a dear friend, would go near to make a man look sad.

HIPPOLYTA Beshrew my heart[9], but I pity the man.

Pyramus stabs himself, and has a prolonged death. As the audience comments on the acting, Thisbe enters.
剧情简介：丕若莫拿起剑刺入自己的胸膛，来了场延时死亡。观众还在点评着表演，这时提兹碧上场。

1 Bottom's great moment (in pairs)

Look back at the suggestions on page 136 for performing Bottom's final speech. When you have read them, take turns with your partner to play Bottom in Pyramus's death scene (lines 275–90). Make the most of the opportunity for physical humour, throwing yourself into the role and going thoroughly over the top. On stage, Bottom often mistakes right for left as he searches for his heart. He takes a very long time to deliver his final line, milking every 'die' for laughs. Usually, actors show how much Bottom is enjoying his moment on stage and how he is loath to leave it and 'die'.

1 **frame** 创造出
2 **vile** 可鄙
3 **deflowered** 破了……的花苞（包臀可能想说devoured [吞食]）
4 **cheer** 欢欣
5 **confound** 毁灭（我）吧
6 **pap** 胸膛
7 **die** dice（骰子）的另一个叫法（此处迪米垂耶用die的这一个意思来打趣）
8 **ace** "幺"（骰子六个面中最小的数字）
9 **ass** （与ace谐音）
10 **mote** 微小尘埃
11 **turn the balance** 打破平衡（一颗尘埃都能使天平倾斜，即这个问题没有所谓的标准答案）
12 **means** 恸哭
13 **videlicet** 如下（拉丁文法律术语，在16世纪晚期已进入日常英语）

Characters 人物分析
An ass by any other name?

Yet again, someone implies that Bottom is an 'ass' (line 294). With a name like Bottom, and having an ass's head at one point, this perception of his character is pretty clear. Think about what Bottom says and does throughout the play, and make a list of reasons why Bottom is – or isn't – an ass. Find quotations for and against.

A Midsummer Night's Dream Act 5 Scene 1
仲夏夜之梦

BOTTOM (*as Pyramus*)
    O wherefore, Nature, didst thou lions frame[1], 275
      Since lion vile[2] hath here deflowered[3] my dear?
    Which is – no, no – which was the fairest dame
      That lived, that loved, that liked, that looked with cheer[4].
        Come tears, confound[5]!
        Out sword, and wound 280
    The pap[6] of Pyramus,
      Ay, that left pap,
      Where heart doth hop:
    Thus die I, thus, thus, thus! [*Stabs himself.*]
      Now am I dead, 285
      Now am I fled;
    My soul is in the sky.
      Tongue, lose thy light;
      Moon, take thy flight;
                             [*Exit Starveling*]
    Now die, die, die, die, die. [*He dies.*] 290

DEMETRIUS No die[7], but an ace[8] for him; for he is but one.
LYSANDER Less than an ace, man; for he is dead, he is nothing.
THESEUS With the help of a surgeon he might yet recover, and yet prove an ass[9].
HIPPOLYTA How chance Moonshine is gone before Thisbe comes back 295
and finds her lover?
THESEUS She will find him by starlight.

                Enter [Flute as] Thisbe.

    Here she comes and her passion ends the play.
HIPPOLYTA Methinks she should not use a long one for such a
Pyramus; I hope she will be brief. 300
DEMETRIUS A mote[10] will turn the balance[11], which Pyramus, which
Thisbe is the better: he for a man, God warrant us; she for a woman,
God bless us.
LYSANDER She hath spied him already, with those sweet eyes.
DEMETRIUS And thus she means[12], videlicet[13] – 305

Thisbe realises Pyramus is dead and kills herself. Bottom asks if the duke wants an epilogue or a dance. Theseus settles on the country dance.

剧情简介： 提兹碧发现丕若莫已死，于是自杀。包臀问大公想看收场词还是跳舞，提修选定民间舞蹈。

▲ Look at the man playing Flute (Thisbe) in the photograph above. Think about whether this image works well, and what Flute might be like if played by very different-looking actors. The actors in the pictures on page 130, for example, look much more feminine.

1 'Adieu, adieu, adieu!' (in pairs)

a Compare and contrast the death scene of Pyramus with that of Thisbe. Consider how costume, props and facial expressions can be used to heighten humour.

b How much sadness or pathos would you like to convey? Discuss how the characters of Bottom and Flute can be developed through their performances as the doomed lovers. In some productions, members of the onstage audience feel more involved at this point and enter into the play more sympathetically than they did earlier.

2 Hot-seat* questions (in pairs, then whole class)

The Mechanicals complete their play. What questions would you like to ask Bottom and Quince at this point about the details of the play, their performances and the audience?

- In pairs, agree on your most important two questions, one for each of these two characters.
- One member of the class plays Bottom, and one Quince. In character, they each have to answer one question from each pair.

---

1 **lily lips** 百合花般的嘴唇（嘴唇是红色的，百合花是白色的，这里显然用词不当）
2 **cherry** 樱桃红（福笛混淆了形容脸色与唇色的颜色词）
3 **eyes were green as leeks** 如扁叶葱般绿色的双眼（绿色一般表示新鲜、青春或者嫉妒，而不是爱。福笛又一次不搭调且滑稽的比喻；颜色的误用是本场喜剧效果的一部分）
4 **sisters three** 命运三女神（见第136页注解4）
5 **hands as pale as milk** （常用于比喻女士白皙的皮肤）
6 **Lay** 放到
7 **gore** 血泊
8 **shore** = shorn（剪断）
9 **shears** 大剪刀
10 **thread of silk** 生命线
11 **imbrue** 刺入；血染
12 **left** 活着留下来
13 **epilogue** 收场词
14 **Bergomask** 贝加莫舞（源于意大利贝加莫 [Bergamo] 的民间舞蹈）
15 **excuse** 道歉，解释
16 **notably discharged** 表演得非常棒

* **Hot-seat** 热座位，一种课堂游戏，玩法是请一位同学坐到讲台上的一把椅子上，其他同学轮番给他/她出难题，哪个问题他/她回答不出就算输。

FLUTE (*as Thisbe*)
          Asleep, my love?
          What, dead, my dove?
     O Pyramus, arise.
          Speak, speak! Quite dumb?
          Dead, dead? A tomb
     Must cover thy sweet eyes.
          These lily lips[1],
          This cherry[2] nose,
     These yellow cowslip cheeks
          Are gone, are gone.
          Lovers, make moan;
     His eyes were green as leeks[3].
          O sisters three[4],
          Come, come to me
     With hands as pale as milk[5];
          Lay[6] them in gore[7],
          Since you have shore[8]
     With shears[9] his thread of silk[10].
          Tongue, not a word!
          Come, trusty sword,
     Come blade, my breast imbrue[11]! [*Stabs herself.*]
          And farewell, friends.
          Thus Thisbe ends –
     Adieu, adieu, adieu! [*Dies.*]

THESEUS Moonshine and Lion are left[12] to bury the dead.

DEMETRIUS Ay, and Wall, too.

BOTTOM [*Starting up, as Flute does also.*] No, I assure you, the wall is down that parted their fathers. Will it please you to see the epilogue[13], or to hear a Bergomask[14] dance between two of our company?

THESEUS No epilogue, I pray you; for your play needs no excuse[15]. Never excuse; for when the players are all dead, there need none to be blamed. Marry, if he that write it had played Pyramus and hanged himself in Thisbe's garter, it would have been a fine tragedy: and so it is, truly, and very notably discharged[16]. But come, your Bergomask; let your epilogue alone.

The Mechanicals dance, the duke instructs everyone to go to bed, and Puck enters. He speaks of the night, the time when the fairies play.

剧情简介：工匠们跳起舞，大公指示各位回去就寝。捣蛋精上场，称黑夜正是仙子们活跃之时。

1 Puck's night-time world (in pairs)

Listen as your teacher reads Puck's speech (lines 349–68) aloud twice through. Individually, draw what you consider to be the major night-time images. Share your final design with a partner. Have you picked up the same images or focused on different ones? Describe the mood presented by your images. The results could be used to make a classroom display.

1	iron … told	（指钟声报时）
2	overwatched	熬夜，睡太晚
3	palpable-gross	明显粗糙
4	heavy gait	沉重、迟缓的步伐
5	A … solemnity	我们有两周婚庆活动
6	behowls	号叫
7	heavy	疲倦，困乏
8	foredone	精疲力竭
9	wasted brands	燃尽的火炬
10	wretch	可怜虫
11	shroud	寿衣，裹尸布
12	sprite	鬼魂
13	triple Hecate's team	希腊神话中司天、地、冥三界的赫卡特女神的马车（triple据说源自月亮的三种月相：满月、亏月及冥月［月食］）
14	frolic	欢腾
15	hallowed	神圣

Language in the play 剧中语言

'*Enter* PUCK [*carrying a broom*]' (in pairs)

> I am sent with broom before
> To sweep the dust behind the door.

Robin Goodfellow was thought to sweep the house at midnight as a good turn (善行), and often maids would put out a bowl of milk as thanks. It is not clear here whether Puck is clearing away the dust or just sweeping it behind the door and then leaving it there. With your partner, discuss the significance and purpose of this metaphor at this point in the play.

Write about it 写作练习

Three worlds – three accounts (in threes)

The mortals have left, and the fairy world begins its entrance. One member of the group chooses to be one of the lovers, another is one of the Mechanicals and the third is a member of the court. Each writes a diary account of the evening. Concentrate on perceptions, thoughts and feelings rather than simply describing events. Take turns to read out your accounts.

[*The company return; two of them dance, then exeunt Bottom, Flute and their fellows.*]

The iron tongue of midnight hath told[1] twelve.
Lovers, to bed; 'tis almost fairy time.
I fear we shall outsleep the coming morn
As much as we this night have overwatched[2].
This palpable-gross[3] play hath well beguiled   345
The heavy gait[4] of night. Sweet friends, to bed.
A fortnight hold we this solemnity[5]
In nightly revels and new jollity.

               Exeunt

Enter PUCK [*carrying a broom*].

PUCK Now the hungry lion roars,
    And the wolf behowls[6] the moon,   350
  Whilst the heavy[7] ploughman snores,
    All with weary task foredone[8].
  Now the wasted brands[9] do glow,
    Whilst the screech-owl, screeching loud,
  Puts the wretch[10] that lies in woe   355
    In remembrance of a shroud[11].
  Now it is the time of night
    That the graves, all gaping wide,
  Every one lets forth his sprite[12]
    In the church-way paths to glide.   360
  And we fairies, that do run
    By the triple Hecate's team[13]
  From the presence of the sun,
    Following darkness like a dream,
  Now are frolic[14]; not a mouse   365
  Shall disturb this hallowed[15] house.
  I am sent with broom before
  To sweep the dust behind the door.

Oberon and Titania enter with their fairies. Oberon instructs them to go through the house, blessing the three couples with loving marriages and 'perfect' children.

 剧情简介：欧博让和提坦妮娅带着仙子们上场。欧博让命令仙子们穿遍房屋，祝福三对新人婚姻恩爱，子孙"完美无缺"。

1 Blessing mortal marriages (in pairs)

Oberon delivers the blessing of the fairy world on the three marriages. He speaks in four-beat rhythm, quite different from the verse of the court and the prose of the Mechanicals. His blessing draws on country myths and folk tales. Every culture has its own blessings, and you may wish to research these. The following is a blessing on marriage and children from *The Book of Common Prayer* (1662):

> *We beseech thee, assist with thy blessing these two persons, that they may both be fruitful in procreation of children, and also live together so long in godly love and honesty, that they may see their children christianly and virtuously brought up, to thy praise and honour; through Jesus Christ our Lord.*

With a partner, decide how Oberon should speak his lines in the script. The mythical and religious connections suggest a serious and reverential (虔诚) approach, but the song and dance imply a lighter tone. Decide as directors how you would advise your actor on his line delivery and actions.

1 drowsy 昏昏欲睡
2 ditty 小曲
3 trippingly 轻盈，欢快
4 by rote 熟记于心
5 warbling note 柔和的音乐
6 grace 喜爱，祝福（也表示动作优雅）
7 stray 游荡
8 best bride-bed （指提修和希坡丽塔的婚床）
9 issue 子嗣
10 blots of nature's hand 自然之手创造的污点（即下文所说的胎记、黑痣、兔唇[harelip]、疤痕、胎记等身体缺陷）
11 mark prodigious 不祥的胎记
12 Despisèd in nativity 生来让人讨厌
13 consecrate 圣洁
14 take his gait 各行其道
15 several 各自，分别
16 Trip away 轻快地飞走

Themes 主题分析

From conflict to 'sweet peace' (in small groups)

Compare the speeches in the script opposite with the conflicts of the opening scene and the conflicts in the wood. The play has dramatised problems in the relationships between women and men. What has brought them to 'sweet peace' now?

a For each couple, describe their conflicts and explain how they have been resolved.

b Write a short dialogue between one of the couples, in which they look back at what has happened to them over the last two days. End their conversation with their thoughts about what the future holds. (You may also want to look at 'Conflict', p. 151.)

A MIDSUMMER NIGHT'S DREAM ACT 5 SCENE 1
仲夏夜之梦

*Enter [*OBERON *and* TITANIA,] *the King and Queen of Fairies, with all their train.*

OBERON   Through the house give glimmering light
     By the dead and drowsy[1] fire;   370
Every elf and fairy sprite
     Hop as light as bird from briar,
And this ditty[2] after me
Sing, and dance it trippingly[3].

TITANIA   First rehearse your song by rote[4],   375
To each word a warbling note[5];
Hand in hand with fairy grace[6]
Will we sing and bless this place.

Song [and dance].

OBERON   Now until the break of day
Through this house each fairy stray[7].   380
To the best bride-bed[8] will we,
Which by us shall blessèd be;
And the issue[9] there create
Ever shall be fortunate.
So shall all the couples three   385
Ever true in loving be,
And the blots of nature's hand[10]
Shall not in their issue stand.
Never mole, harelip, nor scar,
Nor mark prodigious[11], such as are   390
Despisèd in nativity[12],
Shall upon their children be.
With this field-dew consecrate[13],
Every fairy take his gait[14],
And each several[15] chamber bless   395
Through this palace with sweet peace;
And the owner of it blessed
Ever shall in safety rest.
Trip away[16], make no stay;
Meet me all by break of day.   400

Exeunt [all but Puck]

Puck, on his own now, asks for the audience to think of the play as their dream. He promises improved performances and asks for the audience's approval.

🖋 **剧情简介**：捣蛋精独留在台上，请观众将此剧当成自己的一个梦。他承诺会改进表演，并请观众鼓掌认可。

Stagecraft 导演分析

Puck's farewell (in pairs)

a The best thing to do with Puck's farewell is to speak it. Take turns with your partner to deliver the lines. Help each other by suggesting different ways of increasing dramatic effect.

b Think carefully about positioning this soliloquy in relation to the audience. Try a close and intimate approach and then a more distant, formal one. Present your preferred version to the class.

c As Puck's speech closes the play, try to describe the final mood on stage in three words.

1 shadows 精灵
2 slumbered 打盹儿
3 No more yielding 没有更多益处
4 Gentles 贵宾们
5 reprehend = reprimand（责难）
6 mend 改善，改进
7 honest Puck 老实的捣蛋精
8 unearnèd luck 侥幸得来的运气
9 'scape the serpent's tongue 逃避毒舌的嘘声
10 Else = Otherwise
11 Give me your hands 请为我们鼓掌
12 Robin shall restore amends 若宾会用改进表演来报答

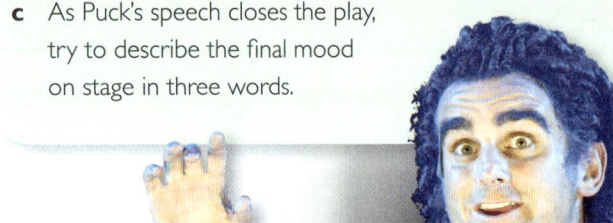

Characters 人物分析

Who else might speak to the audience?

Puck speaks directly to the audience, which in Shakespeare's time would either hiss ('the serpent's tongue') or clap ('Give me your hands') at the end of plays. Plays often ended with a request to the audience to clap (and not hiss). Is Puck the right character to end the play and ask the audience for their applause?

a Suggest why Shakespeare gives him the final word, even though he has been so mischievous and negative about humans in the play: 'Lord, what fools these mortals be', 'The shallowest thick-skin of that barren sort'.

b If you had to choose a different character to speak the final words, who would it be and why? Write a paragraph on your suggestions and reasoning. What might your alternative character say to the audience at the end of the play?

A Midsummer Night's Dream Act 5 Scene 1

仲夏夜之梦

PUCK   [*To the audience*]
            If we shadows[1] have offended,
            Think but this, and all is mended:
            That you have but slumbered[2] here
            While these visions did appear;
            And this weak and idle theme,   405
            No more yielding[3] but a dream,
            Gentles[4], do not reprehend[5];
            If you pardon, we will mend[6].
            And, as I am an honest Puck[7],
            If we have unearnèd luck[8]   410
            Now to 'scape the serpent's tongue[9]
            We will make amends ere long,
            Else[10] the Puck a liar call.
            So, good night unto you all.
            Give me your hands[11], if we be friends,   415
            And Robin shall restore amends[12].   [*Exit*]

A Midsummer Night's Dream
仲夏夜之梦

Looking back at the play 本剧回顾
Activities for groups or individuals

1 Presenting Puck

Compare the photographs on this page with other images of Puck in the book. Talk with the person next to you about what you think works well in each image and what you would change. How would you present Puck in your own production of *A Midsummer Night's Dream*?

2 Puck as symbol

'We cannot possibly deal with Puck as a realistic character.' Say whether or not you agree with this statement, then suggest what issues and themes Shakespeare is exploring through this character. Pool your ideas in a small group in the form of a spider diagram.

3 Important to you – why?

Write down what you consider to be the ten most important quotations in the play. Compare your list with a partner's, giving reasons for your choices.

4 Sixty-second challenge

In pairs, write a quick version of the play, with all the main characters (you may want to cut some of the minor ones), that lasts one minute. You will have to prioritise the key moments and reduce each of them to its fundamental words or message. The class could perform the most successful attempt.

5 What were Shakespeare's views?

What do you think were Shakespeare's own views on his groups of characters? Where do you think his sympathies lie? Does he present one group more positively than another? What attitudes, values and ideas does he appear to be addressing through the construction of his characters? Talk about their behaviour, language, interactions, values and development during the play. Rank the groups of characters in order, from the one Shakespeare presents most positively, to the least, with your rationale.

6 Unpleasant moments?

Although this play falls firmly into the comedy category of Shakespearean plays, it has its bleak and unpleasant scenes and images. Identify particular moments in the play that you think could be seen as disturbing. Present your findings in pictorial or diagrammatic format. Add comments explaining how the examples you have chosen could be played as both nightmarish and comic, and how important messages are being conveyed through these serious and perhaps disturbing scenes.

7 A futuristic all-action movie

You are a screenwriter who has been commissioned by a Hollywood director to write a film version of *A Midsummer Night's Dream*. The director is intrigued by the surreal and mystical nature of the play. He wants it to be set in the future and modelled on such blockbuster (大片) movies as *Avatar*, *Prometheus* and *Cloud Atlas*. In pairs, work on one short scene and invent some suggestions to present at a script conference.

8 And finally …

You have the opportunity to meet William Shakespeare and can ask only one question about this play. What would be your question? Write it down, taking care that it is thoughtful, intelligent and well expressed. Remember that Shakespeare is the most influential and famous playwright of all time.

A Midsummer Night's Dream 仲夏夜之梦

Perspectives and themes 视角与主题

What is the play about?

A Midsummer Night's Dream is a play about love, and it shows clearly that 'the course of true love never did run smooth'. When used as a technical term in drama, the word **comedy** doesn't just mean that something is funny. A Shakespearean comedy is a play where everything starts in chaos but ends in harmony, as opposed to its opposite, the **tragedy**, where a situation that seems harmonious to start with ends in chaos. *A Midsummer Night's Dream* is a comedy, so traditionally should end happily, with problems solved along the way. At times the play presents threatening moments for its central characters, with scenes of dramatic tension, hurt and humiliation interspersed with farce (闹剧) and comedy.

The play begins with plans to celebrate a wedding. Theseus, Duke of Athens, and Hippolyta, Queen of the Amazons, have been at war but now are to marry to ensure future peace. This scene is interrupted by Egeus, a court official with a problem that he demands Theseus should solve. His daughter is refusing to marry the man he has chosen for her. Much of the rest of the play focuses on the attempts of the various lovers to sort out their complex relationship problems.

The play has three main groups of characters:

- Four **lovers** (and Hippolyta and Theseus) live in and around the court of Athens. They are primarily concerned with their love lives and how to achieve happiness. The lovers are very young, and the action of the play will, to some extent, see them grow up and become more perceptive.
- **The Mechanicals** are ordinary working men; friends interested in amateur dramatics who are keen to perform a play before the duke at his wedding. If their play is chosen they will earn respect and 'sixpence a day' for life, ensuring financial security.
- **The fairies** have their foundations in myth, legend and superstition and can be interpreted in a wide variety of ways. They are often the most memorable characters because of the imaginative nature of the characterisation and the richness of their language.

Three storylines run through the play:

- The problematic story of the lovers – Hermia and Lysander, and Helena and Demetrius – that revolves around their dramatic attempts to avoid parental interference and marry happily.
- The Mechanicals' endeavour to rehearse their play: Bottom, their lead actor, becomes involved in the third plot in a relationship with the fairy queen.
- The conflict between Oberon and Titania, the king and queen of the fairies, is presented as a fight for power and control. Oberon and his attendant, Puck, become involved in the lovers' complex interactions.

These storylines all unite in Act 2, as Shakespeare cleverly contrives to have the characters in the same wood on the same night. The lovers are never aware of the fairies, who cause greater turmoil in their relationships before order is restored. The Mechanicals have contact with the fairy world, with Bottom used in Oberon's humiliation of Titania. The lovers do not see the Mechanicals until the final act, when they watch them perform their version of *Pyramus and Thisbe*, which partly parodies the lovers' own situation.

Themes

Another way of answering the question 'What is *A Midsummer Night's Dream* about?' is to identify the themes of the play. Themes are ideas or concepts of fundamental importance that recur throughout the play, linking together plot, characters and language. Themes echo, reinforce and comment upon each other and the whole play in interesting ways. Complex themes are woven through the play and often interconnect with each other – for example, the theme of love is explored alongside that of patriarchy (父权制). Hermia loves Lysander but is being prevented from marrying him by the controlling influence and dominant voice of her father, Egeus.

Perspectives and themes

As you can see, themes are not individual categories but a mix of ideas and concerns that are interrelated in complex ways. When discussing, analysing and writing about the play you should aim to explore the way these themes cross over and illuminate each other, rather than simply listing each of the themes.

You might also like to think about the way the themes work at three different levels: the individual level (psychological or personal); the social level (linked to society and nation); and the natural level (the natural or supernatural world). *A Midsummer Night's Dream* is a play about love and relationships, and this theme weaves together all three levels.

Conflict

Shakespeare dramatises the conflict in each relationship. Egeus attempts to force his will on his daughter, but she defies him. Helena's love for Demetrius is unrequited, and in her hurt and bitterness she betrays her best friend. Driven by frustration, Demetrius behaves aggressively towards Helena. Hippolyta and Theseus's relationship begins with the conflict of war, and Oberon and Titania are at odds, causing disruption to the natural world. The mythical figures Pyramus and Thisbe die for love of each other.

By the end of Act 3, the four young lovers are at each other's throats. Helena and Hermia quarrel in a spiteful, abusive way and Lysander and Demetrius try to kill each other. Their interaction is punctuated by moments of confusion ('I am amazed, and know not what to say'), mockery ('they have conjoined all three / To fashion this false sport in spite of me') and pain ('Can you do me greater harm than hate?').

However, the lovers are all happily united in the end, and the fairies ensure future harmony:

> So shall all the couples three
> Ever true in loving be

◆ Discuss and make notes on how each pair of lovers in the play provides similarities and contrasts, and highlights certain themes (don't forget Titania and Bottom, and Pyramus and Thisbe). You may want to organise your responses in a table so that comparisons and patterns are clearer.

Love and marriage

The play looks at the problems facing lovers and the obstacles placed in the way of true happiness. Shakespeare begins with Theseus's 'nuptial hour' that 'draws on apace', but Theseus's tender comments on his 'desires' and happiness are soon tempered when the audience realises that he has won Hippolyta 'with his sword'. However, although there are lovers' quarrels, misunderstandings and scenes of cruelty and bitterness, the audience is encouraged to laugh at the plight (困境) of lovers and feels secure in the knowledge that it will all end happily. We see how love makes people look foolish, blind, fickle and desperate. At the end we see that 'Jack shall have Jill' and 'naught shall go ill'. Ironically, this is achieved through the intervention of the fairy king rather than the lovers' own good sense.

A closely related theme is the difference between 'doting' and 'love', something like the distinction between fancying someone and loving them. The play also presents love as a kind of madness, showing that 'reason and love keep little company together'. The variety of relationships provides parallels and contrasts. Shakespeare presents the audience with four couples whose relationships need resolving, allowing a range of other themes to be explored – particularly conflict and change.

Order and disorder

The play explores the need for a balance between the rational and irrational, between rules and magic, in the interests of love, harmony and creativity. The order of the Athenian Court, with its cultural restrictions, strict hierarchies and strict legal systems is rejected by the lovers as they escape its limitations to seek freedom and a more accepting world. The Mechanicals also attempt to escape from their secure and ordered lives into the make-believe world of amateur dramatics. When the fairy world meets the mortal world, it creates a fever of disorder and confusion.

A Midsummer Night's Dream
仲夏夜之梦

Appearance and reality

Many of Shakespeare's plays show how people and events are often not as they seem. Puck transforms Bottom into an ass (although Puck's choice does to some extent reflect an aspect of Bottom's nature). Later, Puck meddles with the lover's feelings, causing confusion: 'I am amazed, and know not what to say.' Even at the end, when their lives have been restored to a semblance of normality, neither the lovers nor Bottom understands what has happened and cannot distinguish between their waking lives and dreams. This theme is explored comically in the Mechanicals' flight of fancy in their production of *Pyramus and Thisbe*.

Gender tensions

It is possible to interpret *A Midsummer Night's Dream* as a play about women defying men. The female characters do not conform to the accepted norm of subservience. The action begins with an Amazonian queen who has battled with Theseus and lost. Even though they are betrothed, their relationship continues to show signs of conflict. Hermia stands up to her father and insists on her right to marry the man she loves. Helena proclaims her unrequited love to the world in a way that does not follow expected behaviour, and she spends much of the play chasing Demetrius through the woods at night. The tensions have echoes in the fairy world, where Titania is totally unwilling to submit to Oberon's demands and defies him as long as she is able.

The conventional ending with the women accepting their place as compliant to the will of the men may jar with modern sensibilities, but would have been familiar to Shakespeare's contemporaries in a world where men had more power than women. Elizabeth I was a real exception, introducing a new concept of monarchy where a woman could be a successful ruler.

Motifs

Motifs are recurring elements and patterns of imagery that support the play's themes.

Nature, represented through the magical world of the forest, is placed in contrast with the civilised court of Theseus. The natural world is disrupted by the disharmony between the fairy king and queen: 'And through this distemperature we see / The seasons alter'.

The moon is used to reflect change, disruption and unpredictability: 'Therefore the moon, the governess of floods, / Pale in her anger, washes all the air'.

Sleep and dreams in the play take us to mysterious places. They are states of innocence and vulnerability, and cause confusion and the blurring of boundaries between fantasy and reality: 'God's my life! Stolen hence, and left me asleep! I have had a most rare vision. I have had a dream.'

The **eyes** are signs of perception and perspective: 'Reason becomes the marshal to my will / And leads me to your eyes, where I o'erlook / Love's stories written in love's richest book'. They symbolically provide access to the heart, and are 'windows on the soul'.

Shakespeare uses the idea of putting on a play and **playing roles** to represent magical transformation and the importance of the imagination. It is also an ironic comment that plays are not real: 'you have but slumbered here / While these visions did appear.'

Magic appears in the play as the unseen, the unpredictable, the irrational and inexplicable.

- ◆ Choose five quotations where magic is being performed and explain how the magic develops and shapes some of the themes in the play in each example.

- ◆ Write a paragraph exploring Shakespeare's use of the motif of magic and its impact on the characters and an audience.

The contexts of *A Midsummer Night's Dream*
《仲夏夜之梦》的创作背景

Elizabeth I and her court

A Midsummer Night's Dream was written towards the end of the reign of Queen Elizabeth I. Elizabeth was Gloriana, the Virgin Queen who had taken on an almost mythical significance in the imagination of her subjects. Both Hippolyta and Titania embody certain aspects of Elizabeth's royal mystique (神秘气氛). Hippolyta, as the beautiful 'Amazon queen', evokes Elizabeth's reputation for military prowess, as well as her political refusal to marry. Her navy had conquered the Spanish Armada (西班牙无敌舰队) and she had ruled for longer than any other monarch.

Elizabeth also has much in common with Titania. Shakespeare represents Titania as a great patroness of music, dancing and the arts, as was Elizabeth. Titania, the fairy queen of the play, clearly references the famous epic poem by Edmund Spenser, *The Faerie Queene*, written in 1590, which was an elaborate celebration of Elizabeth and her court.

The fairy 'court' and its rituals and relationships appear in many ways to mimic and perhaps parody those of the human duke, Theseus. Oberon's and Titania's roles as rulers with power, surrounded by their attendants, are strongly reminiscent of (令人想到) the world of mortal monarchs. Whether their conflicts, bitter words, licentiousness (放荡) and jealousy present a commentary on the Elizabethan court is arguable, but this aspect of the play may serve as a cautionary tale (警世故事) on the consequences of immorality and corruption. Their behaviour certainly seems to mimic the worst excesses and spoilt manners of the aristocracy.

Although the play is full of possible references to her, there is no evidence that Queen Elizabeth ever saw *A Midsummer Night's Dream*. Some critics have suggested that the play contains a message to Elizabeth about how responsibility and power must be tempered by the natural laws of feeling and sensitivity.

Greek setting

The play is set in Athens, yet its characterisation and thematic development seems very English – particularly the presentation of the Mechanicals, their working background and their language. The Greek setting is used because the more cultured and educated of Shakespeare's audience would have recognised the allusions to mythological figures and made connections with the legends, which would have given the play serious literary and historical reference points. The historical setting also serves to 'disguise' possible connections with contemporary figures. This was important for Shakespeare who, along with all other playwrights, was dependent on sponsorships (individuals and businesses who contributed financially to the running and upkeep of theatres and theatre companies) and needed to protect himself from political interference and censorship.

Often in Shakespeare's plays, an ancient and cosmopolitan setting suggests order and reason. Certainly, Theseus's court runs on strict rules and social expectations. The forest, which Lysander and Hermia use to escape 'the sharp Athenian law', presents a stark contrast: reason and order have little place there.

Fairies and magic

The characters of Oberon and Puck have their foundations in mythology. The placing of the action on Midsummer's Eve connects them with pagan (异教) celebrations. Much of the play takes place at dusk and at night, when tradition held that fairies were at their most active. It is also the time when witches were said to harvest magical plants: it is during the night of Midsummer's Eve that Oberon instructs Puck to go in search for 'love-in-idleness', with its transformational emotional powers.

A Midsummer Night's Dream
仲夏夜之梦

Puck is the fairy with the most traditional associations with myth and legend. Under Oberon's command, he plays the role of Cupid and attempts to put right the mortals' love dilemmas. Puck is introduced to the audience as 'Robin' at the start of Act 2. Robin Goodfellow was a mythological character who would have been familiar to an Elizabethan audience. However, the name Puck finds its origins in 'Puca', an old English term for a woodland spirit who was much feared by ordinary folk. 'Pouk' was a medieval name for the devil, so for Shakespeare's contemporaries Puck would have profound resonances (共鸣) – most of them ominous. In traditional stories, Robin Goodfellow was known as a 'hairy goat-man, horned and hoofed'. His connection with evil and mischief is clear. (Remind yourself of the image and notes on p. 55, and see also p. 158.)

May Day celebrations and English traditions

A Midsummer Night's Dream is one of Shakespeare's early 'festive comedies'. The play contains a fair amount of commentary on Shakespeare's contemporary English world. The title refers to an English holiday custom, Midsummer Eve – the night of the summer solstice (夏至) at the end of June. On this evening, bonfires were lit and people would sit outdoors. The custom was to tell stories of fairies and witchcraft. The play also refers to 'the rite of May' – a similar English tradition that took place on the first night of May, when young people would sing and dance in the woods outside their towns. This was an occasion for flirtation and romantic dalliances (嬉戏). The play's title and setting recall English social and cultural traditions as well as suggesting superstitions, wild parties and making offerings to the gods.

At the time the play was written, these traditions had come under attack by the English Puritans, who thought that they were inappropriate and ungodly 'pagan' practices that encouraged lawlessness and immorality. The play's happy ending, after all its midsummer madness, implies Shakespeare's defence of rural folklore and customs. They are certainly presented as amusing and harmless. Egeus, the character closest to a killjoy, is silenced by Theseus at the end: 'I will overbear your will.' Philostrate, who disapproves of ordinary men's involvement in celebratory festivities, is shown to be similarly joyless.

The working man

In English towns, the economy did not concentrate on agriculture. Here, the people were either craftsmen or labourers, like the Mechanicals. Men earned their living as butchers, bakers, tailors, weavers, blacksmiths and carpenters. At this stage in the economic development of England, people did everything by hand. Those who did not produce their own goods focused on selling others' goods to earn a living.

Women in Elizabethan England

Although England had a female ruler, women were considered significantly inferior to men. Men held most power in the workplace and within the family. Women had little say about whom they married; a male relative (usually the father) chose a young women's future husband on the basis of status. A man who would bring increased prestige, money or social respectability to a family was considered to be a catch. This was an important fact of life for upper- or middle-class women, and Shakespeare gives this issue prominence by showing Egeus's determination that his daughter will marry the man of his choice. As with men, a girl's fate was bound up in her class and financial situation. A poor rural woman would toil hard on the land as well as bringing up the children and running the home.

A middle-class woman's life may have been more economically secure, but she had no independence and little personal power or control over the family's finances. Like women of other classes, she usually had to endure numerous pregnancies. Infant mortality was high, as was death in childbirth. A woman had no access to divorce and no rights to her own children. A woman was entirely at the mercy of her husband's nature.

The contexts of A Midsummer Night's Dream

Even upper-class women were totally dependent on men, and were used to forge alliances with other powerful or rich families through arranged marriages. If they did not marry, they depended on male relatives to support them. Their main roles in life were to marry well and to bear male heirs. This presented a dilemma for Elizabeth I: convention dictated that if she married, she would have to obey her husband. This may explain why she chose to remain unmarried.

It was, however, customary for upper-class girls to receive a good education. They were tutored at home and were expected to be proficient in languages, the classics, history and music, as well as the more domestic skills of needlework and household management. Elizabeth herself was an accomplished scholar. She shared her brother's tutors as a child and was better educated than most of the men at her court. By the age of eleven, Elizabeth was able to speak fluently in six languages – French, Greek, Latin, Spanish, Welsh and, of course, English.

Shakespeare's depiction of women in the play is interesting in light of this. Hermia is an upper-class girl, clearly intelligent and articulate, who decides to defy her father. Although she has moments of hardship and suffering, she ends up happily married to the man she has chosen.

◆ Work in pairs, with one of you taking the part of Helena and the other Hippolyta. Re-read the scenes where these characters appear, and make notes on how Shakespeare presents them. Think about their language and ideas, the choices they make and the consequences of these choices on their lives. Together, consider whether this research gives you an insight into the lives of Elizabethan women.

◆ As a whole class, hold a discussion on the similarities and differences of life for women in the 1590s and in the early twenty-first century.

Art and theatre

One of the most interesting aspects of *A Midsummer Night's Dream* is that the audience is unsure whether what they have seen is real, or whether they have just watched some kind of dream sequence. They feel the same sense of disorientation as Bottom and the lovers. This is, of course, precisely what Shakespeare wants to make clear – that the theatre is about the power of the imagination, a shared dream.

In the play within the play, the Mechanicals present their interpretation of *Pyramus and Thisbe*, a play they have made up themselves, which makes demands on the offstage audience's suspension of reality. The onstage audience's constant interruptions serve to highlight all that is unreal in a drama. Ironically, the Mechanicals are able to show total belief in their play. Much of the humour in their rehearsals and performance comes from their fumbled attempts to stage a classical, tragic story. Shakespeare focuses much of his plot on this 'theatre within a theatre'. This is partly a structural device to include scenes of pure physical and linguistic comedy, driven by well-meaning and serious but totally inept (笨拙) characters. It also causes the offstage audience to reflect on what makes great theatre and the roles of the actors and the audience in accomplishing this.

The performance of *Pyramus and Thisbe* – however delightful for the real audience at the theatre – clearly does not work for the onstage audience. Watching their reactions to the performance helps us to draw our own conclusions about why this is, and adds to our enjoyment.

A Midsummer Night's Dream
仲夏夜之梦

Characters 人物分析

Oberon

Oberon has his roots in a wide variety of European myths and legends, and it is unclear which of these influenced Shakespeare when drawing up this complex character. There is a fairy elf ruler called Alberich in ancient German mythology; his story, written in the thirteenth century, also revolves around war, love and marriage. The name Oberon was first seen in a thirteenth-century French tale of a fairy dwarf: the story tells of how this handsome dwarf helps the hero to succeed in winning a king's pardon.

In *A Midsummer Night's Dream*, the audience first learns from Puck of Oberon's anger towards Titania, and so is prepared for his dominant and adversarial presence on stage. Thematically, there are links between Oberon and Theseus. Both are powerful men who subdue the women they love. The mortal and the fairy worlds are presented as male-dominated societies. Titania accuses Oberon of amorous interest in a number of mythical women, including Hippolyta, who is described as being his former 'warrior love'. Quite often, Theseus and Oberon are played by the same actor, as are Hippolyta and Titania, which creates a connection in the mind of the audience. Oberon's interest in sexual relationships is a key part of his character. We also learn that he was involved with a country girl named Phillida (a mythical shepherdess known to be in a passionate but unrequited relationship) and disguised himself as a shepherd so that he could pursue her. He involves himself in the lovers' complex relationships and attends the blessing of their wedding beds at the end.

Oberon has impressive magical powers that make him – and Puck – fascinating to watch. The invisibility that enables them to overhear mortal talk can be presented as either amusing or sinister. Oberon's magic and Puck's ability to 'Put a girdle round about the earth' allows for the use of interesting visuals and special effects such as trapdoors, lighting effects, mirrors and hidden wires. The 'love-in-idleness' flower can be perceived as the absolute abuse of power, as it interferes with emotions, or as the ultimate righter of wrongs. The power the fairies have to create storms and ruin crops parallels a monarch's power to affect the lives of others, which emphasises the fact that influence must be accompanied by a sense of responsibility. It could also allude to the Elizabethan view that the supernatural world was able to interfere in the mortal world (good versus evil forces, reflected in chaos and harmony in nature).

CHARACTERS

Titania

Titania is presented as a regal figure, sure of her power and importance. She keeps a rival court to Oberon's, and has her own attendants. During her struggle with Oberon, she defies him and refuses to submit to his bullying. She certainly dominates their first encounter, leaving him spluttering threats after her: 'Thou shalt not from this grove / Till I torment thee for this injury.' She holds the stage dramatically for some time during her famous 'forgeries of jealousy' speech (Act 2 Scene 1, lines 81–117). This is the longest speech in the play, and through its powerful imagery the dominance and force of the fairy world, as well as the violence of their emotions, is made clear to the audience.

After Titania's initial assertive behaviour, Oberon succeeds in tormenting her. Her relationship with Oberon is obviously sexual, with constant accusations of jealousy and betrayal. Her punishment for not complying with her husband's wishes is to be made to fall in love with the transformed Bottom: 'What angel wakes me from my flowery bed?' This relationship is amusing because of the irony of a beautiful fairy queen believing herself in love with an arrogant, ugly labouring man who looks like an ass.

While retaining her authoritative nature – 'Out of this wood do not desire to go: / Thou shalt remain here, whether thou wilt or no.' – she is truly enraptured (狂喜) with her hairy-faced love. Her enslavement to her emotions is so absolute that even Oberon begins to pity her.

Titania has strong links with the natural world (see again her 'forgeries of jealousy' speech), and her language is full of natural and cosmic imagery.

By the end of the play she is reunited with Oberon and her role, with him, appears to be to bless the marriages of the newlywed mortals. However, in order to regain her own marital harmony she has had to suffer a cruel indignity and give in to Oberon's wishes. For a modern audience, Titania's capitulation (让步) to Oberon is surprising. (See 'Women in Elizabethan England', p. 154.)

A Midsummer Night's Dream
仲夏夜之梦

Puck

Puck keeps Oberon amused with his antics: 'I jest to Oberon, and make him smile.' He is an enigmatic character, difficult to read and capable of being presented on the stage in a variety of ways. He is the first fairy introduced to the audience, and is variously described as a 'shrewd and knavish sprite' and 'that merry wanderer of the night'. He has been played by adult actors (male and female) as well as by children. As a character he is certainly a lot of fun; he indulges in great merriment at the expense of the humans with whom he comes into contact. He takes pleasure in people's indignities and misfortunes:

> And those things do best please me
> That befall prepost'rously.

Puck is Oberon's servant and their relationship appears affectionate: 'My gentle Puck', 'Welcome, wanderer.' However, Oberon is well aware of the true nature of his messenger's 'mad spirit' and will happily blame him when things go wrong:

> This is thy negligence. Still thou mistak'st,
> Or else committ'st thy knaveries wilfully.

Shakespeare appears to enjoy Puck, and uses him as a running commentary on the absurdities of the mortals. An audience can feel that Puck is right when he exclaims 'Lord, what fools these mortals be!' He has his parallel in the jesters in a real court, whose job was to entertain the monarch and courtiers with jokes, physical humour and observations on the stupidity of their behaviour. A court jester was often allowed to get away with comments that no one else would dare to voice.

At the end of the play, almost admitting that all his trickery was intentional, he asks the audience not to be 'offended' as all 'is mended'. His final lines imply that the play's premise is a 'weak and idle theme'. He suggests that the audience should treat it all as a dream. Reality and illusion continue to blur. It is interesting that in a play about power and control, Shakespeare gives the final lines to the servant and not to the master.

▼ Puck sending Helena to sleep at the end of Act 3.

Bottom

For many people, Bottom is the funniest and most memorable character in the play. He is magically transformed into an ass, and the queen of the fairies falls in love with him. The humour is generated partly by the situation Bottom finds himself in, partly by his lack of self-awareness and partly by the audience's recognition of his character and his faults. Through all his adventures, Bottom remains very human.

Bottom is pompous (自命不凡). In the 1999 film of *A Midsummer Night's Dream*, he was presented as a character who feels superior to his colleagues. He is fully involved in their play and its rehearsals and, although Quince is the director, Bottom has a tendency to take over: 'let me play Thisbe too. I'll speak in a monstrous little voice'. His self-belief, which is so misplaced, is also infectious and highlights his enthusiasm. His workmates do not appear to resent him, and welcome his reappearance with an ecstatic, 'O most courageous day! O most happy hour!' They are distraught when he goes missing and cannot conceive how they could perform their play without him: 'he hath simply the best wit of any handicraft man in Athens'. Their loyalty to him is endearing.

With the most wonderful irony, Puck places an ass's head on Bottom, making it clear what he thinks of this character. Bottom is the only mortal to have a relationship with a fairy, and this relationship is intriguing. Both Titania and Bottom are the victims of cruel magical tricks, and their brief 'love' affair is the result. When he wakes from his dream, the audience wonders if he has become a wiser man: 'I have had a dream, past the wit of man to say what dream it was.' Here we see a very different Bottom: a thoughtful, articulate and reflective man.

Bottom is the only mortal character who has a role in all three plotlines. He is the Mechanicals' main actor, the lover of the enchanted fairy queen and the main performer for the newly married courtly couples. It is only his fellow labourers who truly appreciate him and his talents.

However, Shakespeare makes Bottom's performance as Pyramus as amateurish and as funny as the audience could wish, and some people's final impression is that he is still 'an ass'.

◆ With a partner, consider how Shakespeare uses Bottom as a thematic linking device. Make notes on your ideas in response to the following questions:

1. How are the harshness of love, unrequited love and yearnings for the impossible explored through Bottom?
2. How does his character develop ideas on fantasy, dreams and magic?
3. How does Shakespeare investigate the fine line between ignorance and wisdom with Bottom?

Quince

Peter Quince is the driving force for the rehearsal and production of the play to be performed at Theseus's wedding. He is the author of *The Most Lamentable Comedy and Most Cruel Death of Pyramus and Thisbe*. At the rehearsal in the wood, he takes on the role of director and is in charge of casting the play. He appears to know something about plays, how they are structured and meant to be performed and asserts to Flute: 'You speak all your part at once, cues and all.'

When performing the play, Quince recites the Prologue. It is an affecting scene as he struggles to fit his lines into the metre (韵律) and make the rhymes work, with both comedic and tragic effect. The stage audience makes jokes at his expense.

Hermia

Hermia is a young woman at a time when a father had absolute authority over his daughter's choice of husband. Unfortunately, Hermia is in love with Lysander and her father is insisting that she marry Demetrius. Although she lacks real power, it is clear from the beginning that Hermia is willing to assert her views, taking centre stage to explain them: 'I would my father looked but with my eyes.' She is also willing to defy and humiliate her father publicly by agreeing to run away with Lysander.

A Midsummer Night's Dream
仲夏夜之梦

Hermia is small – during the conflict Lysander calls her 'bead,' 'acorn' and 'dwarf' – but feisty. Hermia and Helena have enjoyed a close relationship since childhood, but their situation obviously puts a strain on the friendship. now Helena says of her:

> O, when she is angry she is keen and shrewd;
> She was a vixen when she went to school

Helena

Shakespeare presents Helena as a stark physical contrast to Hermia, who calls her a 'painted maypole' in their argument in Act 3. She is obviously tall and slim, and is usually cast as such.

We meet Helena at a low point in her life. She is very much in love with Demetrius, a young man who once courted her. He now wants to marry Hermia and has consequently rejected Helena. This has not altered her feelings, and she cannot understand his change of heart. She is conscious that there is something about Hermia that has attracted him:

> O, teach me how you look, and with what art
> You sway the motion of Demetrius' heart.

Although she makes much of the notion of sisterhood, 'Both warbling of one song, both in one key,' Helena is the only female in the play who is guilty of real disloyalty, with her disclosure to Demetrius of the elopement plan. Her pursuit of Demetrius when he is chasing another woman may seem undignified to a modern audience:

> I am your spaniel; and, Demetrius,
> The more you beat me I will fawn on you

Today, we sympathise with Helena as the victim of unrequited love, but might be doubtful about the way she copes with it. It is interesting that, although she achieves her happiness with Demetrius at the end, this only occurs after he is placed under the influence of Oberon's love potion. Is this a plot device or a comment on Helena's or Demetrius's character?

Lysander

Lysander is confident, despite the problems that he and Hermia face at the beginning. Certain of finding a way out of the situation and sure of Hermia's love, he is not undermined by Egeus's lack of support, Demetrius's competition or Theseus's initial decision.

Shakespeare presents Lysander as a proactive lover. He plans the elopement, but then loses his way in the wood. In some ways he is a stereotype: he tries hard to persuade Hermia to sleep with him, and when confronted with Demetrius's opposition he resorts to violence.

Demetrius

Demetrius appears much less likeable than Lysander. We never discover why Egeus prefers him. He does not say much in the first scene, but what he does say appears arrogant: 'Lysander, yield / Thy crazèd title to my certain right.' He seems rather careless of Hermia's lack of interest. Even less favourable is his rejection of Helena and his indifference to the hurt he has caused her. His behaviour to Helena in the woods is abusive and aggressive.

Egeus

Egeus's complaint against his daughter Hermia dominates the first scene. Shakespeare uses this character to introduce the themes of the law and control versus freedom. Egeus is determined to bring down the full force of the law on Hermia if she refuses to obey him. He seems to be motivated by a desire for control rather than by reason, and in the end Theseus denies his request.

Theseus and Hippolyta

Theseus and Hippolyta are the first two characters on the stage. Through them we are immediately introduced to the play's main themes of marriage, love and conflict: 'Now, fair Hippolyta, our nuptial hour / Draws on apace', 'Hippolyta, I wooed thee with my sword'.

These two characters and their story of war and wooing are based on Greek myth and have parallels with the

Characters

fairy world. However, Hippolyta and Theseus never come into contact with the fairies and are more closely connected to the lovers through the exploration of sexual relationships.

Theseus has been played in various ways: as an autocratic politician, a lecherous (好色) rogue, a battle-weary young man and an elderly general. He is very much in charge in Act 1 Scene 1. It is problematic for an audience to make a judgement about a man who describes his own marriage and Hermia's death in the same short speech. Here, he wholly supports Egeus's demands, and yet a few days later he says 'Egeus, I will overbear your will'. Shakespeare does not make it clear what has caused this about-face (彻底改变). Perhaps Theseus has found himself moved by young love. Some productions show Hippolyta encouraging him towards this more feeling response.

Hippolyta only speaks twenty-eight lines in the play, and may appear passive: she makes no comment on the lovers' plight, leaving all the decision-making to Theseus. But Shakespeare presents her as a confident and thoughtful woman in Act 5. Here, she is willing to stand up to Theseus when discussing the lover's story, and offers her perspective.

Hippolyta comes from a tribe of powerful women, the Amazons. She has had to surrender to Theseus but he falls in love with her so, in effect, also surrenders to her.

◆ In the production pictured here, Theseus and Hipployta are played by middle-aged actors. This would provide an interesting contrast with the much younger lovers. Make a list of the advantages and disadvantages of making the age difference so distinct. Consider which themes a director may wish to highlight by taking this approach.

◆ In groups of four, each choose one of these characters: Theseus, Helena, Quince, Oberon. Prepare a PowerPoint presentation showing your personal reading of your chosen character, and present it to the other members of your group. Each presentation should include the following five slides:

- A picture of the actor that you would cast as your character in a new stage version of the play, with some bullet points to explain your rationale.
- Ideas on how this character should look on stage – their costume, hair and make-up. Consider the symbolism of your choices.
- The five most important quotations that reveal your character and their development. Include some language analysis.
- Some ideas on how this character is used by Shakespeare to move forward the plot and develop the play's themes.
- Your personal response to this character, with an explanation of how you think an audience would respond to them on stage.

161

A Midsummer Night's Dream
仲夏夜之梦

The language of *A Midsummer Night's Dream*
《仲夏夜之梦》的语言

Old language

Shakespeare's language may seem complex and difficult when you first encounter it. With experience it becomes easier, but it can still remain a challenge.

- With a partner, choose a four-page section of the play. Then, working by yourself, divide the words explained on these pages into those that you can easily understand, those that you find difficult and those that seem to have no link with modern English. Afterwards, swap work with your partner so you can see how he or she has grouped these words. Discuss any differences, and try to explain words to each other if one of you finds them easier to understand.

Of all the major writers in English, Shakespeare uses the largest number of different words: more than four times as many as most authors. He also uses many different meanings for the same words – he obviously enjoyed playing with language.

Shakespeare can also be hard to understand because today's world is so different from that of 400 years ago. Some speeches clearly display that difference, as in Act 2 Scene 1, lines 35–8:

> *That frights the maidens of the villagery,*
> *Skim milk, and sometimes labour in the quern,*
> *And bootless make the breathless housewife churn,*
> *And sometime make the drink to bear no barm*

Here, the agricultural England of the 1590s is much in evidence. However, there is little in the play that only a person from Shakespeare's time could understand.

Literary language

Shakespeare's language isn't just old, it's literary. *A Midsummer Night's Dream* draws upon many other types of writing and stories: Greek and Roman mythology, old plays and folk tales and legends. The language is also shaped for the Elizabethan stage. Unlike many of today's writers for film and television, Elizabethan playwrights often used complex and playful language rather than trying to be realistic.

People in Shakespeare's day did not speak like the characters in his plays; they certainly did not speak in rhyme! Shakespeare did not use the ordinary speech of real people – he followed the stage conventions of the time by writing much of the play in verse.

There are times when the language seems to run away with itself, as in Bottom's lines 205–7 in Act 4 Scene 1, where Shakespeare uses the Bible as his guide:

> *The eye of man hath not heard, the ear of man hath not seen, man's hand is not able to taste, his tongue to conceive, nor his heart to report what my dream was!*

Shakespeare also uses **alliteration** to highlight the comedy implicit in the literary limitations of the Mechanicals:

> *Whereat with blade, with bloody, blameful blade,*
> *He bravely broached his boiling bloody breast*

- Watch a TV drama and list some examples of when the dialogue mimics real speech. Do these moments have a distinct purpose – for example, to move the story on, or to reveal something about a character's past? Do any characters speak in a way that you never really hear in a conversation?

Imagery

A Midsummer Night's Dream abounds in imagery (sometimes called 'figures' or 'figurative language'). Imagery is created by vivid words and phrases that conjure up emotionally charged mental pictures or associations in the imagination. Imagery provides insight into character or develops a theme, and stirs the audience's imagination. It also deepens the dramatic impact of particular moments.

Imagery works well when describing love. Lysander shows his love and concern when he says to Hermia:

The language of A Midsummer Night's Dream

How now, my love? Why is your cheek so pale?
How chance the roses there do fade so fast?

Helena, because of her unhappy situation, describes love as 'Cupid painted blind'. And at the end of the play, Demetrius describes his renewed love for Helena with an image that links love and health:

But like a sickness did I loathe this food,
But, as in health come to my natural taste

Problems in love and conflict are also described in terms of storms and bad weather. Hermia describes her tears as a 'tempest of my eyes', and Titania's 'forgeries of jealousy' speech (Act 2 Scene 1, lines 81–117) is filled with extreme images – 'contagious fogs', 'whistling wind' – that create a clear picture of a world in torment because of her 'wrath' with Oberon.

There is a predominance of natural imagery in the play. This is to some extent due to Shakespeare's presentation of the fairies, who are all named after things found in nature. The natural imagery also helps to link the woodland setting to the situations in which the characters find themselves. There was little scenery when the play was performed in Shakespeare's time so the language had to convey clearly the setting to the audience. When Puck torments the Mechanicals (Act 3 Scene 1, lines 89–93), he uses an abundance of frightening imagery so that the audience can picture the scene:

Through bog, through bush, through brake, through briar;
Sometime a horse I'll be, sometime a hound,
  A hog, a headless bear, sometime a fire,
And neigh, and bark, and grunt, and roar, and burn,
Like horse, hound, hog, bear, fire at every turn.

A few lines later (103–6), Bottom responds with his own more comforting natural imagery to show he is not afraid:

The ousel cock so black of hue,
  With orange-tawny bill,
The throstle with his note so true,
  The wren with little quill –

Shakespeare uses the moon as a recurring image in the play, for a variety of effects. Theseus's image 'Chanting faint hymns to the cold fruitless moon' describes Hermia's life if she chooses to become a nun. Earlier, he uses the moon as a marker for the slow passing of time until his wedding day: 'how slow / This old moon wanes!' And in Act 1 Scene 1, lines 9–11, Hippolyta links the moon with night-time and dreams:

And then the moon, like to a silver bow
New bent in heaven, shall behold the night
Of our solemnities.

Most of the play takes place at night, and the language conjures up the image of a place with no light except moonlight, in which the characters stumble around, feeling vulnerable. The natural imagery highlights how the boundary between wisdom and foolishness has blurred. It is an excellent place to explore the complications of mortal love and the whims of human beings. The moon becomes a symbol of inconstancy and infidelity, highly relevant to Lysander's and Demetrius's fickleness. Lysander plans to meet Hermia under the light of the 'silver visage' of Phoebe (goddess of the moon, associated with chastity), but when in the wood standing on the grass decked 'with liquid pearl' he behaves in a less constant way.

The imagery of dreams and reality is fascinating and thought-provoking When she wakes up after her night in the wood (Act 4 Scene 1, lines 186–7), Hermia comments on the experience:

Methinks I see these things with parted eye,
  When everything seems double.

Bottom is also puzzled by his memory of events and thinks it is 'past the wit of man to say what dream it was. Man is but an ass if he go about to expound this dream' (Act 4 Scene 1, lines 201–2). Bottom is trying to be philosophical and reflect upon the meaning of his vision, but his mixed-up imagery makes it even more confusing, and amusing for the audience. This is exactly what Oberon intended when he declared in Act 3 Scene 2, lines 370–1:

When they next wake, all this derision
Shall seem a dream and fruitless vision

A Midsummer Night's Dream
仲夏夜之梦

The play is full of images of dreams. It ends with Theseus commenting on the Mechanicals' play: 'The best in this kind are but shadows; and the worst are no worse, if imagination amend them.' (Act 5 Scene 1, lines 205–6.) And at lines 403–6 Puck tells the audience to think:

> That you have but slumbered here
> While these visions did appear;
> And this weak and idle theme,
> No more yielding but a dream

The Mechanicals view the moon less as image or symbol. They want a physical representation of the moon in their play: a lantern. They cannot comprehend how language can create a moon, making it real for an audience.

Shakespeare's imagery uses metaphor, simile and personification. All are comparisons that substitute one thing (the image) for another (the thing that is actually being described).

A **simile** compares one thing to another, using 'as' or 'like'. Demetrius describes his love for Hermia, 'Melted as the snow'; and Lysander says he will shake Hermia from him 'like a serpent'. Earlier, Helena describes her friendship with Hermia as 'like to a double cherry'. Sometimes inappropriate similes can be used for comic effect. Thisbe, attempting romantic imagery, describes Pyramus: 'His eyes were green as leeks.'

A **metaphor** is also a comparison, suggesting that two dissimilar things are actually the same. A metaphor borrows one word or phrase to express another. In Act 3, when the lovers are in a potion-induced confusion, they use metaphor to put each other down. Lysander calls Hermia 'loathed medicine! O hated potion' and Hermia calls Helena a 'painted maypole'.

Personification is the attribution of human characteristics, such as personality, to non-human objects or abstract ideas.

Antithesis (对偶)

LYSANDER The course of true love never did run smooth;
But either it was different in blood –
HERMIA O cross! too high to be enthralled to low.
LYSANDER Or else misgraffèd in respect of years –
HERMIA O spite! too old to be engaged to young.
LYSANDER Or else it stood upon the choice of friends –
HERMIA O hell, to choose love by another's eyes!

The first of these lines from Act 1 Scene 1, lines 134–40, is now proverbial. The exclamations that follow ('O cross!' 'O spite!' 'O hell') are absurd and comical, but also highly patterned (notice the echoing rhythms of the last five lines). Shakespeare is using one of his favourite language devices, **antithesis** – setting words or phrases against each other to heighten the sense of conflict (high/low, old/young).

- ◆ Try to find more examples of antithesis in moments like this, where the language seems to overwhelm or contradict the emotions.

- ◆ Consider again Shakespeare's use of binary opposition (introduced on p. 98). Look for one example in each act, and think about the effect on the audience at key moments in the play as the characters and themes unfold.

Verse and prose

Although it has a good deal of rhyme, more of the play is written in **blank verse**: unrhymed verse with a five-beat rhythm (**iambic pentameter**). Each line has five **feet** (音步) (groups of syllables) called **iambs** (抑扬), which have one stressed (/) and one unstressed (×) syllable:

× / × / × / × / × /
This man with lanthorn, dog, and bush of thorn

The court and the fairies mainly use this kind of verse, but (apart from their *Pyramus and Thisbe* play) the Mechanicals' speeches are in prose. Thus, the language of the characters reflects their social position as well as creating different types of comedy.

Shakespeare also uses other metres, most obviously four-stress rhythm – as in 'You spotted snakes with double tongue', and in the final sixty-seven lines of the play.

- ◆ Write a modern speech in iambic pentameter. Try to imagine a scene that Shakespeare has omitted, such as a conversation between Helena and Hermia when they return to Athens.

THE LANGUAGE OF A MIDSUMMER NIGHT'S DREAM

Language and character

The language of the characters – the words, patterns and images they use – reflects their personality as much as their actions or the plot do.

◆ Examine the speeches of your favourite character in order to identify the language patterns they use, and to what effect.

◆ Devise some dialogue that the actors could be speaking at the moment shown in the picture below. It can be in modern English or, if you want a real challenge, try to write dialogue in the style of Shakespeare himself!

◆ Create a poster that concentrates on the language of the play. Present some of the most important features of Shakespeare's language. Include some of the following ideas:

- famous favourite lines from the play
- examples of different kinds of wordplay and humour, with modern versions or interpretations
- words and phrases no longer used today that you find interesting

Display your ideas around the classroom. Look at each other's posters, and leave two comments on each: WWW (What Went Well) and EBI (Even Better If).

A MIDSUMMER NIGHT'S DREAM
仲夏夜之梦

A Midsummer Night's Dream in performance
《仲夏夜之梦》的演出

There is little clear evidence about when and where this play was originally performed. Shakespeare's earliest plays were performed at The Theatre, an open-air playhouse in Shoreditch, London. His company, The Chamberlain's Men, then moved their performances to the Globe Theatre. The theatre burnt down in 1613, and was rebuilt in 1997 as a copy of the original. The modern Shakespeare's Globe replicates to some extent the experience of Shakespeare's contemporaries, both as actors and audience.

When *A Midsummer Night's Dream* was first performed on stage, all the female parts were played by boys. This issue is amusingly explored through the character of Flute and his response to being cast as Thisbe: 'Nay, faith, let not me play a woman: I have a beard coming.'

There were few props and little in the way of sets. The audience had to imagine the contrast between the first scene in the palace and the night scenes in the wood. Most performances took place during the day. In this they were greatly helped by Shakespeare's imagery and the actors' responses.

◆ Look at the picture below. What do you notice about the building, the staging and the audience in the modern Shakespeare's Globe? How is it different from other theatres you have attended? How might the audience experience differ?

This 1900 production is in the lavish Victorian style, in which each scene resembles a living picture. The action of the play was in danger of becoming secondary to the setting.

The ways productions of *A Midsummer Night's Dream* have been staged over the years have to some extent been informed by changing social attitudes to marriage. For example, a Victorian audience may well have had a very different view from a modern one towards Hermia's refusal to yield to her father's wishes and her decision to elope with Lysander.

A production would also reflect the audience's perception of the whole notion of fairies, magic and the supernatural. Prior to Elizabethan times, fairies were considered to be evil. Shakespeare, along with other writers at the time, redefined fairies during this time period, turning them into gentle, albeit mischievous, spirits.

◀ Northern Ballet Theatre's production of *A Midsummer Night's Dream*, 2007.

Ballet and opera

A Midsummer Night's Dream has inspired ballets and operas. Operatic versions of Shakespeare's plays cut the language very heavily or rewrite it.

In 1692, Henry Purcell wrote the music for a spectacular operatic version called *The Fairy Queen*. David Garrick's operatic version, *The Fairies* (1755), dismissed all the characters except the lovers and the fairies. Fewer than 600 lines from Shakespeare's original remained, but there were an additional twenty-eight songs, some from other plays by Shakespeare and some from other poets, such as Dryden.

An opera with music by Benjamin Britten premiered in 1960. Britten connects his music to the three groups of characters. The Mechanicals are given folk-like 'simple' music, the lovers have a more romantic sound and a more ethereal music is used to represent the fairies. All of the action takes place in the woods and the fairies dominate, which is appropriate as Shakespeare associates them throughout with music and dancing. Britten focuses on the innocence and romanticism inherent in the lovers' story, rather than the sexuality. Puck is a naughty, acrobatic child.

All the action and characterisation in a ballet are interpreted through music and dance. George Balanchine choreographed a ballet version of the story using Mendelssohn's music written in 1843. The ballet tells the story in dance in two acts. The first act tells the story of the lovers and fairies, and the second focuses on a dancing marriage celebration. The ballet was first performed in 1962.

Music and dance have always played a large part in productions of the play, and continue to do so. Directors often commission composers to write original scores for new productions.

- ◆ In groups of four, compose a short piece of music and choreograph a dance sequence for Act 4 Scene 1, from line 80 ('*Soft music plays*') and line 83 ('*They dance*') up to line 99 ('*Exeunt Oberon, Titania and Puck*'). Try out your ideas and show the result to another group.

▶ Oberon and Puck enter the stage from above in Peter Brook's 1970 production of the play.

Modern productions

In contrast to the lavish productions and the focus on dance and musical set pieces so beloved of Victorian audiences, Peter Brook's production of the play in 1970 presented a radical new interpretation. The stage was spartan, the set a stark white box, the costumes simple and in primary colours. The fairies were shown suspended above the stage on trapeze-like swings and were lowered up and down for their interactions with the mortals. The magic in the play was interpreted through circus tricks and acrobatics. Many of the relationships were presented in crudely sexual terms. It proved to be an influential production, and many companies, directors and costume and set designers have imitated these ideas and developed them further in the last forty years.

▼ This Korean production used music, movement-based acting, mythology and mime to create a fun and energetic interpretation of the play.

A Midsummer Night's Dream
仲夏夜之梦

Shakespeare is often thought of as English through and through, and *A Midsummer Night's Dream* particularly so, yet successful and well-received productions take place all over the world.

Tim Supple directed a successful production using dancers, martial arts experts, musicians and street acrobats from across India and Sri Lanka to reproduce the mysterious and surreal world of the fairies. The production toured India to great acclaim, and had a successful run at the Swan Theatre in Stratford-upon-Avon in 2007 and 2008. It used traditional live Indian music, bright and beautiful costumes and was performed in six Indian languages and English. *The Times* newspaper described this production as 'Shakespeare brilliantly reimagined'. There are other photographs of this production on pages 44 and 50.

▼ The fairies tumbling down acrobatically in Tim Supple's vision of *A Midsummer Night's Dream.*

Presentations of the fairy world

Titania and her fairies have been presented in many different ways. The photograph below is of a 2001 production. It shows Titania surrounded by her fairies, who are presented as childlike creatures.

In contrast, the image on the right, from a 1992 National Theatre production, shows a very different Titania. Here, the imagery is much darker and more sinister. Bottom appears as the captive of the fairies, who look like they have emerged from the underworld.

◆ Compile a list of the dramatic gains and losses of presenting the fairies as these two productions have. Which do you prefer? Why?

A Midsummer Night's Dream
仲夏夜之梦

A 2001 production had an all-female cast playing the Mechanicals. The comedian and writer Dawn French played Bottom. This gender role-reversal is the opposite of that in Shakespeare's day, when all the characters – including the female ones – were played by men or boys.

◆ In a group, discuss the considerations you think influenced this casting decision and the effects it might have had on characterisation and the development of the relationships on stage. What challenges might it present to the actors involved? How are they similar or different to the challenges for an all-male cast playing both genders in Elizabethan theatre productions?

▶ 'Let me play the lion too. I will roar'.

Set design（布景设计）

No Shakespearean comedy offers wider scope to the imagination of directors, designers, and actors.

(David Richman, *Laughter, Pain, and Wonder: Shakespeare's Comedies and the Audience in the Theatre*, 1990)

This play is indeed a set designer's 'dream'. It includes a duke's palace and the magical world of fairies, all contrasted with a group of unworldly and comical amateur dramatics. Much of the action takes place at night, and the imagery encourages a creative response to Shakespeare's vision.

When studying or acting in a Shakespeare play, one question always arises: 'What does it all mean?' The answer is that it means different things at different times and also many things at once. *A Midsummer Night's Dream* has been acted for over 400 years and people are still debating and exploring its different meanings and interpretations. The complexity of the play and its language is part of its appeal. It is an exploration in which there is no final, complete and 'right' explanation. Perhaps Bottom was right:

I have had a most rare vision. I have had a dream, past the wit of man to say what dream it was.

- ◆ The striking school setting shown on this page will have been the combined vision of a director, a set designer and a lighting designer. In threes, each taking one of these roles, combine your ideas to create your own vision of a key moment in the play.

- ◆ As much of its action takes place in the woods at night, *A Midsummer Night's Dream* is popular for outdoor evening productions, often in parks or country house gardens. What type of outdoor space would you consider using, and which aspects of the play would it enhance?

A Midsummer Night's Dream 仲夏夜之梦

Writing about Shakespeare 笔论莎士比亚

The play as text

Shakespeare's plays have always been studied as literary works – as words on a page that need clarification, appreciation and discussion. When you write about the plays, you will be asked to compose short pieces and also longer, more reflective pieces like controlled assessments, examination scripts and coursework – often in the form of essays on themes and/or imagery, character studies, analyses of the structure of the play and on stagecraft. Imagery, stagecraft and character are dealt with elsewhere in this edition. Here, we concentrate on themes and structure. You might find it helpful to look at the 'Write about it' boxes on the left-hand pages throughout the play.

Themes

It is often tempting to say that the theme of a play is a single idea, like 'death' in *Hamlet*, or 'the supernatural' in *Macbeth*, or 'love' in *Romeo and Juliet*. The problem with such a simple approach is that you will miss the complexity of the plays. In *Romeo and Juliet*, for example, the play is about the relationship between love, family loyalty and constraint; it is also about the relationship of youth to age and experience; and the relationship between Romeo and Juliet is also played out against a background of enmity between two families. Between each of these ideas or concepts there are tensions. The tensions are the main focus of attention for Shakespeare and the audience, and they also happen to be how drama operates – by the presentation of and resolution of tension.

Look back at the 'Themes' boxes throughout the play to see if any of the activities there have given rise to information that you could use as a starting-point for further writing about the themes of the specific play you are studying.

Structure

Most Shakespeare plays are in five acts, divided into scenes. These acts were not in the original scripts, but have been included in later editions to make the action more manageable, clearer and more like 'classical' structures. One way to get a sense of the structure of the whole play is to take a printed version of the play (not this one!) and cut it up into scenes and acts. Then display each scene and act, in sequence, on a wall, like this:

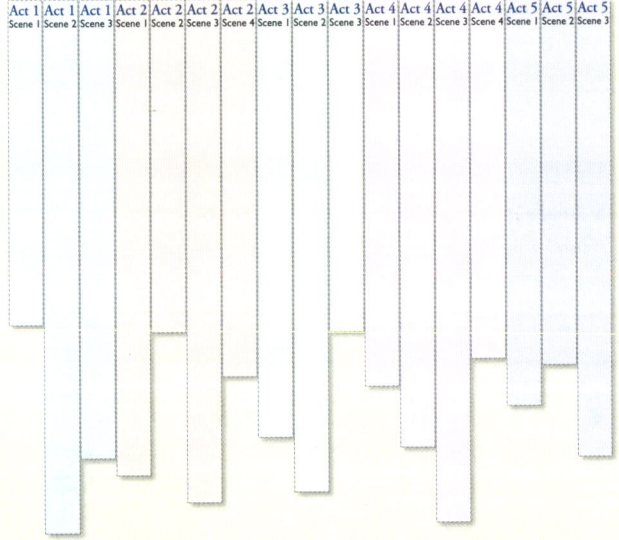

As you set out the whole play, you will be able to see the 'shape' of each act, the relative length of the scenes, and how the acts relate to each other (such as whether one of the acts is shorter, and why that might be). You can annotate the text with comments, observations and questions. You can use a highlighter pen to mark the recurrence of certain words, images or metaphors to see at a glance where and how frequently they appear. You can also follow a particular character's progress through the play.

Such an overview of the play gives you critical perspective: you will be able to see how the parts fit together, to stand back from the play and assess its shape, and to focus on particular parts within the context of the whole. Your writing will reflect a greater awareness of the overall context as a result.

The play as script

There are different, but related, categories when we think of the play as a script for performance. These include *stagecraft* (discussed elsewhere in this edition and throughout the left-hand pages), *lighting*, *focus* (who are we looking at? Where is the attention of the audience?), *music and sound*, *props and costumes*, *casting*, *make-up*, *pace and rhythm*, and other *spatial relationships* (e.g. how actors move across stage in relation to each other). If you are writing about stagecraft or performance, use the notes you have made as a result of the 'Stagecraft' boxes throughout this edition of the play, as well as any material you can gather about the plays in performance.

What are the key points of dispute?

Shakespeare is brilliant at capturing a number of key points of dispute in each of his plays. These are the dramatic moments where he concentrates the focus of the audience on difficult (sometimes universal) problems that the characters are facing or embodying.

First, identify these key points in the play you are studying. You can do this as a class by brainstorming what you think the key points are in small groups, then debating the long-list as a whole class, and then coming up with a short-list of what the class thinks are the most significant. (This is a good opportunity for speaking and listening work.) They are likely to be places in the play where the action or reflection is at its most intense, and which capture the complexity of themes, character, structure and performance.

Second, drill down at one of the points of contention and tension. In other words, investigate the complexity of the problem that Shakespeare is exploring. What is at stake? Why is it important? Is it a problem that can be resolved, or is it an insoluble one?

Key skills in writing about Shakespeare

Here are some suggestions to help you organise your notes and develop advanced writing skills when working on Shakespeare:

- Compose the title of your writing carefully to maximise your opportunities to be creative and critical about the play; or explore the key words in your title carefully. Decide which aspect of the play – or which combination of aspects – you are focusing on.
- Create a mind map of your ideas, making connections between them.
- If appropriate, arrange your ideas into a hierarchy that shows how some themes or features of the play are 'higher' than others and can incorporate other ideas.
- Sequence your ideas so that you have a plan for writing an essay, review, story – whichever genre you are using. You might like to think about whether to put your strongest points first, in the middle, or later.
- Collect key quotations (it might help to compile this list with a partner), which you can use as evidence to support your argument.
- Compose your first draft, embedding quotations in your text as you go along.
- Revise your draft in the light of your own critical reflections and/or those of others.

The following pages focus on writing about *A Midsummer Night's Dream* in particular.

A Midsummer Night's Dream
仲夏夜之梦

Writing about *A Midsummer Night's Dream*
笔论《仲夏夜之梦》

Before embarking on an extended piece of writing, it is important to think carefully about how it is structured. This play is a comedy and complies with the comic conventions of Elizabethan theatre. The plot is typically arranged into five acts, with an accepted formula:

Act 1   A situation with tensions or conflict
Act 2   Conflict is developed
Act 3   Conflict reaches a climax and often an impasse
Act 4   Problem or conflict begins to be sorted out
Act 5   Problem is resolved and loose ends are tied up

◆ With a partner, look at each act and consider:
   - the development of the main characters and the outcome for each one
   - how the main themes are developed and how and when each is concluded
   - how Shakespeare introduces and develops the imagery
   - the tone and mood, for example the moments of dramatic tension, empathy, humour and happiness.

Extended writing on a Shakespeare play is a challenge. It is important that you have had the opportunity to develop a personal response. The next two activities test your ideas, help you to build your argument and see how you can you use the text to support it.

◆ In groups of four, take one question each and write down your ideas in full, using quotations to support your ideas:
   - What is the turning point in the play?
   - What is the most memorable moment?
   - Which is the most important line?
   - Who is the most important character?

◆ In turn, take one minute to explain your ideas to your group. As the others in your group are speaking, make notes of their ideas and write down questions. Don't let each other off lightly; ask your questions so that each individual has to explain their response and justify it with quotations.

◆ In pairs, consider the following readings of the play. Divide them into three categories: Yes (those you agree with), No (those you don't agree with) and Maybe (those you are not sure about). It is very important that any argument you construct is supported by appropriate quotations. Share your responses with another pair.

1   Shakespeare is presenting men as fickle and women as constant and true.

2   Shakespeare believes that the patriarchal society must not be changed. Men must make all the decisions.

3   Shakespeare presents love as involving more suffering than pleasure; more of a nightmare than a dream.

4   Shakespeare believes that love will not last forever and will always change.

5   Shakespeare thinks that true love is beautiful and the imagery in this play is evidence of this.

6   Conflict in the play is the more dominant theme. Romance is secondary. This is a dark play where we are laughing at the characters.

7   The tone of the play is so light-hearted that the audience never doubts that things will end happily, and is therefore free to enjoy the comedy without being caught up in the tension of an uncertain outcome.

8   Shakespeare is interested in imbalance in relationships; he enjoys exploring unrequited love and arguments.

Writing about A Midsummer Night's Dream

Essays

You may have some choice in your essay title for *A Midsummer Night's Dream*. However, it is likely that coursework, controlled assessment or exam practice essay titles will be suggested to you. The best essay titles are those that encourage you to formulate a line of argument. A quotation or statement can be useful starting points. For example:

Sigmund Freud said: 'You are always insane when you are in love.' Analyse this statement in relation to Shakespeare's presentation of the lovers in Act 4 Scene 2 of A Midsummer Night's Dream.

'Helena is presented by Shakespeare as a desperate character with whom the audience has little sympathy.' Analyse the presentation of this important character in light of this statement.

It is better to focus on a precise area of the play – for example, the interactions in one particular scene, the presentation of a character, the development of a theme or Shakespeare's use of imagery and its impact on the audience. This tight focus allows for a more thoughtful and profound exploration.

Structuring your essay

The introduction needs to fulfil two main functions: to address the question, and to launch the line of argument you will construct in response to the question.

First impressions count, and you will need to leave your reader keen to find out how you develop the ideas you have introduced. If this is an examination essay, your assessor will, from the first sentence, be judging your skills and evaluating how well you are addressing the assessment objectives.

Just as Shakespeare has structured his play into acts, you will need to structure your ideas into paragraphs, so that your reader experiences your essay as a journey. Each paragraph will explore a particular focus or analyse an idea. The first sentence of each paragraph, sometimes called a topic sentence, is important. At the end of your first draft, reread all your topic sentences. They should stand alone as an outline of your argument and give a direction to your work. A useful analogy is to think of these opening sentences as the skeleton of your essay, with the development, textual support and analysis as the flesh, or meat, of the essay.

◆ Consider how you would answer the following essay questions. Which one would you like to write most and which least? Which would allow you to show your skills and ideas?

1. Explore Shakespeare's use of setting in *A Midsummer Night's Dream*. Focus particularly on the opening scenes in Athens and the move to the woods at night for Acts 2, 3 and 4. What effect do these scenes have on the development of themes and character?

2. Lysander's line, 'The course of true love never did run smooth', is one of the most famous in the play. Analyse how Shakespeare presents love in Act 1 Scene 1 of *A Midsummer Night's Dream*.

3. How does Shakespeare use language in Act 3 Scene 2 to explore love and hate?

4. Consider the ways that Shakespeare explores the ideas of dreams and reality in Act 4.

5. 'Oberon is a dangerous character using illusion and magic purely for control.' Respond to this statement by analysing Shakespeare's presentation of Oberon in *A Midsummer Night's Dream*.

6. Explore the way that the play *Pyramus and Thisbe* is presented. What themes and ideas are explored by the dramatic device of a play within a play?

◆ Plan a response to two of these titles. Then choose one of them to research further and draft into an essay.

A Midsummer Night's Dream
仲夏夜之梦

William Shakespeare 莎翁年表
1564–1616

1564	Born Stratford-upon-Avon, eldest son of John and Mary Shakespeare.
1582	Marries Anne Hathaway of Shottery, near Stratford.
1583	Daughter Susanna born.
1585	Twins, son and daughter, Hamnet and Judith, born.
1592	First mention of Shakespeare in London. Robert Greene, another playwright, described Shakespeare as 'an upstart crow beautified with our feathers'. Greene seems to have been jealous of Shakespeare. He mocked Shakespeare's name, calling him 'the only Shake-scene in a country' (presumably because Shakespeare was writing successful plays).
1595	Becomes a shareholder in The Lord Chamberlain's Men, an acting company that became extremely popular.
1596	Son, Hamnet, dies, aged eleven. Father, John, granted arms (acknowledged as a gentleman).
1597	Buys New Place, the grandest house in Stratford.
1598	Acts in Ben Jonson's *Every Man in His Humour*.
1599	Globe Theatre opens on Bankside. Performances in the open air.
1601	Father, John, dies.
1603	James I grants Shakespeare's company a royal patent: The Lord Chamberlain's Men become The King's Men and play about twelve performances each year at court.
1607	Daughter Susanna marries Dr John Hall.
1608	Mother, Mary, dies.
1609	The King's Men begin performing indoors at Blackfriars Theatre.
1610	Probably returns from London to live in Stratford.
1616	Daughter Judith marries Thomas Quiney. Dies. Buried in Holy Trinity Church, Stratford-upon-Avon.

The plays and poems

(no one knows exactly when he wrote each play)

1589–95	*The Two Gentlemen of Verona, The Taming of the Shrew, First, Second* and *Third Parts* of *King Henry VI, Titus Andronicus, King Richard III, The Comedy of Errors, Love's Labour's Lost,* **A Midsummer Night's Dream**, *Romeo and Juliet, King Richard II* (and the long poems *Venus and Adonis* and *The Rape of Lucrece*).
1596–99	*King John, The Merchant of Venice, First* and *Second Parts* of *King Henry IV, The Merry Wives of Windsor, Much Ado About Nothing, King Henry V, Julius Caesar* (and probably the Sonnets).
1600–05	*As You Like It, Hamlet, Twelfth Night, Troilus and Cressida, Measure for Measure, Othello, All's Well That Ends Well, Timon of Athens, King Lear.*
1606–11	*Macbeth, Antony and Cleopatra, Pericles, Coriolanus, The Winter's Tale, Cymbeline, The Tempest.*
1613	*King Henry VIII, The Two Noble Kinsmen* (both probably with John Fletcher).
1623	Shakespeare's plays published as a collection (now called the First Folio).

Acknowledgements 鸣谢

Cambridge University Press would like to acknowledge the contributions made to this work by Rex Gibson.

Picture Credits

p. iii: Chichester Festival Theatre 2004, © Donald Cooper/Photostage; p. v top: Royal Shakespeare Theatre 1999, © Donald Cooper/Photostage; p. v bottom: Chichester Festival Theatre 2004, © Donald Cooper/Photostage; p. vi: Royal Shakespeare Theatre 2005, © Donald Cooper/Photostage; p. vii top: Royal Shakespeare Theatre 1958, © Getty Images; p. vii bottom: Ludlow Festival 2006, © Donald Cooper/Photostage; p. viii left: Royal Shakespeare Theatre 2002, © Donald Cooper/Photostage; p. viii top right: Royal Shakespeare Theatre 2005, © Donald Cooper/Photostage; p. viii bottom right: Crucible Theatre 2003, © Donald Cooper/Photostage; p. ix top: Shakespeare's Globe 2008, © Sheila Burnett/ArenaPAL; p. ix bottom: National Theatre 2002, © Donald Cooper/Photostage; p. x top: Barbican Theatre 1995, © Donald Cooper/Photostage; p. x bottom: Chicago Shakespeare Theater 2012, © Liz Lauren; p. xi top: Open Air Theatre Regent's Park 2012, © Marilyn Kingwill/ArenaPAL; p. xi bottom: still from 1999 *A Midsummer Night's Dream* movie, dir: Michael Hoffman, © 20th Century Fox/The Kobal Collection/Mario Tursi; p. xii top: Ludlow Festival 2006, © Donald Cooper/Photostage; p. xii bottom: Royal Shakespeare Theatre 2011, © Geraint Lewis; p. 4: Chichester Festival Theatre 2004, © Donald Cooper/Photostage; p. 12: Royal Shakespeare Theatre 1994, © Clive Barda/ArenaPAL; p. 16 'Cupid's Arrows' by Léon Bazile Perrault, Wikimedia; p. 18: Open Air Theatre Regent's Park 2004, © Donald Cooper/Photostage; p. 22: Ludlow Festival 2006, © Donald Cooper/Photostage; p. 24: Stratford Shakespeare Festival, Ontario 1977, © Zoë Dominic; p. 25: Shakespeare's Globe 2002, © Geraint Lewis; p. 28 'Cottingley Fairies' photograph, © National Museum of Photography, Film & Television/Science & Society Picture Library; p. 30: Royal Shakespeare Theatre 1999, © Donald Cooper/Photostage; p. 34: still from 1999 *A Midsummer Night's Dream* movie. dir: Michael Hoffman, © 20th Century Fox/The Kobal Collection/Mario Tursi; p. 40: Ludlow Festival 2006, © Donald Cooper/Photostage; p. 42 top: Britten Leeds Grand Theatre, Opera North 2008, © Clive Barda/ArenaPAL; p. 42 bottom: © Dreamstime, Goce; p. 44: Roundhouse 2007, © Geraint Lewis; p. 48 © Fine Art Photographic Library/Corbis; p. 50: Roundhouse 2007, © Donald Cooper/Photostage; p. 52: Ludlow Festival 2006, © Donald Cooper/Photostage; p. 54–55: © Robbie Jack/Corbis; p. 55: Illustration from 1628 book *Robin Goodfellow: His Mad Pranks and Merry Jests*, 1628 © Mary Evans/J. Bedmar/Iberfoto; p. 56: Royal Shakespeare Theatre 2002, © Donald Cooper/Photostage; p. 58: Ludlow Festival 2006, © Donald Cooper/Photostage; p. 60: Britten Leeds Grand Theatre, Opera North 2008, © Clive Barda/ArenaPAL; p. 62: Open Air Theatre Regent's Park 2004, © Geraint Lewis; p. 64: Ludlow Festival 2006, © Donald Cooper/Photostage; p. 66: Royal Shakespeare Theatre 1989, © Donald Cooper/Photostage; p. 68: Courtyard Theatre 2008, © Donald Cooper/Photostage; p. 70: Open Air Theatre Regent's Park 2004, © Johan Persson/ArenaPAL; p. 74 'Puck' by Sir Joshua Reynolds, 1789, © Bridgeman Art Library;

p. 76: Ludlow Festival 2006, © Donald Cooper/Photostage; p. 78: Barbican Theatre 1995, © Donald Cooper/Photostage; p. 80: Novello Theatre 2009, © Donald Cooper/Photostage; p. 82: Royal Shakespeare Theatre 2011, © Ellie Kurtz/Royal Shakespeare Company; p. 84: Royal Shakespeare Theatre 2005, © Geraint Lewis; p. 86: Royal Shakespeare Theatre 2005, © Geraint Lewis; p. 88 Royal Shakespeare Theatre 2002, © Donald Cooper/Photostage; p. 90: Royal Shakespeare Theatre 2011, © Geraint Lewis; p. 92: Salzburg Festival 2007, © AFP/Getty Images; p. 94: Willamette University Theater 2008, © Chris L. Harris; p. 96: Royal Shakespeare Theatre 2011, © Geraint Lewis; p. 99: 'The Nightmare' by John Henry Fuseli, 1781, Wikimedia; p. 100: Ludlow Festival 2006, © Donald Cooper/Photostage; p. 102: Rose Theatre, Kingston 2010, © Nobby Clark/ArenaPAL; p. 104: Open Air Theatre Regent's Park 2006, © Donald Cooper/Photostage; p. 114: Intiman Theatre 2011, © John Ulman; p. 116: Open Air Theatre Regent's Park 2006, © Marilyn Kingwill/ArenaPAL; p. 118: Open Air

A Midsummer Night's Dream
仲夏夜之梦

Theatre Regent's Park 2012, © Marilyn Kingwill/ArenaPAL; p. 120: Great River Shakespeare Festival 2004, © Alec Wild; p. 126: Royal Shakespeare Theatre 2005, © Donald Cooper/Photostage; p. 130 top: Barbican Theatre 1995, © Donald Cooper/Photostage; p. 130 bottom: The Roundhouse 2007, © Donald Cooper/Photostage; p. 132: Watermill Theatre, Berkshire 2003, © Colin Willoughby/ArenaPAL; p. 134: Opera London 1990, © Clive Barda/ArenaPAL; p. 136: *Romeo and Juliet*, Royal Opera 2000, © Donald Cooper/Photostage; p. 138: Ludlow Festival 2006, © Donald Cooper/Photostage; p. 140: Brookside Theater, New Hampshire, USA, © Waterville Valley, NH/Shakespeare in the Valley; p. 142: Barbican Theatre 1989, © Donald Cooper/Photostage; p. 144: Barbican Theatre 1987, © Donald Cooper/Photostage; p. 146: Chichester Festival Theatre 2004, © Donald Cooper/Photostage; p. 148: Courtyard Theatre 2008, © Nigel Norrington/ArenaPAL; p. 149: Linbury Studio Theatre 2005, © Johan Persson/ArenaPAL; p. 156: Glyndebourne Festival 2006, © Donald Cooper/Photostage; p. 157: Chichester Festival Theatre 2004, © Donald Cooper/Photostage; p. 158: Glyndebourne Festival 2006, © Donald Cooper/Photostage; p. 161: Chichester Festival Theatre 2004, © Donald Cooper/Photostage; p. 165: Shakespeare's Globe 2002, © Donald Cooper/Photostage; p. 166: *Richard III*, Shakespeare's Globe 2012, © Franz-Marc Frei/Corbis; p. 167: 1900, His Majesty's Theatre, © V&A Images; p. 168: Northern Ballet Theatre 2008, © Merlin Hendy; p. 169 top: Royal Shakespeare Theatre 1970, © Donald Cooper/Photostage; p. 169 bottom: Arts Centre Melbourne, 2010, © AFP/Getty Images; p. 170: Roundhouse 2007, © Donald Cooper/Photostage; p. 171: National Theatre 1992, © Donald Cooper/Photostage; p. 172: Alberry Theatre 2001, © Donald Cooper/Photostage; p. 173 top: Open Air Theatre Regent's Park 2012, © Marilyn Kingwill/ArenaPAL; p. 173 bottom: London Coliseum 2011, © Sisi Burn/ArenaPAL.

Produced for Cambridge University Press by White-Thomson Publishing
+44 (0)843 208 7460
www.wtpub.co.uk

Project editor: Alice Harman
Designer: Clare Nicholas
Concept design: Jackie Hill